LITTLE EVE

NIGHTFIRE BOOKS BY CATRIONA WARD

The Last House on Needless Street
Sundial

LITTLE EVE

CATRIONA WARD

NIGHTFIRE

A TOM DOHERTY ASSOCIATES BOOK

NEW YORK

LITTLE EVE

Copyright © 2018 by Catriona Ward

Reader's Guide copyright © 2022 by Tom Doherty Associates

All rights reserved.

A Nightfire Book
Published by Tom Doherty Associates
120 Broadway
New York, NY 10271

www.tornightfire.com

Nightfire™ is a trademark of Macmillan Publishing Group, LLC.

Library of Congress Cataloging-in-Publication Data

Names: Ward, Catriona, author.
Title: Little Eve / Catriona Ward.
Description: First U.S. Edition. | New York, NY : Nightfire,
a Tom Doherty Associates Book, 2022. |
Identifiers: LCCN 2022011403 (print) | LCCN 2022011404 (ebook) |
ISBN 9781250812650 (hardcover) | ISBN 9781250879028 (international,
sold outside the U.S., subject to rights availability) | ISBN 9781250812667 (ebook)
Classification: LCC PS3623.A7315 L58 2022 (print) |
LCC PS3623.A7315 (ebook) | DDC 813/.6—dc23
LC record available at https://lccn.loc.gov/2022011403
LC ebook record available at https://lccn.loc.gov/2022011404

Our books may be purchased in bulk for promotional, educational, or business use.
Please contact your local bookseller or the Macmillan Corporate and Premium Sales
Department at 1-800-221-7945, extension 5442, or by email at
MacmillanSpecialMarkets@macmillan.com.

First published in Great Britain by Weidenfeld & Nicolson,
an imprint of the Orion Publishing Group Ltd.

First U.S. Edition: 2022
First Nightfire Book International Edition: 2022

Printed in the United States of America

0 9 8 7 6 5 4 3 2 1

*For my nephew Wolf Alexander Ward Enoch,
born May 17, 2018*

AUTHOR'S NOTE

I never thought any novel would challenge me more than *Little Eve*. It's my second novel, the follow-up to my debut, *The Girl from Rawblood*. I spent seven years writing and rewriting that one, and I had no idea how to approach a new book—how to create a new world filled with living, breathing characters; how to make their hearts beat, conjure their loves and fears and desires.

So, I started with the landscape. My mother was born in Ayr, a town on the west coast of Scotland, the birthplace of beloved Scots poet Robert Burns. When she was three, her family moved to Zimbabwe. Many years passed before she returned to the UK's most northern—and perhaps its most beautiful—kingdom. Yet she, along with her brothers and sister, still retains traces of her Scottish accent, especially after a wee dram. There's a yearning in them for the old country, a homeland they barely knew but missed with a deep and resonant longing. That longing has made its way down to me. The hills and heather and sea have travelled in our blood. It's strange to feel such a bond with a place you haven't lived. I thought a lot about that feeling while writing *Little Eve*. It made its way into the book, that sense of love, longing, and family, all anchored to place. So did its dark mirror-twin: the feeling of always being a foreigner in the place you call home.

My parents have always been adventurers. My father worked as a water economist in developing countries, and my sister and I grew up in the US, Kenya, Madagascar, Yemen, and Morocco. When we started school in Washington, DC, my sister was asked where she was from. She insisted that she was from Madagascar, where we'd been living for the past four and a half years. The question didn't make sense to her. My parents told her to say she was from Devon, UK, where we had spent some summers. She didn't remember it very well.

We never lived in a home or indeed one country for more than a few years, which meant that the four of us became each other's home.

Family is at the heart of *Little Eve*. I love my family. That love remains one of the strongest forces in my life. So one of the greatest fears I could draw on for this book was the possibility of that love going awry. I wanted to explore that sometimes contradictory feeling of being deeply reliant on those you love and are related to, as well as being isolated with them. Trapped with them, one might put it. These conflicting, powerful feelings are the engine that hums beneath the hood of this troubling book. And it is troubling. I wanted it to be. How close is too close? When does love become dependence? Or, as an editor once asked me, "What is it with you and sisters?"

Little Eve took me a long time to write. I chipped it out of the rock, a millimetre at a time. I missed deadlines. I took long, terrible detours that ended in the rockface. Still, I struggled on and on. When it was finally published, it attracted scant attention and only sold a couple hundred copies. I became convinced it was a terrible book and that my career was over.

But a year later, *Little Eve* won the Shirley Jackson Award and then the British Fantasy Award for Best Horror Novel. I dared to hope that maybe I'd written something worth reading and that there might be another chance for this strange dark flight of imagination I'd committed to the page. Now, it has been given another life, with this, its first US publication. I still remember how emotional I felt, hearing the news that it had this shining second chance.

My first novel gave me the tantalising hope that I might be a writer. *Little Eve* made me into one. I've finished three novels since, and I am lucky enough to do this for a living nowadays. I want to write many more books, though I've found that during each one, there always comes that moment when I wonder whether I'll ever be a writer. And I will always keep a special place in my heart for *Little Eve*—certain parts of me are here, in these pages, caught forever in time like a fly in amber.

Catriona Ward
February 2022
Devon, UK

A 'nighean mar a máthair
"Like mother, like daughter"

Highlands proverb

LITTLE EVE

DINAH

1921

MY heart is a dark passage, lined with ranks of gleaming jars. In each one something floats. The past, preserved as if in spirit. Here is the scent of grass and the sea, here the creak of wheels on a rough path, here a bright yellow gull's beak. The sensation of blood drying on my cheek in the wind. Abel crying for his mother, Uncle's hand on me. Silver on a white collarbone. The knowledge of loss, which comes like a blow to the heart or the stomach. It does not reach your mind until later.

She is there, too, of course. Evelyn. Somewhere along the rows, behind glass, she floats in the dim air. I do not seek her out. My survival depends on that.

After everything, and against all odds, I have been given a chance. A life. Never mind what kind. I have people who depend on me and I on them. Never mind who they are.

I am filled with memory. I must make room in the dark passage. So I cast it forth, this day. I give it to you. This is the day I became what I am.

* * *

On the morning of 2 January 1921, James MacRaith was roused by silence. The storm that had raged across the coast for three days had passed. Thrushes and waxwings sang in the silver birch trees that lined Loyal's narrow cobbled street. It was half past six, and there would be no dawn in these northern reaches for some hours.

Jamie was twenty-eight years of age, in good health, and had never married. He dressed by the light of a candle in front of the small square of glass that hung on the wall above the chest of drawers. A vest, thick woollen socks with gaiters, the collar of his cotton shirt tied together with a bright red kerchief, a sheepskin waistcoat smelling strongly of lanolin. He painstakingly worked up lather from a sliver of shaving soap and stropped his razor. He put in his dental plate, filling the dark gap on the left side of his upper jaw with a white incisor and canine. The teeth had been lost in a blast in France. Last of all he put on with care the cufflinks his father had left to him. These were battered silver, inlaid with yellowing ivory, and Jamie MacRaith had always loved them. When he held them in his hand he felt the sway of a long trunk, the gentle tread of a great foot on dusty earth; he caught the scent of flowering hibiscus. The cufflinks also made him recall his father's death.

The upstairs of the cottage comprised two bedrooms, one occupied by Jamie. The other had been his father's and now lay empty. Sometimes he still heard his father moving about in there.

Jamie ate some preserved apricots from a jar. He smoked Woodbine cigarettes while drinking strong tea. He buttered two slabs of white bread and sprinkled them with sugar before wrapping them carefully in wax paper and slipping them into his jacket pocket for later. He read a few pages of *Tarzan and the Ant-Men* by Edgar Rice Burroughs. In this story, Tarzan was taken prisoner and enslaved by a race of tiny people who put him to work in the mines. Jamie

MacRaith was fond of reading, particularly stories of adventure and murder. The other books he had out on loan from the travelling library on that January day were *The Mysterious Affair at Styles*, and an instruction manual for building a carburettor engine.

Jamie locked the cottage and stowed the keys in a pile of slates by the back door. Locked doors had been unknown in Loyal until three years earlier, when Jamie MacRaith's father was murdered. He fetched Bill the pony from the paddock behind the henhouse. Bill's shaggy mane was filled with ice crystals.

The village of Loyal is one street lined with whitewashed houses that sits on the northernmost edge of Britain. Settled in the nineteenth century by Highlanders fleeing the fire and blood of the Clearances, Loyal was a kelp town until there was no more kelp. The War had taken most of the young men and now it was a village of cripples and old women, bearing the names of long-destroyed royal clans. MacRaith, McRae, Buchanan. They grieved for the past. They held the memories of their grandfathers and grandmothers close.

Jamie led Bill the pony down the dark street by Loyal's tiny harbour. The oily salt scent followed him in the cold air. During the storm, the boats had been pulled high above the waterline, into the cobbled street, masts unstepped and lashed down with rope. The boats now lay sprawled on their sides, putting Jamie in mind of beached sea monsters.

At ten to eight, Jamie was unlocking the shop. He had been the butcher in Loyal for two years, since he came home from the War. He went to the cellar, unhooked a large side of beef, and wrapped it in a sheet. He dragged it out to where Bill was tethered at the front of the shop. Jamie had spent several months training the pony not to fear the scent of blood. Still, Bill sometimes balked at it. The beef had been ordered by the Castle of Altnaharra for New Year's Eve, known as Hogmanay in those parts. It was now three days late, owing to the storm, and Jamie was uneasy concerning payment.

He loaded the side of beef onto Bill using a harness and clips of his own design, then set off along the path which followed the sea.

He did not meet or see a living soul on the road. At nine o'clock, the hour of winter sunrise, the world began to reveal itself. Birds circling in the brightening sky; the hills painted in russet brown and grey, rolling on and on into the deep north. Out to sea the sun was a burning ball, casting its shattered light across the water.

The Castle of Altnaharra sat on the isle of the same name, a quarter of a mile off the western shore of the peninsula. In 1898 Colonel John Bearings returned from India and travelled north into the Highlands to take up his inheritance—a dilapidated ruin on a wind-struck island. He repaired the castle, planted gardens, set up beehives. Two women joined him, Alice Seddington and Nora Marr. They took in four infants, foundlings plucked from the many destitute communities that litter the Highlands. The inhabitants of Altnaharra came into the village every now and again to buy bootlaces, or to have a harness mended. They were considered odd by the local population but were left alone.

After the murder, in 1917, a great steel gate appeared across the stone causeway that connected Altnaharra to the mainland. The children stopped attending the school in Loyal. The women no longer came to the village for bootlaces, no longer gathered driftwood on the shore. They retreated into themselves.

The only signs of life within were the polite notes left for tradesmen in the wire cage that hung from the gate. *Pale green wool, the shade of a cabbage heart. Knitting needles (x 3). Three sharp flensing knives and a ball of string (large). Beef for Hogmanay, please. Hung for at least three weeks.* The people of Loyal were accustomed to check the basket as they passed Altnaharra and left the goods there when next they happened by. Payment was left in the cage in the same fashion, always correct to the farthing.

It was said in Loyal that the residents of Altnaharra opened the gate at night under the autumn moon and ran wild over the moor, painted blue, looking for souls to take. Some said they were all long dead, and that the isle was now populated by ghosts. Jamie did not set any store by this. Ghosts and fairies did not use such things as lamb mince or wool.

The walkway to the isle lay before him now, under an inch of gleaming water. He congratulated himself that he had timed his journey so well, for the tide would soon turn and start coming in again. Altnaharra could only be reached at the ebb, and if he had dallied, the sea would have been lapping at his thighs by the time he came to cross.

But Bill balked at the causeway. He planted his four legs firmly and showed that he would not get his hooves wet. Jamie tried to persuade him with the piece of sugared bread which he had meant for his own lunch. He petted and threatened, all to no avail. The pony would not go across. Rather than argue with five hundred pounds of stubborn Highland, Jamie unhooked the side of beef, took it resignedly onto his own back and waded precariously out to the isle.

A stiff wind blew in the wake of the storm and more than once the weight of the beef nearly toppled him into the sea. He heard the distant bark of seals. He did not relish the idea of falling into deep water with a hundred pounds of steer strapped to him. The pods which overwintered at Altnaharra were grey seals: vast, ugly and strong. They had been known to attack if they caught the scent of meat.

As Jamie came close the wind sang strangely through the steel gate. It was fifteen feet tall, hung from vast posts. Heavy chains held it fast. Jamie put the beef in the wire cage with a thump. As he turned to go, he stumbled in the shallow water and steadied himself by grasping a crossbar of the gate. At his touch it slowly swung open and Jamie went with it, falling to his knees with a splash.

Before him was a small blue pebble beach. A path led up the hill through yellowed winter grass. Sheep scratched mournfully at the hard earth. Above, the tumbledown silhouette of the castle was stark against the sky.

Jamie straightened quickly. He called a hallo. The sheep leapt in alarm, but no answer came.

"I thought they wished me to bring the meat up to the castle," he told the inquest later. "And that they had left the gate open for me."

Jamie shouldered the beef once more. He climbed the narrow stony path. The sky was clearing to the sharp blue of a cold day. The sea rippled and shone. Behind, to the west, the land was bathed in light. To Jamie, each step felt like trespass.

The castle was surrounded by a motte, old and crumbling. The rusting portcullis was half-descended. In the courtyard beyond, scraps of white paper or handkerchiefs tossed violently in the wind.

The spikes on the portcullis were sharp and Jamie "did not want to put himself under, as it looked as if it might go all the way down at any time, and into me." He called out to the house. There came no answer.

He rolled the beef under the metal spears and then, reluctantly, with his eyes tightly closed, he wriggled through, waiting for the old iron to hurtle earthwards and pierce his ribs.

Once inside the courtyard he called again. Still no reply came. Jamie was put out—he thought that perhaps he was being mocked, or that there was some game being played.

He saw as he approached the kitchen door that the white handkerchiefs were in fact five or six gulls, squabbling over scraps of something. As he raised his fist to pound on the oak, one gull, pursued by its fellows, barrelled into his legs. It dropped what it was holding in its beak at Jamie MacRaith's feet. This proved to be a human thumb, severed neatly at the joint.

Jamie's heart began to beat hard. He put the side of beef down quickly, then wrapped the thumb in his handkerchief and put it in his pocket. The gulls pecked angrily at his fingers as he did so. Next, he removed the metal hook which had been lodged in the meat for hanging. With this in his hand, he opened the door and slipped quietly into the high-beamed kitchen.

He said later that knowledge swept over him the moment he entered Altnaharra. Standing in the silence and breathing the air, he knew that they were all dead. He looked about the room with its scrubbed table and iron range, four times the size of the little one in his cottage. The stove was cold to the touch, which told him that no one had stoked it that day. A heavy cleaver lay on the floor, a slit bag of flour slumped by it. The wind had blown a fine dusting across the room. In the flour were two sets of footprints. He followed them, taking care not to disturb the tracks. He was, after all, a reader of detective fiction.

In the passage, the flagstones were caked with black mud, great swathes of filth described across the floor, not quite dried. Jamie saw with a feeling like falling that the mud was tinged with red. From somewhere above there came what sounded like a shot. Jamie told police later that everything "went cold and came to a stop." After a few moments the sound came again and reason reasserted itself. It was only a door flung hard by the wind in some upstairs room.

He went to the entrance of the Great Hall. The tall windows overlooked the sea to the east, and the reflections of the water played across the walls and beams of the vaulted ceiling. There was a sweet, fermented smell. Chairs were pushed back as if in haste and the candles were all burnt down to nothing in the sconces. In the corner of the room, two chickens pecked hungrily at the cold flags. Upstairs the door crashed again in the wind with an almighty sound. After a moment, Jamie MacRaith swallowed his heart back down. He went on through the house, following the trail of mud and blood.

He came to the door that gave on to the east of the isle and greeted the air and the sky with relief. But the lintel was marked with a rusty handprint. The path at his feet was spattered with dark drops. It led towards the sea. He followed as he knew he must, a question and answer repeating in his head like a nursery rhyme or a half-remembered song. *What has happened here? A terrible thing.*

He crested the hill, a smooth slope of green descending to the warm grey huddle of a ruined church. Beyond it were the standing stones. They reached like wise fingers to the sky, casting long shadows on the sward. The largest stone, known as Cold Ben, lay on its side, beside a gash where it had been torn from the earth.

Then Jamie saw them.

In the centre of the stone circle lay five shapes, arranged in a star. They were attended by gulls, feeding busily. As Jamie crept closer the gulls lifted off, beating white wings.

The shapes were people, lying peacefully as if in a children's game. Their feet pointed to the centre of the circle and their heads radiated out; bodies telling the points of the compass. They were wrapped in fine white wool. Jamie saw their faces, and he saw that they were dead.

Jamie MacRaith's first instinct was to turn and run. He mastered it. His second impulse was to vomit and for a few moments he crouched on all fours. When he had recovered, he went quickly to the circle. He checked each cold wrist for a pulse. Their hearts were still. Their right eyes had been neatly removed. The sockets gaped red.

Elizabeth's corpse was laid east to west, pointing at the sea. Her head rested by the fallen stone. She had been fourteen. The wind tossed her curls. Next to her was John Bearings, his flesh like marble, stiff with rigor, hair spilling back from his brow. His thumb was neatly severed at the knuckle. By him was Nora. Her single large grey eye stared. Dinah lay on the far side of the circle. Beside Dinah lay

Sarah Buchanan, a village girl. What ill fate had drawn her here to Altnaharra, Jamie could not imagine.

The inhabitants of the isle were all present save one: Evelyn was not among the dead.

The gulls cautiously began to return. One landed on Dinah's face and drove its beak into the place where her eye should have been. Jamie shouted in horror and ran at it. It fluttered a few feet out of his reach and landed lazily on Nora's foot. He lunged again at the gull, sobbing, but when he turned ten more had descended. They tore and picked with greedy beaks.

Jamie ran about the circle waving his arms. The gulls rose and settled and rose and settled in white-feathered waves, easily avoiding him. They filled their bellies with the soft flesh of the dead.

Jamie was screaming, and so he did not at first hear his name spoken in a weak voice. Dinah called to him again. She fluttered her fingers. Her face was ghastly pale, her words slurred, her head lolled drunkenly and a thin line of blood trailed down her cheek. But she was alive. Jamie cradled her and wept.

"Where is Evelyn?" she said. "Oh, I remember. She took our eyes."

Jamie MacRaith stared about him as if Evelyn might be lurking behind the stones or in the long grass, but there was nothing save the bright morning.

Jamie came galloping into Loyal. The pony trembled with exhaustion, his long shaggy coat drenched with sweat. They were greeted with astonishment by Mrs. Smith, who had come out to sit on her doorstep to repair a fishing net. She tried to take Jamie inside to give him a nip and settle him but he would not go. He pointed again and again with a shaking finger: over the moor, to the east, to the sea, as if those things had done some great wrong.

"They must get to Altnaharra," he said. "The police. They have all been murdered. Only Dinah is alive."

What has happened here? A terrible thing.

* * *

So I lived, although I did not wish to at the time. They brought me back to Loyal on a stretcher. I stared up with my remaining eye. The clouds wreathed above me, forming and reforming. In it were the faces of the dead.

People came from houses and from fields as we neared Loyal. We became a procession. There were eyes and hands everywhere. They seemed to lick their lips as they looked at me. A small boy touched a bloodstain on my sleeve with a dirty finger. I screamed. I did not stop until we were inside the inn and the door was bolted. I could still hear them breathing behind the door. All those people. I had not left the isle in years.

They put me in a room above the bar where they stored broken things awaiting mending: a hand plough, a tankard, a box of smashed plates, a stirrup leather, a spinning top with flaking red and blue paint.

An old doctor from Tongue dressed my eye. He smelt of tobacco and camphorated oil and I wept all the while. Strange that a missing eye can still weep.

"My name is McClintock," he said.

I asked again for Uncle, Nora and Elizabeth. I said there must have been some mistake, for they could not be dead. He said that they were. I tore out my hair by the roots and clawed at my face. He gave me milk with something in it. Knowing no better, I drank it. The stuff sent my mind spinning, crashing softly into itself.

"Why did she take the eyes?" the old man asked me.

"She thought it would give her power," I said. "She put her own eye out three years ago. It was not enough."

He made a disapproving sound in his throat. "That is the sort of nonsense they will seize on. Out there they are already telling the old tale, saying it was the *Eubha Muir.*" The old man rose with a creak.

"I have tended to the living, now for the rest." Nonsense or not, he wanted to be away from me.

I said, "I must be with them."

Despite his protests I went with him across the road in my bare feet, through the watching crowd. The bodies were in Jamie Mac-Raith's cellar with the beef. I followed him down the stairs. When I saw them all I wept again. I tried to climb onto the slab to lie next to Elizabeth. The doctor would not let me. "I am one of them," I said, "I am dead, too."

"Get down," he said. "Let me do my job. There are things that I must do—the corpses must be aired. It is the old Parisian method. You will find it upsetting."

"I cannot go back to the inn. All those eyes and hands."

He looked at me with impatience and some sympathy. "There is nothing to fear," he said.

"There is Evelyn."

"Och, they will catch her and hang her," he said. "Or she will die in the cold. There is none in these parts will shelter her. She is not the *Eubha Muir*, merely an evil woman."

"Let me stay."

The old man shrugged as if to say, "It is your choice. I still have work to do." He went to Uncle's body, white on its slab. He made a small incision in the flesh, scalpel winking in the dim light. There was a hiss from the corpse, as of gas escaping. He scratched a match alight and set it to the wound. The incision began to burn with a blue-green flame. He repeated this operation on the lungs and abdomen, making candles of the dead.

I lay down in the doorway of the cellar. The dose was working in me. The scene shimmered, the corpses burned like votive offerings. All around, the carcasses of cows swayed gently on their hooks. I was changed.

* * *

Here is the jar with its pale contents. It is yours now. I hope it haunts your nights. I think it will.

Perhaps I will never send this. If I do, I will post it from another town. Do not look for me. You owe me that.

D

EVELYN

1917

THE door swings closed behind me with a long, high note. I make a silent screaming face. Surely Dinah will wake. But she sleeps on, hair tangled over her parted mouth, arms spread wide as if falling through the air from a great height.

I watch her. She is white, flesh poured over fine bones like wax, lashes like long shadows of saplings at dusk. She is damp at the temples, hair a slew of burnished pennies spilling across the bed. She has become all lips and eyes this summer, and sometimes I think, *who is that woman?* As if a stranger has always lived inside her and is now being revealed.

Through the open window the night is dying. Dark air full of the promise of light, the heavy pause before dawn. Below, the sea is hung with mist, which is His breath on the water. Somewhere beneath the waves His slow, heavy coils are moving in the deep.

"Do not come to Dinah today," I pray. "She does not wish for it."

Dinah gasps in her sleep. She has powerful dreams and waking is hard. She crosses the border slowly.

If left, Dinah will sleep until Uncle comes. She will wake, dazed, to his disappointment. I will be quick and bright as a knife. Uncle will put his hand on my head and the warmth will spread right down through me. *Eve, awake betimes!* Uncle will see at last that I am his favourite.

I sigh. I pinch the inside of her pale thigh. "Wake up, slug."

Dinah grasps my arm with surprising force, five nails digging in. "Eve." Her voice is thick, far-off. "We were white rabbits. We were shut in, we could not get out. The reekling was among us with its needle teeth. We did not know when it would strike." The reekling is Dinah's own monster. It has come to her since first her mind made dreams.

"It is time, Dinah."

She sits wearily, returning, then groans and stands, her bare feet blanching on the freezing flags. The match fizzes in her hand; the candle warms the dark.

Dinah stares at her reflection in the little cracked square of glass on the wall, as if at a great mystery. She has begun to suspect that she is beautiful but is not sure yet. She probes her bruised upper lip with her tongue and winces. "Do you think that this will go by school day? I hope it will." When Dinah is afraid she slows almost into stillness and her attention narrows, finds some small focus.

I watch her divide her dark red hair into rivulets and plait. When she has finished she is crowned with a coronet of braids. Nora taught Dinah how. My fingers would not learn it. Or perhaps it was that Nora would not teach me. We are not fond of one another, she and I.

"Come here, slug," says Dinah.

Her fingers are quick and deft, binding my hair to my skull. It is her way of thanking me. I could have left her to sleep.

She takes the knife from her cuff and cuts a loose thread from her skirt. She binds the end of the plait. "Where did you go in the night?"

"I was asleep by you," I say.

"No," she says. "You went somewhere and then you came back. The door made a noise like a sick lamb."

"You and your dreams, Dinah!"

She just looks, dark eyes wide. "I wish the trying was over," she says.

Uncle is in the doorway. His monocle winks in the candlelight. Uncle is slight, shy. He walks about in a cloud of diffidence. His eyes are very young, his brown beard and moustache burst in thickets from his face, the scars beneath only glimpsed, like river stones through running water. As ever, the world realigns with his presence. It takes on colour and detail.

"Awake betimes, Dinah. And ready." His approval is a caress. I see it pass over her, leaving her cheeks hot, a shy smile on her lips. How silly she looks. Longing makes a sour taste in my throat.

"And Eve awake, too." Uncle opens his arms.

We both run into them. It is like being held by a friendly tiger, the brush of its muzzle.

"Quickly now," says Uncle. "Dawn is upon us." He goes, humming.

The turret stairs are worn smooth by centuries of feet, the old arrow slits are serpent's eyes, fringed with fern and moss. The blasted courtyard is surrounded by canting battlements, eaten away as if by giants. Above us, the sky is steely and full of birdsong. Little black rabbits scatter over the bare grass, showing their white heels.

We duck under the rusted portcullis, out of the protection of the castle's crumbling arms. The wind hits like a blow. It is a constant on Altnaharra. The whine, the cold battering of your ears. Ahead of us, the stones are black against the brightening sea. Some are tall, notched, others broad and flat, smoothed by time. They cant and reel at ungainly angles. As we approach each stone pulls on me, little tugs of power. Cold Ben leans in on the eastern side. He is not the largest stone but he is the most powerful. His will hovers in the air.

We run to our places in order of age. Dinah stands beside Abel. He is fifteen turns but I am nearly as tall as him, which he hates. His face is pale under a shock of white-blond hair. Abel is elusive all through. He stares ahead but his hand gently brushes Dinah's, little finger to little finger. She shivers, grateful.

I take my place on Abel's other side. Baby Elizabeth swings on Alice's hand. She dandles a wooden spoon and strokes it like a soft creature. The faint light makes a nimbus of her hair. Elizabeth has seen eleven turns of the seasons but she will always be everyone's baby. She does not speak. Two turns ago she simply stopped.

Nora and Alice are encased in creamy linen from head to toe. Beneath the peaks of their caps their faces are removed and lovely. In their rippling white they look like two great birds, feeding tranquil among humans. We girls will all wear the white, some day.

The air is full, waiting for colour.

Uncle gives Alice honey from his hands. He raises a pearl of blood on her thumb. He comes to each of us with honey and the knife. We hold the trembling red globes on our fingertips. The sweet dizziness of bloodshed moves through me.

A burning finger falls across the bay and the air comes alive. The stones are silhouetted against the blazing sky, the sea a field of shattered glass.

We let the blood fall to the earth.

Uncle beckons Dinah to the centre of the stones. She goes, looking dazed and stupid. Her lips are parted, she takes little sips of air.

Uncle opens the rush basket at his feet and tips it gently. Hercules pours out, silver stripes flowing like a river as he moves. His red eyes stare. Uncle takes him in his bare hands. I watch the placement of his thumb behind Hercules' jaw.

Hercules writhes then goes still. Uncle holds him aloft, an offering to the sky. "Take him," Uncle says.

Dinah breathes deeply. Her face is frozen. She reaches for Hercules with trembling hands. Dinah takes him by his tail, his neck. Her lips move. She stares at the snake. She tries to go inside him.

Hercules flips, showing his white belly. His head is a dark blur. There is a sound like the snap of a green twig. Dinah cries out.

Uncle tuts and takes Hercules back gently, then places him in the basket.

"It is ended," he says. "He did not let Dinah see with his eyes."

Altnaharra settles about us again. Birdsong and the wind. Dinah is beginning to sweat. She clutches her arm and winces. Two glistening punctures. The flesh around them swells as I watch.

Uncle picks up Hercules' basket and starts up the rise towards the castle. "Come," he says to Nora and Alice. "The day marches on." They hurry after him in a bustle of skirts, each holding one of Elizabeth's hands.

Dinah sits among the stones making a high needling sound. Her shoulders tremble. I start towards her but Abel pushes me aside. He puts his thin arms around Dinah and whispers something in the voice they use only for one another.

"Dinah," I say. "Do not cry!"

"Go away, Eve," Abel says, shrill. He strokes Dinah's cheek, shiny with tears. She does not look at me.

Something rises in my throat, hot. Dinah is the fixed point. I take shape around her. When she does not notice me I fade at the edges and do not know what to do.

* * *

In the grey light of the kitchen Uncle rests a hand on my head. "Do not be sad for Dinah," he says. "That is in the past."

Alice laughs at something Nora says under her breath in her rich voice. Strange vowels from somewhere else. Their cheeks flush. When Uncle looks they become serious, dark eyes flickering. He smiles at them. Nora has grown very fat in recent months. Her stomach sticks out like a boulder. Sometimes she holds it as if she loves it or as if it hurts. The sea has come into Nora lately and left a child in her.

We cast our eyes down and join hands. "To Him we give thanks," says Uncle. "May He coil about the world."

Nora spoons out porridge and honey. Five mouthfuls. We eat as a serpent does, little and seldom. Hunger brings us closer to Him.

When Uncle's porridge is finished, Nora brings him bacon and mushrooms. The scent fills the air, rich and savoury, and my mouth waters. I wonder if meat tastes as it smells, like both comfort and pain.

Alice and Nora are talking of the circus. They heard about it at market. Orde's Circus comes through Loyal some years, on the way south to England. They camp under Ardentinny.

"A palmist," says Nora. "A bearded lady! A *psychic*!"

"What is psychic?" I ask. I like the word. "Psychic, psychic, *psychic*."

"Stop that," says Nora. "It means someone impure who pretends to have the power of the eye and exchanges it for money."

"You are too young to remember the last time they came through Loyal," Alice says. "They have elephants, poor things, and they put winter coats on them, like the ones worn by those silly little dogs old Edinburgh ladies own . . ." Nora looks at her in warning and Alice flushes. She covers her hand with her mouth. "Forgive me," she says to Uncle.

"How big are elephants, Uncle?" I ask quickly. "Are they *this* big?" I spread my arms wide to make him laugh.

"Much bigger," he says, smiling. "Now to your tasks."

I know, of course, that *Loxodonta africana* stands up to fourteen feet and *Elephas maximus* up to eleven feet.

It is feeding day for Hercules. Hercules is Uncle's task as the chickens are mine and the ewes are Abel's and Haystack the pony is Dinah's, and Alice patches us up when we fall and Nora tends the bees. Hercules' tank is by the kitchen range. On warm days Uncle will move him into the sun for the daylight hours.

Uncle holds a big, shining frog. Its throat moves. He drops the frog into Hercules' tank and closes the lid.

The frog stares and leaps with powerful legs. Hercules strikes, his thick coils unleash. The frog is caught in his jaws mid-air. Its legs continue to kick. Hercules dislocates his lower jaw and swallows the frog. His red eyes stare into me.

I will be ready when my time comes, I promise him silently.

* * *

When I have fed the chickens and collected the eggs, I go to the western shore. The tide is out and stranded water gleams in pools on the rock. I find him easily, as if he has come at my call. His smooth, rounded carapace is delicate orange, pink, edged with green and blue. The colours of bruised flesh. I lift him carefully. His ten armoured legs stroke the air. We call him a shore crab but he has another secret name.

I climb with him to my hidden place above the sea. It is surrounded by boulders, covered with lichen and gull droppings and old seaweed thrown here by storms. There is a strong odour of dead fish. It is the haunt of many sand fleas. No one comes here but me.

From beneath a stone I take out the parcel, wrapped in brown oilcloth. It is heavy and I can scarcely lift it. My hand strokes the cracked leather. *Classes of the Kingdom Animalia and Plantae*, the lettering reads in faded gold, carved into the skin of the book.

The names make such good shapes in the mouth. Shellfish become *Brachiopoda, Crustacea, Chordata, Loricifera*. The *Kingdom Animalia* tells of things I know. Seals and snails and worms and sheep, everything that lives beneath the glassy ceiling of the ocean. It also tells of creatures I do not know, forged by heat and sand and air.

I turn the pages until I find him. There. *Carcinus maenas*. I shape the words with my lips.

I found the book in a chest in a room where books were once kept.

We store fishing nets there now. We have no need for books, Uncle says. Truth and knowledge are in the ocean. But cannot truth be found in two places at once?

The book is not like school, which makes me feel cold and alone. The little white house in Loyal where we listen to Mr. MacRaith's lessons. Uncle says we must go, must do just enough to seem like others. On school days we are orphans. Charity children, taken in by Uncle. I hate this lie. It burns my mouth. It is like hiding a great light under sackcloth.

I set the crab down and he makes for the cliff edge.

"*Carcinus maenas*," I say in a low breath.

For a moment he stops, caught by the power of his name.

* * *

Nora blows out our candle, then goes shuffling along the corridor. I hear her groan. She is so fat; no wonder.

Beside me Dinah says, "Eve."

"I am doing it." I ease out of bed. I go to the window and open it a crack. The wind whistles, pokes its eager, freezing finger in. I go to the door. I wedge it open with a stool. "Better?"

"Yes," Dinah says, relief running through her voice like a vein. It is cold. In winter we wake with ice on our lips. But the window must be open. Dinah cannot bear to be shut in.

I get into bed shivering and hold her tightly as she sinks into sleep. Soon it is like holding a warm corpse.

I release her slowly, then slide from the bed and go down through the dark castle to where Hercules sleeps in his glass prison.

Someone must be the Adder after Uncle, to care for us as he does. Dinah does not want it. Abel has deep currents in him. He loves and hates too hard, so it cannot be him. Elizabeth—something is broken in her, not just her voice. It must be me. I realised that soon after Uncle began the trying.

How many times have we tried? A hundred, perhaps more. Never have we succeeded in seeing with his eyes. We are bitten each time.

Hercules is part of Him who will come from the ocean. But he is also a snake, *Vipera berus*, a common European adder. I know both his natures.

Uncle always holds Hercules the same way. He supports Hercules' body two-thirds of the way down. This makes Hercules feel safe. He does not swing in space. With the other hand Uncle gently takes him behind his head so Hercules cannot turn and bite. His head is held still, so he does not wish to strike. His body is calm, so he is calm. And he knows Uncle's scent. That is why he does not bite him.

The glass walls of the tank gleam in the scant light. Is Hercules awake or asleep? His red eyes do not close.

I slip my knife from my cuff. I cannot see him in the dark interior, but something shifts, a long, dry rustle. A feeling seems to come from him. Curiosity, perhaps.

I prick my finger with the knife. It is hard to stop, to shed only a few drops. The good feeling comes, mingled with unease. Only the Adder may shed blood on the isle. But I remind myself it is not true bloodshed. Abel grazes himself climbing on the rocks. I sliced my hand open with a knife last summer. Dinah and Alice and Nora shed blood when they have their time and they are hot and angry. This is no different.

I slide back the lid of the tank. I picture Hercules waiting below, black tongue flickering in the dark. Tasting me on the air. I let blood fall from my finger.

He hits the glass like a punching fist as he strikes. I throw the lid of the tank into place. He strikes again, upwards. His head hits the glass with a crack.

For thirty-two nights in a row I have left my bed to do this. Hercules shows no sign of becoming accustomed to me.

I do not go straight back to bed. It is some time before I can stop shaking.

* * *

Alice and Nora are going on mission. We gather by the causeway to send them off. They have removed their white linen. They wear homespun clothes and sack aprons. They look like fishermen's wives. Haystack the pony chews at Nora's sleeve, his eyes mysterious behind a shock of black and brown forelock. She shoves him away and cradles her great belly. Uncle embraces them. He does not leave the isle.

He says, "Be back before nightfall."

Alice and Nora nod. They do not need to be told.

The world changes at night. Bad things from the beginning of the earth roam in the dark. We must always be safe on the isle by the time the sun falls into the sea.

The tide is out and the stony path leads straight to the shore. Alice goes on foot with Haystack beside her, pulling the little cart. Nora rides atop a barrel of salt fish. There are urns of sheep's milk, yellow cheeses wrapped in linen, baskets of peat, ranks of shining summer preserves, all to be sold in the square in Tongue this market day. My mouth waters a little at the sight. Sometimes it is hard that most of the food we make on Altnaharra must go to market. But that is the way of things. We watch Alice and Nora until they are part of the horizon.

"To your tasks," Uncle says.

Dinah is pale. My insides flutter. We have fasted for two days and a night. We must be pure for the morrow. It is good that we are gathering pears, not diving for clams like Abel or chopping wood.

* * *

"That one is bad," Dinah says.

I press the amber flesh with a gentle thumb. "It is good." I make to put it with the others. The pears are conversing, each rustling in its brown paper caul. White scent rises from the crate, making my mouth sing. I sip water from the clay jug. It helps somewhat.

Dinah takes the pear from me and points. "The grub has entered there. See? We cannot save it. There will be eggs laid."

It is a tiny mark no larger than the footprint of an ant.

"That is weather-scald." I take the pear from her. "It is nothing, Dinah."

"I hope it is you and not I who gives Uncle a rotten pear to eat."

I feel protective of the pear. "It is good." I slip it into the pocket of my pinny. When we break the fast I will eat it and show Dinah the clean white flesh. The pear sits against my hip, humming with expectation.

Dinah turns away with a shrug.

"Dinah, Dinah," I sing. "Your hair is made of weeds. Dinah, Dinah, Dinah, you smell of apple seeds!" I tug a strand of dark copper where it spills over her shoulders. She will tell me off but anything is better than not noticing me. Dinah swats at my head but she is trying not to laugh.

The old tree creaks in the salt breeze. The branches touch the ground in places, leaves tickling the earth. The pears are plentiful and golden, plump on the branches. These days before midsummer have been sunlit. Good pear weather. But something is in the air. A faint scent under the breeze.

"A storm is coming," I say.

"That box is full. Any more and they will spoil. Take them down now."

"No," I say, to scare her. "I will stay here and pick more. You take them down."

Dinah shudders with her whole skin. "Please, Eve," she says simply. "I cannot."

I take up the crate and pick my way over the ruined hill. A church stood here once. The Impure built it. They planted the pear tree.

Now they are gone and it is tumbled, the grassy nave lying open to the sea air. Upslope the castle rears, topping the island like a sentinel. The beehives are over the rise. Inside them honey lies in waxy combs. My mouth longs for it. I am so hungry. But honey may only be taken from the Adder's hands.

My foot catches. I am suddenly the wrong weight and shape in the air. The earth tips, there is no such thing as balance. I will fall, the crate will break and the pears will burst forth screaming.

I right myself, skin tingling, and kick hard at the fibrous roots. A shrub with glossy dark leaves, flowers the hue of clouded dusk. It seems to wish to strangle the earth. I call it the crawler. Uncle brought the crawler from very far away and planted it here on Altnaharra. It is not like any other plant on the isle. It speaks of distance, cold mountains where the air thins out and only goats go with their clever, clinging feet. I have never liked it. It means that once there was a time before Uncle came to the isle, before the Children, before I existed. A terrible thought, like stepping into space.

By the seven stones I put the crate down and lay my palms on Cold Ben. There were people here before the Impure. The old people, who knew of Him. They made the circle. But they vanished long ago. Many turns later, when the purpose of the stones was forgotten, the villagers brought witches here to burn them, waist-deep in barrels of pitch. If I am quiet, under the breeze I can hear the crackle of hair catching in flame. The stones do not care for mortal things. They do not think well or ill of us. But they remember.

Many lives have been passed on Altnaharra. We will be the last.

* * *

The cellar is a bite of dark on the castle wall. I go down the steps cut into the rock. The wooden door is barred with iron and the walls gleam damp in the narrow sunlight. Cheeses hang like dead men in the cold air. There are pots of Altnaharra honey, trays of salt taken from the sea, preserves gleaming in rows. All ready to be taken to market in Tongue. I finger the pear in my pocket. I think of the juice running down my chin. I think of sinking my teeth into crumbling white ewe's cheese. But Uncle would know.

In the centre of the floor is the trapdoor. It is flung back, revealing the gaping dark beneath. Why is it open? I should close it. I do not like it here. I only come because Dinah cannot. Quickly I stack the crate of pears on top of its fellows.

Above, the castle sighs and shifts. Creaks, cracks, sound and movement as if with the passage of vast dark coils. The thing from Dinah's dream is down here, too. It crawls up through the trap-door.

I turn and run for the air, the light. I take the stairs three at a time. I race through the afternoon, drawing the clean air deep into my lungs. I do not stop until I see the bent tree like a black spider against the sea, until I catch the scent of broken pear flesh rotting on the ground, until I throw my arms about Dinah and feel the surprise run all the way through her.

"Goodness," she says. "Do not knock me about."

In unguarded moments fear runs through me. Will He be terrible when He comes from the ocean?

* * *

"That is the last." Dinah wipes her brow. The day is fading and night things stir, preparing for their time. To the west the clouds are boiling dark against the sky. The storm is nearly upon us.

Alice and Nora are tiny on the land below. They run, skirts held high. Haystack canters, head nodding. In the channel the waves are building into towers. Out to sea, the clouds are lit in white blasts as the storm races in.

Dinah and I run as rain falls in cold scatters, faster, harder. Abel holds the great castle door. The wind tries to seize it, to slam it closed.

Nora and Alice plough across the causeway, waist-deep in water. Half an hour longer and they would have been too late. I shiver at the thought.

Alice helps Nora from the sea. Water sloughs from their skirts, their hair, their sleeves. Lightning blinks out everything and Haystack screams. The little cart bounces up the hill, then into the castle. We run in after them. Haystack's hooves clatter on the flags. Dinah unharnesses him and he trots into the Great Hall, lead rope trailing. He rolls a wild eye at the tall windows which show lightning over the sea. Abel and Dinah charge out again into the grey downpour. They fetch in the tools and Nora dries them quickly with her apron. They must not rust. Abel hauls the door shut with a slam to rival the thunder. He is just in time. The storm hits in earnest, blasting the walls and shuddering the old timbers. Hail cracks and shatters on the panes.

We run about, placing cans and pots to catch the leaks while Dinah tries to pull the pony towards the door.

Alice says, "Leave him. He has earned time by the fire."

Haystack nips vengefully at Dinah's arm. She squeaks and releases him. He trots to the dying hearth where Elizabeth puts her arms about his neck and sighs as though she has been missing him all day. Perhaps she has.

Alice tosses an armful of dried grass before the pony. He eats, velvet lips parting to show strong brown teeth.

Elizabeth tugs Alice's sleeve. She points to her mouth and makes a mewing sound.

"No, darling." Alice strokes Elizabeth's head. "Tomorrow. You know that."

Uncle sits in his chair, arms outstretched, eyes closed. He communes with the storm.

I take off my pinny, storm-wet, faintly scented with pear, and hang it to dry before the hearth. The warm afternoon seems a year ago. I bank the fire, stoke the dying embers. Abel pumps the bellows furiously and together we coax heat from the coals. Flame leaps up against the dark.

Thunder strikes as though the world is breaking open. Abel and I scream and cling to one another. The electric air speaks; everything is alive.

"I think we're going to *die*," says Abel. We giggle. It is somehow a hilarious thought.

A cry. Nora's face collapses in pain and she clutches herself. Alice drops the pile of blankets she is holding and runs to her. Nora's belly ripples, she is wet about the thighs.

"Oh, it is coming," shouts Dinah. We have been waiting for this for so long. Nora groans and leans on Alice.

"It is early," says Uncle.

"I am well," says Nora. She grits her teeth.

Uncle says sadly, "Too soon."

Alice shouts, "You would send her out into this, John?"

Uncle looks at her.

"No," says Alice.

Alice and Uncle stare. It is a battle. For a moment they seem evenly matched. Then Uncle grows slightly taller, something golden hangs about him.

"It is too small to live," he says in the voice of the Adder. "It may not die on the isle."

Alice bows her head. The Adder cannot be denied. She takes Nora's arm. Nora walks doubled over, moaning. There comes the crash of the great door and then they are gone into the violent night.

Dinah makes a high sound. She points with a trembling finger.

Baby Elizabeth is a thin shadow before the red hearth. In one hand she holds my wet pinny. The other hand holds the pear she took from my pocket. Elizabeth thrusts the fruit into her mouth, eyes dreamy. The flesh writhes and white grubs spill from her lips, curling on the flags at her feet.

Elizabeth fights and grunts as Uncle seals her mouth. He carries her from the hall towards the Wane place. Over his shoulder her blue eyes bulge with fear.

* * *

When I go down to Hercules that night it seems to me that he does not strike the glass as hard as he did before. But perhaps he is like us, frightened by the storm.

Later, I have the bad dream. In it someone stands over me, humming a tune. The tune seems to make its way into my bones, my skull. A hand is on my head, another pulls a blanket up about me. A word that my mind will not form. The shape of that word hangs in the darkness; I breathe it in and out. The humming rises and fills the night, becomes a voice which weaves through the air, up my spine, piercing my heart. Singing.

I wake shuddering, my face wet with tears. The reekling is Dinah's worst dream. This is mine. The feeling it brings will be with me for days, bitter in my throat.

* * *

We go to the stones in the red midsummer dawn. The circle is strewn with blown branches. We clear it in silence. Dinah puts out bowls of honey. Alice dabs oil on the stones, so that they gleam in the new light. Below, seals call, dark heads bob in the sea.

Nora groans as she moves. She and Alice are sombre. Alice keeps one hand on Nora at all times as though afraid that Nora will disappear. They returned in the wake of the storm. Nora is the colour of cheese curd. Her eyes are empty.

Uncle comes round the circle and brings our blood to the air with our knives. Hercules is coiled like a gauntlet around his wrist.

Uncle beckons to Nora and she goes limping to him. He takes her in his arms, bends to her ear and whispers. I cannot hear what is said but Nora weeps and sags. Uncle holds her upright. His lips move. Nora nods and sobs. When Uncle releases her, Nora's face is shining, the sadness gone. "I am seen," she says.

Alice goes next, and then Dinah, Abel, Elizabeth. One by one we are cleansed. Some he holds close for minutes. To others he utters only a sentence and then releases them. It is always different, the seeing. He does what is necessary.

I am last. Uncle's arms close about me. He smells like lightning and the earth. "You are Eve," he says, breath warm in my ear. "No one knows your worth except I. I test you harder than the others. You have great power in you."

I am overcome. I gasp, tears welling.

"Are you seen?" he asks.

"I am seen." *I will be worthy*, I tell him in my mind. *I will not disappoint you.* I go reeling back to my place.

He gives the isle our blood. As he does the Adder comes into him, the old one who touches the power at the centre of the world. He says, "We honour Him in the water."

My soul speeds towards Him over the ocean while a part of me remains in the circle. I see it in the others' eyes, too. We are here, and not-here.

We are swept away into the great light beyond the world.

* * *

I come to, weak and drunk, in the evening. Dusk lies all about, gentle on the land. The others are beside me, spitting grass from sticky mouths. We go back to the castle in ragged pairs, leaning on one another.

Nora lays out bread, cheese, apples and butter in the kitchen, crying all the while. "The Adder told me that she would come again," she says to Alice. "Now I feel better, for I know that I have not lost her for good, my little one. Next time, perhaps, she will stay." I smell the bitter cheese, the rosy skins of the apples. The bread calls to me in a warm voice. My stomach knots. Not long now.

We gather before the hearth in the hall. Alice helps Nora down onto the flags, wraps a blanket about her.

Uncle sits in his great wing chair. "I will tell the Tale," he says. He strokes the lush brown whiskers that cover the scars on his face. He says, "Altnaharra has always been a place of worship. Even as the Impure built their so-called churches here, even as the priests mumbled their heresies, they were preserving His tale. His shadow can be traced in all their legends. Their Book records that the world began with a great serpent who changed the course of mankind . . . No, they cannot forget. He is in everything.

"I spent my life in the Eastern campaigns. I saw much that appalled. In the year 1898 by the calendar of the Impure I was brought news in Tirah of my father's death. I returned to these shores, glad to leave War behind. War is a hungry beast, my Children. It must be fed boys, and when it spits them out they are no longer the same.

"How cold it seemed to me here! I was strange to the English—to my own people. I was brown, as brown as the soles of Abel's feet!" He tickles Abel's heel and Abel writhes in ecstasy. "I did not know my relations—they were fat, soft strangers. As for me, the face they recalled was hidden by scars and they could not find there any love or memory of a youngest brother.

"The portion my father left me was fair but without fondness. A wreck in the wastes of Scotland. I came north to inspect the ruin that was my inheritance and make arrangements for its disposal. I travelled up through the country. As I went, the English summer fell behind, the sky grew larger, the air cooler. Spring crept over the land again, as if this place had dominion over time. I feared it. The strange vowels of its savage people, its unknowable hills.

"I walked the miles from Loyal on a cold and blustery afternoon. I was slow, my wounds pained me and I leant on my stick. I had nothing to eat. I looked often over my shoulder, thinking that I was followed. There was nothing but the blue hills. That is the way in these parts. You are never alone. The land is always watching you.

"When I came in sight of the isle I was shaking with hunger and fatigue. I felt every old break in my bones, each old wound was opened afresh. Altnaharra was silhouetted against the dusk. It put me in mind of a corpse, lying in the shallows. As I crossed the causeway, an eerie keening noise came from the dark waters about me. I had never heard a seal's cry before.

"You would not have known the castle then, my little pups. The roof was torn away in places and the stars showed through. Spiny seagrass grew in the hall where we now sit. Gulls and bats had made their homes in the rafters, and their droppings were everywhere. Ivy throttled the walls, inside and out, and the panes of the windows had long ago been shattered.

"I had in my pack roots and bulbs of various flowering bushes that I had known in India. The climate of the Western Ghats is similar to this, and some species can flourish in both places. I had thought to plant them in the soil here, but I ate some of the roots, I was in such desperation. They were dry and bitter and I could not persevere. I found gulls' eggs and ate them too. I was so hungry that I ate seaweed, grass, little toadstools. A sleeping beehive filled the dead hearth. I stole a comb from the little sisters.

"Then there came a soft noise from the place where that door is now." He points into the black beyond the firelight. "From the shadows came three men. They were thin to breaking point—I could see their skulls beneath the skin. How long had they watched?

'*Sassenach*,' one said. '*Mac na galla*, give us what you have.' These men had hidden on the isle, perhaps for many years, and they would not easily give up their haven. They unsheathed the sharp little *sgian-dubh*, daggers, which were strapped to their legs. I saw that they would not let me live.

Give your flesh to the isle. Be one with it, and with me.

"I took my flesh from the bone with a knife and the Adder came into me. There was a great brightness and the benison sang in the air. I stood and saw the isle laid out in time before me, burning in the light of ages. I saw Him through the water, His coils sending waves halfway across the world. The men were gone, as if they had never been."

Uncle pulls up his trouser leg to show his wasted calf. It is as thin as a child's, mottled as if badly burnt. It does not look like a leg at all, but like a twisted root. Uncle never shows his leg unless he is telling the Tale. It is a sacred thing and we sigh at the sight of it.

"Did it hurt?" asks Dinah.

He smiles at her. "The pain was nothing. Each drop of blood I spill in His name lends Him power. Meanwhile the Impure destroy one another in the Great War. This is His work, too. He grows, they diminish. Soon He will coil Himself about everything."

"What will it be like?" asks Abel. "When He comes?" He has a toothache. His jaw is swollen and he tries not to touch that side of his face. He is afraid that Alice will take it out with the pliers, so he is pretending that it does not hurt.

32

"The Impure tell of a great flood that consumed the world," says the Adder. "So it will be. He will be everywhere, and the world will be full of power, as it is on Altnaharra."

"When He comes Uncle's leg will be mended," says Dinah.

"When He comes Baby Elizabeth will find her voice again," says Alice. "I hope she is all right down there, John. She is not strong."

"Perhaps when He comes Eve will grow some inches!" says Abel. "Won't you, little Eve?"

I feel I could kill Abel, kill him quite dead. Why must he always call me that? It makes no sense! He is barely a finger's breadth taller than me.

"I will see the babies again when He comes," says Nora. "All my lost babies."

"How will we breathe in the ocean, Uncle?" I ask. "Will we gain gills? Will we have a subcutaneous layer of fat for warmth, like seals?"

The silence that follows is thick. I put my hand slowly over my mouth, as though that could undo it.

Uncle says, "Where did you learn such words?"

"At school," I say.

"You will not break the fast with us," says Uncle. "You are shunned this night."

Abel and Dinah turn and begin to whisper. Alice's eyes go blank. I become a hole in the world; I cease to be. No one will look at me or speak to me until dawn breaks. I could scream and shout, I could hit them and they would pay me no mind. It makes me feel mad. I begin to doubt my existence.

* * *

The others are in the warm, lamplit kitchen, breaking the fast. I listen as they tear open soft loaves of bread and cut slices of cheese and apple. They clatter their knives, shout through mouthfuls of bread and honey. They are all bathed in the light of Uncle's love.

I go from the hall. The cold night air puts its fingers into my joints. The moon moves across the sky, leaving its gleaming path on the sea. *You*, I think. But I cannot hear Him. Uncle said that I may not break my fast with them. Well, I will not.

In the hen coop sleepy noises greet my hand, reaching under feathered bellies. Three eggs. I break them into my mouth. My throat accepts the slippery mass with difficulty, but I force it down. In time the trembling in my legs subsides.

I go to the cliff, to the stones. I put my arms about Cold Ben and rest my cheek against his granite skin. He is dark and still. He gives no comfort.

In the ruins of the old chapel the leaves of the crawler are glossy, its blooms night-scented. I kick at it, moody. My foot meets something that is not a stone. It rings hollow. It is wedged into a crevice between two broken pillars. An old tin, of the kind used to keep tea. The surface is blackened with wear. This tin has been here for a long time.

I pry it open. Inside there is a small book bound in mouldering cloth. It says 1903 on the front. Fourteen turns ago.

I sit and strike a match. Out on the hill the wind whistles but here in the lee of the old walls the flame hardly wavers.

The pages of the book are cotton-soft from much handling. There are stories in it, under dates. It is a diary of sorts. Most entries are only a line long. They are about a baby named Amy. *Today she ate a strawberry mashed up. Amy cried at all the lullabies but the one I made up for her. Amy is restless today.* And then: *I cannot stand this much longer.* I know the writing. I have seen it on jars of blackcurrant preserve. It is Nora's wavering copperplate. This baby must have died a long time ago. Perhaps it was the first.

There is a poem in the book.

So we sit alone we two at break of dreadful day
And so I vow to you my dear, love will find a way

Over the mountains fearful cold,
And in the restless running streams,
Love will find a way
Wherever we do turn, whatever they will say,
Your heart and mine will burn.
Love will find a way.

Perhaps it is not a poem but a song. I hum as I turn the pages. A tune comes. I stop when I realise that it is the song from my dream. I do not want to think of that.

A grainy black and white image, folded into the pages. Eyes shadowed by long-ago sunshine, a faded, plump face, a lick of dark hair, barely there. I stroke the picture. I have seen photographs before. There is one in the schoolhouse, of the Impure King. But I have never seen one of someone I know, or almost know. How strange that Nora's little baby can be here, where the Altnaharra breeze sings and also somewhere else, many turns past. *Love will find a way.*

There is a lock of fine dark hair and a ribbon. When I hold it near the match it leaps into colour—pink, faded brown and watermarked.

Whether she speaks of it or not, Nora thinks about the past. And like me, she hides a book. It is as though the sky has been peeled back to reveal another colour. I put Amy's book back in the tin. I wedge the tin among the stones, trying to make it look just as it did when I found it.

There is a whine in the air, or in my head, as I make my way back to the castle. Eggs were not enough.

Dinah is curled under the table, snoring. Abel's white head rests on his neatly crossed arms. Nora and Alice are on a pile of blankets in the corner. Uncle is gone. The seeing takes his strength. It is the way of things. Everything has a price.

There is nothing but crumbs left on the table. I sweep those into my hand and lick my palm. In the glass tank eyes gleam atop dark coils. Hercules watches as I open the lid. He does not stir when my blood falls in. I wait. Nothing.

Slowly I put my hand into the tank. I tremble. Every fibre of me resists. I keep my hand where it is. I feel him sliding gently. His tongue flickers on my palm. He will bite now, now will come pain, the crunch of fangs in flesh.

But he does not bite.

I take him gently behind the head. I support his body with my hand. I lift him slowly, pulse racing. He is heavier than I expected. He settles comfortably in my grip. "We are ready," I tell him.

I do not wish to be inside, tonight. I sleep curled up among the owl pellets and the glossy leaves of the crawler, on the old, cracked stones of the chapel floor. I dream of the dead baby.

* * *

Mushroom day. Dinah and I go through the beech wood after rain.

My back aches as if I have fallen or been beaten. Sleeping on stone is not good.

"Would you rather be a fish or an otter?" I say to Dinah.

Dinah hums. She does not like this kind of game, but she feels bad for me because of last night. "Otter," she says. "They are nice with their little hands and their tails."

"They are not nice. They are angry and hungry all the time. I would be a fish. You wouldn't have to walk, ever again!"

"Otters are better."

"They are rats that swim," I tell her. I tug on her hair. "Fish belong to the water, otters only borrow it."

"Go on," says Dinah. "Be a fish. See if I care. I'll catch you and eat you." She reaches for me and I scream and run. She pinches me in the soft places under my arms and I am weak, crying with laughter.

"Don't," cries Dinah as I tickle my fingers along her ribs. "Don't, I shall drop it!" The basket of mushrooms swings, precarious.

We dawdle by the stream, the water running clear over our feet. Overhead the branches hold back the sky with interlocking fingers. The forest is alive, redolent of sap. Sun dapples the woodland floor, the bright grass, the waxy little heads of buttercups.

I see a flash of bronze in the cleft of a mossy rock. I catch him with sure fingers, the long body shifting in my hands like a stack of coins.

"How do you always find such creatures?" asks Dinah. She shivers with delicate revulsion. "Wherever you go."

I look into the black round eyes, the clever face. A slow-worm. *Anguis fragilis.* I do not find them, they find me. I let him slide through my fingers, away through the nodding blades of grass.

"Always frowning," says Dinah. "You could be pretty, Evelyn, if you didn't pout like a fighting dog." She means a bull terrier. Dinah doesn't know the names of animals. She strokes my brow, her fingers cool.

"You are hot," she says. "Maybe you should go back, Eve."

"It is just the sun." I do not want the day to end.

She looks at me with her lip between her teeth, considering. "I have a secret," she says in a rush. "Can you keep it? Look." She takes something from the neck of her shirt.

"What is it?" I have never seen anything so beautiful. A shining star.

"I cannot let you hold it," says Dinah. "It is too precious. Jamie MacRaith gave it to me." The schoolmaster's son.

"What is it for?"

"I do not know," says Dinah. She slides a nail into a hairline crack in the silver oval, and right before my eyes the front swings open like a little door. "It is called a locket. He says you put hair in it."

"Well," I say. "That is stupid."

"I know," Dinah says. "But that is what he says."

"Whose hair?"

"Mine, I suppose. It is my locket. Look." *D.B.* is inscribed on the silver in fanciful letters.

Dinah looks up, takes in the height of the sun. "Eve," she says. "You mushroom without me for a while."

"Where are you going?"

"I have an *appointment*." Not her word. Someone else's, it sits clumsy on her tongue. She stands, pinching her flushed cheeks. She strokes the locket with a finger.

I want her to stay. We could talk through the afternoon. She would touch my face again and tell me I could be pretty. I wish I had a locket to give her. But I am just boring little Eve, and she is leaving.

I slide my little knife out from my cuff and take Dinah by the hair. Dinah screams as I saw off a copper strand.

"Now you have something to put in it," I say, offering the lock of hair.

"It never pays to be nice to you," Dinah says with tears in her eyes. "I won't forget that again." She takes the hair with a sniff.

I put handfuls of mushrooms in my mouth. Their cool white flesh is perfumed by the earth.

"That is not safe," Dinah says. Disapproval makes her voice gruff. We only eat on the isle.

"You cannot tell," I say. "Or I will give account of you."

Dinah makes a cross *ugh* sound and goes. I watch her slender form disappear into the green. Time is driving us apart. When did it begin? Four turns ago, perhaps, when Dinah had her first time and Uncle began the trying.

No wonder Uncle does not like us to speak of the past. It is painful.

I get up and go after Dinah through the beech wood. She is easy to follow. She walks slowly, held in a dream, her hand touching a tree branch here, there taking a leaf between her fingers. She sings something low under her breath.

The wood opens into a meadow. Boulders, acid yellow with lichen, lie about as if tossed by giants. Clouds of small white butterflies rise like spume. The old blackhouse sits squat among the young grasses, a lump of stone thatched with reeds and marram. Once there was a village here named Forth. But that was long ago.

Jamie MacRaith sits on a stone, his face strange and solemn. He rises when he sees Dinah. When she reaches him they do not touch or speak but stand very close together. Each searches the other's face. His hand moves towards her ear. He takes her earlobe and pulls it gently downwards. She makes a little grimace, and their heads meet.

I press the point of my knife into the fleshy part of my forearm. My fingertips and thumb are too sore now, covered in tiny cuts. I raise a few drops of blood, and as the red beads rise, so does the warmth. It rushes through me.

* * *

Alice took Abel's tooth out yesterday and now he has a fever. His face is still swollen and it smells bad. She feeds him broth through a piece of straw. He cries all the time, even in his sleep.

I go to my special place on the cliff, swatting at the sand fleas. I weigh down the pages of the *Kingdom Animalia* with stones. The wind shrieks along the cliff, mourning. Above it the voices of the seals. Leopard seal, *Hydrurga leptonyx*, grey seal, *Halichoerus grypus*, the harp seal, *Phoca groenlandica*. Their skin like the surface of the water, their happy round eyes. What would it be like to be a seal? To swim all day and rest on the rocks at night, always among those you loved.

For a time after midsummer I had resolved not to look at the *Kingdom Animalia*. I know that it is impure. Uncle would be disappointed. I should leave it to rot in its place above the sea. But what good would that do? I cannot remove the knowledge from my head. I cannot forget the beautiful names of whales or the classification of herons.

A sound that is neither the wind nor a seal. Voices beyond the stones on the cliff. How did they come so close without my noticing? A stiff white flicker of skirts. Laughter. I peer through the scrub.

Alice and Nora sit in a little patch of shingle on the cliff. They have taken off their caps and shoes. Nora's brown hair ripples free, her bare feet are white and vulnerable. Alice blows her hair away from her mouth, impatient. I have always thought Alice and Nora to be the same age as Uncle but perhaps that is not true. Now they seem younger.

"Oh, love," Nora says. "You know our duty. To let the sea come in and increase us. It will be all right."

"I do not think that I can do it all over again," Alice says. "Altnaharra is changing. It is not as it used to be. John is not. He should not have made you leave in the storm."

"He sends us no more than we can bear. I understood."

"This is too hard a life for children," says Alice. "He permits only bandages. Iodine and honey for disinfection! I was a volunteer RN for a month, only because the other debs were doing it." I hear the tears welling in Alice's voice. "Abel's tooth," she says. "It would not come. I am not sure I got it all out, Nora. He will not stop crying."

"Come," Nora says. She settles on the rock. "Come here." She takes Alice in her arms and holds her. "Let us speak of the past," she says. "Just this once. Do you recall, Lady Alice, the night you left your home? Slipped out the front door, in the dead of night and all the house abed? I heard the latch, and when I came out to see who was robbing us, there you were, going off into the dark with your case."

Alice laughs. "You said, 'Do you know how to hail a cab for yourself?' And I didn't!"

"I was only a second housemaid. It was so pert of me to speak to you. You said, 'I am going to meet the most marvellous man who is going to change everything.'"

"We were both such silly girls," says Alice. "But you were kind.

Not sixteen, and in trouble yourself, and you wouldn't let me go alone. You came to the station in the cab with me, and I explained about this place. John met us at Euston."

"He said he would buy me a ticket for the sleeper," said Nora. "And that all I need do was listen to his ideas, and if by Preston I did not think that he was right, I should have my fare home, no questions asked. He told me I should have my child here, and the isle would resound with joy. There would be no shame, no poorhouse. I was his by Watford."

"You were so dignified. It was sweet. You said . . ."

"'I do not believe I shall be returning to my post,'" says Nora. "I have never regretted it for a moment since. I am even grateful to that knife boy, who I thought I loved at the time. We are free women, beholden only to the earth and the sea."

"Oh, Nora," says Alice, "I left because I did not want to marry some silly man and have an awful great house and push out children year after year. Girdles and ironed newspapers and afternoon tea! I thought the rules were wrong. But it seems that the rules have come and found us here. Are we really so free?" Alice takes a little shuddering breath. "Last week I told him that I was taking Haystack to be shod. Instead I rode to Tongue, then took a train to Inverness. I walked past our house, where we spent those summers away from London. Orme Place. Do you recall? I go to look at it, sometimes. I don't know why. It is always empty, boarded up." She pauses. "This time, the shutters were open. My mother and father are in Scotland again. Why would they come back after all these years? The only answer I can think of is that they are still hoping to find me. Oh, Nora, it does such things to my heart."

"Alice," says Nora, seriously. "They may be looking for you, just as they would seek a ring, a bracelet or any mislaid property. But they do not love you. You are not doubting John—or me?"

"Of course not," says Alice. "Forgive me, I am foolish."

Nora kisses her. "All will be well."

The undergrowth crackles with Nora's departure. She approaches my hiding place. I make my mind a rock, my body still earth. I hear her skirts as she passes; they almost brush my cheek. Then she is gone. A kittiwake screams and I turn, skin thrilling. A tall white figure stands over me.

"You have been listening, Eve," says Alice, quietly.

"You were speaking of the past," I say. My tone sounds accusing, childish. I feel like a child. She is Alice who paints our cuts with iodine, but now she is also someone else I do not know.

Alice comes close to me. She puts a warm arm about my shoulders. With one hand she turns the page of the *Kingdom Animalia* which lies beside me in the sunshine. "You like to read about animals?"

I put a protective hand on the book. Will she tell?

She sighs. "Do you ever wish that you were a normal little girl with a mother and father? That you lived in a house and had dresses and books and . . . jam sandwiches? Things like that?"

"I am a normal girl," I say. "I love Him and Uncle and you and Dinah and Baby Elizabeth. I would die if I was made to live anywhere but here."

Alice laughs. "He is right," she says. "You are a true child of Altnaharra. Very well. But it is not always easy for you. I see that." She touches my cheek with a white finger. "We are good friends, you and I. Are we not?"

"Yes," I say. Though truthfully I am in awe of Alice, whose long bold stare and aquiline nose make her seem powerful like a stone.

"Then I wish two things. One, we agree that neither of us shall mention our meeting here. It is, after all, now in the past. We shall not speak of it!"

The words have a furtive gleam to them. If I did not know better, I would think Alice was mocking our ways. But no one would mock Uncle's word.

I nod. If Uncle knew he would take away the *Kingdom Animalia* and I do not wish for that.

"Secondly, I want you to remember these words. Number fourteen, Orme Place, Inverness."

It sounds like nonsense to me. I shrug.

"Will you remember?"

"Yes. What is it?"

Alice takes my face between her hands. "It is a secret," she says. Her blue eyes hold an expression I do not know. It is not quite sadness, and it is not joy. "If you ever feel . . . differently about your place here, perhaps it will prove a useful secret." Alice glances at the sun. "Run along. You have the hens to feed." She turns and walks away briskly.

* * *

Evening. We stand in a line on the clifftop, in order of age. We crouch and each muscle sings its expectation.

"Go," shouts Uncle. We dive. A rush of air and then the water hits like stone. Cold salt fills my nostrils, my mouth. I hear the others about me. Sometimes at this moment the joy is so fierce that I think I will dissolve into the ocean, be carried away on the currents, flow into Him. We carve through the deep, our wet skin gleaming. Uncle watches from the cliff like a mast.

Once round the island, a full circle, back to where Uncle stands. Then the rope ladder. The first one to the clifftop is the winner.

Elizabeth makes peeping sounds and begins to swim in circles. She watches the gulls, the seabirds. She doesn't seem to understand that it's a race. We leave her, carving through the water.

Ahead of me Dinah swims. Above the smack of waves in my ears I hear her grunts. Somewhere behind, Abel's lungs are whistling. The ocean is all about me, beneath me, in me.

We pass the place where the ruined belfry rises. My arms are seizing and cold has yielded to hectic warmth. A furnace burns in me, uncertain and bright. A haze falls across my eyes. I find my last reserves and push level with Dinah. We are all three gasping. Now I am past them. My heart is in my throat. We are in the channel between the isle and the mainland. Somewhere beneath us is the drowned walkway. I am almost there. The world blazes. I call on Him. I feel Him beside me, supporting me. The water is my cradle. I am of the sea. I find a burning core of strength and pull from it.

I grasp the rough rope swollen with seawater and pull myself up. Suddenly my foot is seized as if by a strong mouth. I kick out hard, but the hand around my ankle pulls me down and I swallow cold salt. Above me the mirrored underside of the ocean ripples.

When I surface, Abel is a thin white shape halfway up the rock face. He climbs with trembling hands, his breath sawing in and out. At the top of the cliff Uncle takes him in his arms.

I hope Abel enjoys his win. Tomorrow is my trying.

*　*　*

The stones hum about us, gleaming with power. The taste of honey is sweet and slick between my teeth.

Uncle holds Hercules before my face. His fierce red eyes look into me. He sways gently in Uncle's grasp. I will win and Uncle's love will cover me.

Hercules hisses. He is afraid. I am afraid, too, despite my preparation. His flat head, the ancient line of his jaw, his needle fangs, his vertical, slitted pupils. My flesh shrinks. The fear reaches back in time beyond me; it is the old dread of all those who look into the eyes of a snake.

Uncle puts him into my arms. Time slows almost to stillness. His body shifts. Cool, smooth skin, longing for the sun. Each scale perfect like plated armour. Everything in me wishes to stay as far as possible from the broad, spade-shaped head. I take his narrow neck in my hand. He swings, questing. He is trying to turn. To bite? Does he recognise me? There is some sound in the distance, a far-off drum. I shake my head to clear it. My grip tightens and Hercules thrashes. He does not like to be held tightly, I remind myself. Against my instincts I loosen my hold. Hercules calms. He becomes a cooperative weight on my forearms. It worked, all those nights of giving him my scent.

The drum grows louder.

"Please," I say to Uncle. "I cannot think straight. Please, that noise, make it stop."

He looks surprised and his mouth opens, but nothing emerges. Instead he goes away and the world becomes a silver tunnel filled with soft thumping.

*   *   *

My tongue slips in and out of my mouth, black. I see through it. I taste the world. Each tiny current of air is a brushstroke. It paints a great ringing canvas. The sea a cauldron of minerals and rot. Bruised grass rising green, each flint buried in the chalky earth a dark exclamation. The splintered scent of a grasshopper, the fizzing of midges in the air.

The drumming goes on. It is the cold beat of my heart, buried between my ears, behind my brain.

I have a name in the old tongue from when the world was young and my fathers ruled the earth, taking aurochs whole into their bellies, leaving acres of forest crushed by their passage. My name is not rendered in sound, but in tiny movements of my head, a delicate, precise secretion of chemicals. It means something like *dark-soil-and-mouse-blood*, my name.

I swing in air, my body a long muscle. Something warm and meaty is clasped about my middle. Too close. I do not like it. The earth is too far below. Old inherited memory stirs, of vast copper wings, great claws and the cruel hook of a yellow beak. I cannot taste *eagle* in the air, but my body tells me I am caught. I feign death, waiting for the moment to strike.

* * *

My mouth is thick and my breath feels strange in my whistling nostrils. It is hard to remember how to use my eyes or my voice. In my arms, Hercules lies quiet. I thought that it was a trial of logic and of cunning but I was wrong.

I say, "Uncle, I saw. His grace was in me."

Uncle regards me. He will embrace me now, or touch my head in benison.

Uncle flicks Hercules' head out of my loose grip. Hercules twists and spirals in the air. His head swings around on his powerful neck. He wraps himself about my wrist and the twin needles of his fangs sink into my flesh. There is sharp pain but the sight of it is always worse, the dark head fastened on the web of my hand as if suckling, caught between finger and thumb. I scream and shake my arm. His muscular body writhes, furious in the air. He falls, twisting, to the turf.

Uncle picks up Hercules tenderly. Hercules opens his mouth in distress. It is pink and empty.

"You have been practising, Eve," Uncle says. "The flecks of blood in Hercules' cage each morning. Did you think I would not know? I, the Adder?"

The wounds are dark, two little tunnels filled with blood. Something gleams in the red depths. Hercules has left his teeth in me. The broken ends of two ivory needles.

"But . . ." I say. "I saw with Hercules' eyes, I was in him . . ." My lips are growing numb, sickness rises as the poison works its way in. The world tips and I sink with it. I must make him understand.

Uncle raises his voice. "Eve is a cheat. She has dishonoured the trying, so it is at an end. She is shunned. I set no limit on the time."

He looks through me as if I do not exist. I will not be real again until he decides that I am.

"Please, Uncle." Abel's face is desperate. "Please, no." It was his turn to be tried next. He screams, "I hate you, Eve!" Then he stops seeing me.

Dinah is white, aghast. "How could you, Eve?" I see myself fade in her eyes too.

* * *

Breakfast, porridge, six mouthfuls. No one speaks to me. Nor during our tasks, nor at the noonday meal, bread and cheese, six mouthfuls, nor at supper. One potato, dried herring. It has been three days. I begin to think I will die of it.

"I am sorry," I say to Uncle over and over. "Forgive me!" His eyes gaze ahead, serene. Perhaps I am already dead.

After supper Alice changes the dressing on my hand. It is the first indication of my existence that I have had all day. She paints the bite with honey and purple iodine. She cannot remove the fangs. They are broken beneath the surface, hooked into my swollen flesh.

"Perhaps they will work their way out with time," she says, as if to herself.

At bedtime Dinah will not look at me. After Nora douses the candle, I slip out of bed, the chilly floor biting my feet. I open the window. I prop the door with the stool. "I have done it, Dinah," I say.

Dinah rolls herself up in her blanket and puts a pillow behind her so I cannot hold her as we sleep.

I lie awake. When I move my fingers the adder fangs move with me, a spirit adder under my skin.

* * *

A school day. We line up on the causeway in order of age. Dinah does not need to come to school; she is of age. But Uncle will not have us go alone.

"Who do you watch while you are in the impure world?" Uncle asks Dinah.

"I watch myself and others for signs of corruption," Dinah says.

"Abel?"

"I watch myself and others for signs of corruption."

"And when others ask you of your birth?"

We each have a story. Abel was taken from a house of ill repute, whatever that may be. Dinah's mother was addicted to spirituous liquors. Elizabeth and I were abandoned on the shores of Altnaharra by frightened girls. But Uncle does not ask me for my story today. His eyes bore through me.

The wind tangles my hair. The causeway lies beneath a fine skin of water and the sea laps about our feet as though we are growing from the waves. Dinah holds Elizabeth's hand, drawing her away when she wanders near the edge. Sometimes Elizabeth does not know the difference between safe and dangerous.

"Do you think Jamie MacRaith will be there today?" I ask Dinah.

"Do not dawdle so," Dinah says crossly to Elizabeth. She does not look at me.

We take the sandy coast road which forks inland, across the grey and green moor, to Loyal and Mr. MacRaith and the impure world.

It is a few moments before I realise that Abel is not with us. I turn. He is marching away down the coast, small against the land.

"Abel!" Dinah calls.

He turns, shivering in the wind. "I am not going to school. I am going to Tongue."

We stand, mouths agape. We go to the woods, or to the hills, or to school. We do not go anywhere else. Abel is talking about going off the edge of the world.

"You cannot," says Dinah. Then, "Why?"

"That is where Nora and Alice go on mission," says Abel.

Dinah smiles. "The sky is blue," she says. "Sheep eat grass. He comes from the ocean."

Abel does not smile back. "Tongue is probably where Uncle got us from. Nora and Alice go and come back in one day. It cannot be too far. If we follow this path, I bet we'll find it. Maybe the ladies who were our mothers are there."

Dinah says quietly, "That is impure, Abel. Uncle lifted us from the sea."

"Do you *really* believe that, Dinah?" Abel sounds world-weary. How did he come by these thoughts?

"We do not speak of the past," Dinah says, stubborn.

"We speak of the past *all the time*!" he shouts, pale face twisted. "Everything is in the past. They do not wish to speak of their lives before the isle. We do not *have* that kind of past."

"You do not have a mother either," Dinah says.

"I remember her, Dinah, so there. She had nice hair and we lived in a little room in a tall house with lots of ladies."

"You are making it up," says Dinah.

"There was a kitten with a notched ear. I played with it on the stairs."

"Mothers do not give up their children," says Dinah. Her mouth sets in a little line. "So we must come from the sea."

"Maybe they did not give us up," says Abel. "Maybe we were took. Anyhow, I'm going to find out."

Dinah goes to Abel and takes him in her arms.

He struggles and his face crumples. "I want to go, Dinah," he says through tears. "I want to find her."

"What would you want with a mother?" she says. "You have me."

He screams and raises his fist as if to strike her.

Dinah catches Abel's fist. She unclenches his fingers, one by one.

"Come," she says gently. "We will be late for school." She takes him by the hand and leads him towards Loyal.

* * *

The little room in Loyal is white and smells of pine. Mr. MacRaith stands at the front, blade-thin in his blue suit. He is speaking of the Impure Book. "An eye for an eye," he is saying.

On my right Abel appears to be writing everything down. But he is drawing dragonflies. Elizabeth watches. She has eaten most of her pencil.

I feel the weight of a look. I catch the tail of Jamie MacRaith's stare.

Once when Jamie thought everyone was in the schoolyard I saw him combing soap through his hair to make it lie flat. He flushed when he saw me reflected in the glass. I do not know what the point of him is.

Sarah Buchanan's breath is warm on my neck. The children from Loyal and the farms do not talk to us. There is a circle drawn clear as if in chalk. But Sarah is not above copying from my exercise book.

Her tongue protrudes, her pencil strikes hard through the paper. She looks like custard or a sweet in her yellow dress, her white ankle socks, a yellow Alice band in her shining yellow hair, which seems to be made of some immortal substance. She sees Jamie looking in our direction. She smiles at him, her smile hanging warm in the air. Beside me, Dinah stirs.

Jamie swallows, then fixes his eyes upon Mr. MacRaith, who is describing a beheading. His father, his teacher.

There are twenty children in the room. There were more once. The older ones are all girls. The boys have gone to be eaten by War.

Sarah leans in once more. Even her breath smells of butter and sugar. I cover my exercise book with both hands.

* * *

All around the yard, children eat from pails. Pasties and bannocks kept warm in cloth, hard yellow cheese, baked potatoes. I go to where the others huddle against the fence.

"Eve has chalk dust all over her knees," Dinah says to Abel. "Have you noticed?" Her tone is disdainful. I am so relieved to be mentioned. I brush the chalk dust from my skirt.

Jamie is across the yard leaning against the far wall, his hands in his pockets. He watches Dinah. Pink creeps over her skin.

"Dirty foundlings. Creeping about, *spying*." Sarah Buchanan's eyes are cold marbles in her head.

"We are not dirty," I say. "We are pure."

Sarah Buchanan laughs behind her hand. "Aye, pure," she says. But she makes it sound like *poor*. There are two girls behind her who laugh too. They have rainwater hair and whey faces. I wonder if that is why Sarah chose them; because they are the colour of mouse fur and beside them she shines like gold.

Dinah comes to my side. "You are nothing to us," she says to Sarah.

Sarah's porcelain cheeks turn a high pink. She flicks her nails almost lazily down Dinah's forearm. A long crimson score appears, running from wrist to crook, winking with beads of blood.

The wound glistens, unseemly. It is as if Sarah had pulled up Dinah's skirt or torn open her blouse.

"You shed my blood," Dinah whispers.

It happens so quickly that she does not seem to move. One moment they are five feet apart and the next Dinah is atop Sarah, punching her face. The mouse girls try to hit Dinah.

I pull Elizabeth away from the fight. I push her back against the wooden fence. "Stay there, Baby," I tell her. She looks at me with shining eyes. "Do not move."

I turn back to the fray. Abel is beside me. We do not do anything to join the fight; it enfolds us like the sea. Someone has their hand about my neck. I crush a finger in my teeth. Jamie MacRaith is here, too, pushing the mouse girls off Dinah.

I have blood under my nails and a handful of yellow hair. Shedding my own blood was one thing—this is different. No wonder Uncle keeps this power for himself. It is wonderful. I do not know how long we have been fighting. We are all deep in a world of heavy breath and colour and flesh on flesh.

When the eye comes it is not like the last time. There is no silver tunnel, no muffled heartbeat. Instead I am inside Sarah, standing in the dark. It looks like the inside of the cupboard in the corner of the schoolroom. A scent of paste, chalk and the lye they swab the floors with. In Sarah's mind the cupboard has no back. Beyond the mops and old bottles it opens into an endless night.

Sarah is gleaming in the dark, giving off light like a star. There is someone in the cupboard with her. He is tall and still. I am afraid, but my feelings are faint, drowned by Sarah Buchanan's. He says, *Come here.* She says, *But it is wrong.* Sarah and I move towards Mr. MacRaith. Sarah becomes smoke and winds herself all about him, burning brighter and brighter . . .

The schoolyard is welcome, cold and real about me. I am shaken by strange sensations. I elbow Sarah hard in the ribs for making me feel them.

I am grasped firmly by the sleeve, pulled aloft and everything seems to fall apart. I blink in the watery autumn day. Mr. MacRaith is holding Abel by the elbow. Dinah is red, glowering. Abel looks with interest at Sarah Buchanan, who is crying. Her friends have made themselves scarce. Her white ankle socks are covered with mud, her fancy yellow dress is torn at the hem, and not in a way she can repair. Sarah's mother will have wanted to let it out for turns yet. Now it's only fit for scraps.

Mr. MacRaith looks at his son with stern eyes. Jamie looks back. He is pretending that he is not afraid. "Father," he says. "It was not Dinah's fault."

"After school," Mr. MacRaith says. "All of you."

Sarah Buchanan continues to cry. "Please," she says. "I have never been kept after school." I catch Abel's eye and we smirk a little. The things the Impure care about.

Mr. MacRaith pays Sarah no mind. He walks like a thin bird into the schoolhouse.

Abel is not looking at me any longer. He is watching Dinah and Jamie. They stand face-to-face, close enough to breathe one another's breath. Dinah stands on her toes. Her lips move by Jamie's ear.

Abel's eyes continue to stare but he has gone. There is no one behind his face. He did not know about Dinah and Jamie Mac-Raith.

* * *

When children are doing nothing, says the blackboard, *they are doing mischief. When children are doing nothing, they are doing mischief. When . . .*

The chalk squeaks as I write. Beside me, Abel shakes his white hair out of his eyes. His handwriting is ornate, crossing over my neat letters.

Mr. MacRaith is caning Sarah Buchanan across her palm. She is crying, of course. I did not cry, nor did Abel or Jamie.

Sarah sobs as he delivers the last blow, then comes to stand beside me at the chalkboard. Her shoulders judder with tears. She turns her pure blue gaze on me and says in a low tone, "I'm going to get out of this godforsaken place. I will have furs and a car and go on the stage." Her eyes look through me into a time and worlds that have not yet come to pass.

"Shut up," I say. "You talk too much." I suck my stinging hand and wonder about what I saw in Sarah Buchanan's mind. Sarah thought that Mr. MacRaith would not punish her because she burst into stars all over him in the darkness of the cupboard. She was wrong.

Mr. MacRaith says, "Dinah Bearings."

Dinah comes forward, eyes large, lips bloodless. Dinah will not cry either. She has pride.

"You are to have a hundred strokes," Mr. MacRaith says.

I had fifty and my hand is swollen like salt beef. "That is twice the number of strokes we had," I say to Mr. MacRaith.

Everyone in the room looks at me in surprise, as if a chair had spoken.

"It's not right to give Dinah more," I say reasonably. "We all fought."

"Father," says Jamie.

Mr. MacRaith says, "One more word from you, my son, and it will be double again."

I understand, then, that he too saw Jamie and Dinah in the schoolyard. He takes up the tawse, its double-tongued strap.

Dinah puts out her hand, biting her lip.

Mr. MacRaith says, "You will take the stripes across your back."

"That is not . . ." I say. His hand meets my mouth sharply, the skin of my lip breaks on my teeth.

"Bare your back," he says to Dinah.

Dinah unbuttons her frock and bends forward. Her skin is milk-pale beneath the older bruises, yellow and green, and her spine stands out like rocks above the sea. She does not look like a person now. She looks like something to be punished.

Mr. MacRaith draws back his arm. The tawse whistles through the air, lands with a *crack* like winter twigs breaking. He puts his weight behind each blow, gives a little grunt as each one falls. Beating Dinah gives Mr. MacRaith a feeling like bloodshed.

"Keep away from God-fearing souls," he says, matching each word to a blow. Dinah clutches her thin cotton dress to her chest. Tears well up in her eyes but do not fall.

It seems to go on for ever.

* * *

On the walk home we are quiet. Elizabeth stays so close to Dinah and me that she bumps into us, burying her nose in my back. She waited by the school gates and did not see the beating, but she knows that something is wrong.

Dinah touches Abel's shoulder. "Abel," she says. He shrugs her off and walks ahead into the dark.

"What will we tell Uncle?" Dinah asks. "He will see your lip, the new bruises."

"We will have to lie," I say. "Otherwise . . ." I do not need to finish the sentence. Dinah shivers.

"We will say Baby Elizabeth climbed a tree to reach a blackbird with a broken leg," I say. "You know how she likes birds. We climbed after her and the bough could not take our weight and we all fell."

Dinah considers. "Will he see?"

"I do not think he sees what happens away from the isle," I reply. "Why must we give account of one another if he does?"

"Uncle would not like what happened today," she says, shivering. "Not at all. He would not like that we broke your shunning, that we were all in trouble, together. I will have to shun you again."

"I know." I take her hand and squeeze it. "Mr. MacRaith is a slug."

Dinah smiles. Her lips are thin with pain. "It was nice of you to try to stop him, Eve."

I swing her hand in the air and she laughs a little. Our locked fists are dark against the grey dusk and the first stars are blooming. My lip hurts where Mr. MacRaith broke it; my hand sings with his blows. But I cannot help a little spurt of gladness. It is nice to be seen once more and to have Dinah to myself.

* * *

Altnaharra. The castle's broken, beloved shape. Candles are lit in the windows. Home. Uncle is there. He waits on the isle at the head of the causeway. The light of his torch falls warm across the water, on our faces. We stand before him in order of age, the evening sea kisses our ankles. My heart swells under his gaze.

"It is nearly dark," the Adder says. "Your lip, Eve. Tell me."

I wait, gazing at him.

"I lift your shun," he says after a moment. Sudden irritation needles me. All that misery and he had forgotten my shun.

"We were walking from school," I say. "Elizabeth saw a blackbird with a broken leg . . ." It is surprisingly easy. As I tell it I feel the forest light on my face. See the orange beak of the blackbird, hear its anguished trills.

Uncle puts a hand on my head. "My pups," he says. "The impure world is dangerous indeed. Alice will clean your wounds. But first, come to me." Uncle's arms are warm.

Abel does not come into Uncle's arms. Torchlight flickers upon him. His eyes are hollow caves. "I must give my account, Uncle," he says. "Eve is lying."

* * *

Nora heats pine tar in a bucket over the fire in the Great Hall. It fills the air with its sharp green scent.

"Do not cry," Uncle says to us. "It is not your fault. It is mine. I have been too sparing with you all. Love has guided me, not duty."

Dinah's head droops as if it is too heavy for her neck. She moves very slowly, as she does when she is afraid. She takes Abel's sleeve. I hear her whisper, "You did not mean to tell about Jamie, did you? You did not mean to put me on Wane." He sits in the corner, arms wrapped about his knees and will not look at her. He does not seem pleased by his victory. A touch of the eye lingers in me. In Abel's mind two pictures are laid over one another: a woman holding a kitten with a notched ear, and Dinah with Jamie MacRaith. Two sides of the same thing.

Dinah and I will go on Wane for three days and three nights for attracting the notice of the Impure. But I will have an extra day and night for the lie. Four days, Four nights. My knees are weak. None of us has ever done longer than two days and two nights.

When the bucket has been warmed by the flames, Dinah and I pick it up. It swings heavy in our trembling arms.

Uncle says, "Abel, come."

Abel starts up. "But I gave true account, Uncle," he says.

"That is why you shall have only one day and one night," Uncle says.

Abel looks ill. He does not argue.

We go out of the great door to the eastern wall, down the steps cut into the rock, through the foundations of the castle to the wooden door barred with iron. Dinah breathes fast at my side.

The stone cellar is cool. Torchlight flickers on the cheeses hanging in their waxy skins, the wooden barrels, the bags of wool. In the centre of the room is the trapdoor.

Uncle dips his fingers into the warm pitch. He gently daubs my lips, covering them with a layer of pine tar. My eyes water at the stink. The tar hardens quickly in the cool air. I always feel panic at this moment, that I will suffocate. I breathe slowly as Uncle seals Dinah's mouth, then Abel's. He opens the trapdoor to the Wane place.

I climb down the iron ladder affixed to the wall. Dinah follows. The light of the world recedes. We are in a recess hewn of rock, below the cellar. The dark chamber is large enough for four to lie down at once. We have discovered that over the years. A freshwater spring runs silent along one side. The castle and the isle are named after it. *Allt na h-Eirbhe*, "the stream that runs under the boundary wall."

I do not know when the Wane place was made, but it was designed for punishment. There are old marks chiselled on the walls. Strikes, counting off days. An elaborate drawing of a ship with sails. Someone has carved with great effort the word *Marguerite* into the stone.

Uncle touches us each on the brow and then he is gone. Far above, the trapdoor closes. The sound of the bolt going home. We are alone in the dark, alone with our breath. Dinah's heart drums at my side like a rabbit running. Abel cries. The cold seems to stun my thoughts, my blood.

Wane is fasting. Our mouths are sealed. We may not eat or drink. Wane is cleansing. It releases the benison and washes away impurity, as the moon must wane to darkness so that it may wax silver once more. Wane is reflection. We may not talk or sleep. If we lie still and listen, the sea will speak and His voice will come into our hearts. Wane is absolution. At the end, Uncle will purify us.

Time quickly drifts into nothing. Hours and nights and days roll on, but here in the cellar they are all the same. Day can be glimpsed only as fine cracks around the trapdoor. The air is thick with the stink of pitch and with our fear. The hunger is bad but the worst thing is the loneliness; drifting for so long in the shadows of my mind. I recite the names of elephants to myself. *Loxodonta, Sumatranus, Maximus.* I claw my belly. It seems to be sticking to my spine.

Beside me Dinah moans through her covered mouth. She has entered a kind of half-dream in which she thinks that the reekling is here in the dark with us. But when she goes quiet, in her clear moments, I know that she is thinking of Abel. Hurt radiates from her. How could he do it?

The trapdoor opens, releasing the scent of rain on the earth. A day and a night gone. Abel is taken away.

The flame of my anger is white. It burns small and fierce at the heart of me. This is all Mr. MacRaith's fault. Uncle had no choice, I can see that. And Abel is Abel. Mr. MacRaith must suffer. I cannot harm him with my hands, so I must find another way. How to do it? As the light of summer blooms and fades and blooms again in the crack around the trapdoor, I think. But everything is clouded with hunger and thirst, with fear. My thoughts run purposeless and wild, gulls scattered by a stone.

I begin to lose the names of things. What is that little round object on my cuff which holds the ends together? Who is with me in the dark, breathing hot tears into my neck? Whoever it is, I must protect her. Someone must suffer for this. For what? There is an answer, I know it—if I could just recall the question.

There is blinding light and the other one is taken away into the world. She cries out, and then I am alone.

After that, my mind becomes useless, liquid. I spin through space, not separate from the rock or the air but part of it. I have always been here. I will always be here. My mouth is sour and poisonous. I cannot breathe. I will die. Perhaps it has already happened.

I take my little knife from my cuff and thrust the tip into my thumb. The blood rises. It courses through me, wonderful, like food or warmth. My limbs still ache with confinement and my head sings with thirst, but I am back. I know where and when I am.

* * *

Uncle releases me early on the fourth morning. I cower in the scant light and my hands are weak on the cold rungs of the ladder. In the end he pulls me up like a fish on a line.

A late moon hangs low in the brightening air. I greet the sky with a sob and try to quiet my shaking limbs. The others are all there, strange, wavering shapes. My eyes cannot make sense of things.

I smell ash and fat, the paste Alice uses to gently lift the hardened sap. My skin burns as she peels it away. I gasp. The fresh air is cold, sweet on my dry tongue. Alice tips water into my cracked mouth, forces me to take tiny sips. I would swallow it cup and all if I could.

The clay knocks against my teeth, soft in my gums. They are always loose after Wane.

Uncle says, "I must speak to Eve alone."

He takes me up the rise to where the ruins sit amid the twining embrace of the vines. The bees are awake. They crawl busily through the purple petals.

"The flowers feed the little sisters, just as the root of this plant nurtured me when first I came to Altnaharra," Uncle says. He sighs. "It came to you again."

"Yes," I whisper. "I am sorry."

He offers me honey on his fingers. "Give me your blade."

I take the honey. He points to a fat bee, busy in the heart of a blossom. "Here," he says. "Look at her. Do not take your eyes from her." He raises blood on my arm. More than usual, a thin stream running eager to the earth.

The bee takes wing. She flies towards my face. I gasp and flinch.

"Do not move," says Uncle.

The bee flies into my skull as though my eye were made of cloud. Or is it me who flies into her?

I am in a room made of a thousand panes of glass. I see shapes and colours I have not dreamt of. My gossamer wings whir; I rub my furred legs against one another.

A screaming begins. The cacophony of a hundred thousand voices shouting instructions in an alien tongue. I have no choice; my blood and nerves have become the voices. If they told me to fly into an open fire I would do it. I am not one but many, feeding the great, combed entity of the hive. Always following the flow, full of needs and commands I cannot understand. Even as I try, the language is changing me. It is like being abandoned on a distant star.

I struggle against the tide of bee song. There is a series of cracks, deafening, and I lie panting and wretched on the sandy cliff. The friendly hum of the hive is all about me.

"What did you see?" he asks.

"I was trapped." My teeth chatter and I can hardly say the words. "I could not get out. They were all screaming, screaming."

"That is power," he says. "Do you still want it?"

"Yes."

He sighs. "You are at war with yourself, Eve. The impure world has its hooks in you. You must choose. Follow His signs."

The metal song of the bees stings my mind long after.

DINAH

1921

ON her first birthday, I will take my daughter to the forest.

I know that Rose will say "no," or "let us go together on my day off," or "it is raining." So after breakfast, while Rose is elbow-deep in dishwater, I put what I need in my pockets. I take Mary from the crib and wrap her in woollens, in oilcloth to keep her dry. I put her little rain hat on her. I put on her mittens and socks. I want to see her in a forest for the first time. It is an old forest. Perhaps I will know who I am, there. I do not recognise myself in this soft land of fields and neat coppices. I want the sea, but a forest will have to do.

The garden gate clicks shut behind us. We run down the little lane to the station. On this grey Sunday the platform is empty, and as we board the train, I am filled with the vertigo of freedom.

Two stops only. The name of the station half-obscured by a branch of rowan. We follow the lane, which turns into a track. The fence ends, and here we are, in the woods.

We walk in light rain through a deserted cathedral of turning leaves. Mary talks to the trees, she reaches for them. They are the thing that has been missing. Her pleasure changes everything and the grey day comes alive. Mary pushes her hat off with an impatient hand. She does not seem to care that the rain is falling on her silken head. I put the hat back on and her face crumples with misery.

I give her a spray of yellow beech leaves on a delicate stem. She puts them in her mouth. Are beech leaves poisonous? I take them from her.

We walk on and on, Mary heavy on my hip. I did not bring the pram. I wanted to walk in the wild with my daughter in my arms. I am still new to this, motherhood, and I did not consider how tired I would become, how my arms would ache. The earth pulls at my limbs. How long have we walked? We take shelter at the foot of a spreading oak.

"I do not have a birthday," I say to Mary. "I will make sure that you have everything I did not have." She touches my face with a mittened fist. I am breathless with love and exhaustion. During the first months I could not let her out of my sight and slept with one hand always on her foot or some other part of her.

I change Mary, then wrap her up again in her cocoon of oil-cloth and flannel, making her warm and dry. I feed her spoonfuls of chicken mashed up with bread and broth. I forgot to bring anything for myself so I eat what she leaves. I am not good with food. It slips my mind. When I do eat I cannot stop; my body never learned how.

A deer emerges from the undergrowth, legs slender as young branches, muzzle dark and delicate. She catches our scent and leaps away, disappearing into the amber wood. Blackbirds sing sharp against the rainfall. At length sleep comes, borne on these sounds.

A looming shadow. Altnaharra is all about me in the storm, and she is there, death in her hand. She holds it high, shining in the night. I feel it as if it has already happened, the piercing pain, the sudden silence of my heart, the sweet decay that begins to spread in me as I die. The isle lies atop everything—then it is gone. Yellow wood, soft rainfall.

* * *

In the here and now a man is leaning over me. His breath smells of rot. He is thin. Odd parts of him are missing: the top of his left ear, some of his cheek, a portion of his eyebrow, as though he is gradually being eaten away.

Wet leaves slide beneath my feet as I start up. Mary begins to cry. I hold her fast to me, close to my thundering heart. The battered locket gleams silver on my collarbone. I always wear it hidden, next to my skin. Did he touch me?

"Penny for an old soldier," he says. Autumn leaves cling to him all over. He must sleep here. Perhaps this is his place and I have taken it.

"No," I say. There are three shillings in my purse—enough to buy cocoa, milk, bread and butter for supper. There is nothing to spare.

He looks me over. His gaze rests on my darned skirt, my mended cuffs. On Mary's small face. It lingers longest on the black patch that covers the place where my right eye once was. It is the one thing I cannot disguise. In his gaze is a kind of recognition. We have both seen things we should not have seen. I see in his look how dangerous the world is for a woman alone with a child.

I make to slip the knife from my cuff, but the place where the blade should sit is bare. I stopped carrying it after I left Altnaharra. What good is a knife? She killed us anyway.

"It was in the papers," he says. "A girl with one eye. She was a murderer, I think. No, that wasn't it. She was the only one to live. A soft, pretty sort of girl, much like you."

"Leave us be," I say. What will happen, here?

Something moves in his face. He holds up shaking hands. "I mean you no harm," he says. He is older than I first thought, by thirty years or so. "I have a daughter and a granddaughter, too. May I walk you somewhere?"

"No." I gather Mary and hurry away from him through the tunnel of golden leaves. Dusk is coming and the woods are alive with shadow. I look behind every few paces but no one is following. He is just an old man. It is not him I fear, really. I am waiting for her to step from the trees and stride towards me, gleaming silver in her hand.

She is dead. She cannot hurt me. But I take her with me wherever I go.

I reach the station as the train roars in. Third class is welcome, smelling of face powder, engine oil and warmth. I feed Mary rice soaked in milk.

The conductor comes, his face red and pouched. When I reach into my coat pockets I find them empty. My purse is gone and with it my ticket. He had already taken it while I slept, the eaten-away man. Or perhaps I am wrong and my purse is lying beneath the oak tree, covered by fallen leaves.

*   *   *

The clouds have parted, the lane is filled with moonlight. I am nearing home. Each blade, each leaf etched as if on glass. I do not recall how I got here. What passed between the train and now is gone. This happens. My mind has too much in it and there is no room for new things. Mary is so very heavy in my trembling arms. She cries harder with each step. The dead are with me, too. In the shadows beneath the hedge, in the sky, in my own shadow behind me, at my ear. I want to run, but who or what would give chase?

The windows of home are blurred stars. Rose is there, black against the lamplight.

She runs to us. "Dinah! It is gone seven. Do not ever do that again. Where have you been?"

"I don't know," I say. Mary screams and writhes in my arms. I try to explain about the woods, how tired I was, the trees, the man. I can tell by Rose's face that I am not doing well.

"Where is the bread, the milk? There is nothing in the house."

"The man stole the money," I say.

I hear in her silence how little we have; how precious those three shillings were.

"Can I not have peace," I shout. "A walk, by myself?" I cannot see her through my tears.

She takes Mary from me. "What have you dressed her in? She needs changing."

Rose unwraps a weeping Mary on the kitchen table.

"I wanted to make a new memory," I say. "One without her in it."

Every day is full of a thousand perils. Light glancing off window-panes, a white apron flickering, the taste of honey. Innocent-seeming, but all a violent transport to the past.

Mary quiets as Rose undresses her. Her skin is flushed. Rose draws cool water into a saucepan. I broke all the bowls last week. I dimly recall doing it.

"I did not want her to be cold," I say.

"She wasn't cold. She was too hot. Couldn't you tell?" But every-thing feels too warm to me. The house, the air outside, the rain.

"I wanted her to have a birthday," I say.

"She's a baby," Rose says. "She doesn't know about birthdays. She won't remember. She needs a roof over her head and not to be smoth-ered in oilcloth, out sleeping in the rain. Neither of you should be doing those things."

"Did I do her harm?" My throat is closed, I cannot breathe.

Rose's hand on my back. "No," she says. The edge is gone from her voice. "I don't think so. But you cannot run off like that."

We hold tightly to one another.

"You should leave us," I say. "I have such things in me and I can barely keep them caged."

She shakes her head.

I say into her shoulder, "I won't do it again."

"You won't mean to," she says.

Mary sleeps in her crib in the corner. The fire crackles in the tiny hearth. Rose is mending, fingers nimble in the firelight, rough with work. Sometimes I wonder how to forgive her, for putting me so in her debt.

Rose is tireless. She milks cows at the dairy down the lane. She cares for Mary. She does the board and the planchette for the ladies in the village. Half an hour for a shilling, but she won't take the shilling if the dead don't talk. And they are a silent lot. I am no help to her. Everything must be done in her name. Bills, the cottage.

How I burned for freedom once. Now I hold it in my hands, useless—like wanting a kitten and being given its corpse.

The needle draws the thread high, gleaming in the warm light. I shiver; it is too like the other thing.

"You are safe here," Rose tells me when I wake in the night. "You are safe," she tells me when I cower in a storm. But my body knows different. I am always in danger.

"On the isle we did not believe in such things as ghosts," I say. "But we were wrong. She is here. She touches me."

Rose glances up, her green eyes unreadable. "If she is walking, it is because you won't let her rest."

"Do you feel her?" I ask.

"No."

I go to the iron-bound chest in the corner. I take the planchette and the board from their red velvet box. I have never liked these things. They belonged to others before Rose. The letters of the board are faded, worn away by desperate fingers. It has a hateful feel. Too much hope has been dashed on its pocked surface, years of lies have soaked into the wood.

"Ask her to come," I say.

Rose takes the objects from my hands. She wraps them in a blanket and puts the bundle on the windowsill behind her. She turns to me. "I will not," she says. "If I ask, anyone may answer."

"But . . ."

"If you do not leave it be," Rose says, "I will take that child from her cradle and walk out with her into the night and you will never see me again. Do you understand? I will *not* try. Swear you will not either."

"I swear," I say.

"Mean it."

"I swear on the dead. On all I have."

"We c-can't go on as we are." Rose's stammer chases through the words. It comes rarely now. Usually she is too tired to stutter. "This is no life for me or for you. It will be no life for Mary."

The anger rises, smouldering. "It has not been a year yet. Am I not entitled to some patience?"

"It is not a matter of patience," she says. "It is what I can take."

"I do not know what to do," I say. Time is like standing in the rain. All the moments. I can't grasp each raindrop in my fists.

"You must find a way," she says. "It did not happen only to you. I live with it too. You make sure of that." Rose rises, folds her mending and gently lifts Mary from the crib. "Come to bed," she says.

I shake my head. Thoughts are strongest in the darkness; they stroke me, cold-fingered.

Rose turns without a word and goes.

I sit before the fire. In its flames I can see faces and people. She is there among them, of course. Evelyn is never far away.

"I must shed you," I tell her. "Like a skin."

The usual words go through my mind. Noose, river, powder, cliff. None of them is any good. I do not want to die, but I do not know how to live. I cannot lose any more of Mary's childhood.

If there is no room left in my head, I must make some. The thought makes me breathless and I laugh a little.

I fetch paper and a pen. Only he will do. There is no one else left.

My heart is a dark passage, I write, *lined with ranks of gleaming jars.* I write of the day I was found by Jamie MacRaith in the dawn.

Memory, that shaken, jagged thing, captured by words. I give him the fear, blood, doubt. The sound of the blade piercing my eye. The day my imprisonment ended. The years contained as if by walls; dark days when the wind in my ears was the very sound of madness. Altnaharra nearly killed me more than once. I don't know which is worse—suffering or the memory of it. Memory, perhaps, because it does not end.

Now it is he who will not rest. I imagine him sitting, reading. I picture his face as my words burrow into him, fuse with his blood and nerves, become little snaps of electricity exploding in his head. It is not just a letter. It is an act of power. Uncle taught us that.

Something begins to ease with the scratching of the pen. A strange, still feeling steals through me, rib by rib. It is a moment before I can name it: peace.

Light is dawning in the east when it is done. I put the lamps out, wearier than death, and feel my way up the rickety stairs. I am so tired I seem to disappear as I go. I do not feel my head touch the pillow.

EVELYN

1917

SOFT mist pats the walls, looking for entry. The windows are filled with white whorls, moving.

I kneel before Uncle. Outside the circle of firelight the air is so cold I feel that I am breathing in ice. But I will not show it. I grasp the pen hard so that the shivering does not reach my hand. He is showing me power.

"MacRaith had no right to touch you," says Uncle. "Any of you. He must be held to account." He looks so sad that my anger wants to burst through my chest. Mr. MacRaith hurt Dinah and now he is hurting Uncle.

I write as Uncle speaks. We put down what Mr. MacRaith and Sarah Buchanan do in the cupboard. How she bursts into stars all over him. He tells me the words to use. I have seen these words carved into the schoolyard fence. Uncle tells me to write that Sarah has a baby in her.

In the corner Dinah pauses over her mending. She feels it as I do, the transmission. The paper becomes one with Uncle's will.

"Do not be seen." Uncle holds the door open. The mist reaches white fingers over the threshold. Like a person, it has ideas.

"I could go when it lifts," I say.

"He tests us in many ways," Uncle says. "This is meant. Look for His sign."

I put the note inside my shirt beside my heart.

The sea is black and hungry on the causeway. The walk to Loyal is long; twice I lose the path and am left alone in the muffling white. All I can hear is my breath. I think I will die out here. People do. I move step by step until I feel the stony way beneath my feet again. The four miles seem like a lifetime spent in a dead world.

In Loyal the mist lies along the street like sediment. The small white houses are blinded with shutters and the boats and rigs in the harbour are faint drawings in the gloom. No one is abroad. That is why Uncle wished me to go now.

I count the houses. Three to the left of old Irish Dromgoole's shop is the Buchanans'. I lift the letter flap and slide in the note. Doing it gives me a strange feeling, as if I have dropped a part of myself into their house. I ease the flap back down. A tiny click as it settles. I shut the gate behind me. It is done.

The note is addressed to Hamish Buchanan, Sarah's pa. I wonder how long it will take for something to happen. Sarah may recognise my writing. Part of me hopes that she does.

"What are you doing here?" Sarah is very close to me. Her eyes are cold globes.

"I came to make amends," I say. "I am sorry for the fight." Did she see me deliver the letter?

She looks at me without feeling. "I do not care about your apology," she says. "You are the devil's brood, Pa says. You worship the snake from the garden. You will all burn in Hell."

"We will not," I say, despite myself.

"I hope it hurts. I hope your skin cracks and goes black and your hair catches fire. I hope you have to watch your own insides being boiled before your eyes."

What will Sarah's punishment be? Perhaps her pa will whip her. Perhaps he will lock her up without supper, like Wane.

As I leave the village the mist lifts like a curtain. Flags of cloud race in the high blue sky. I have never known mist to vanish so. In these parts it usually lingers for days.

I run back along the shining sea.

* * *

In the kitchen Dinah is peeling potatoes. Abel hovers nearby. He offers her a piece of shortbread pastry he has scavenged from Uncle's lunch. My mouth waters at the sight of it.

"Dinah," Abel says. "The blackberries may be ready under Arden-tinny. Shall we go and see? Let's ask Uncle if we may have a black-berry day."

Dinah loves blackberries, but she stares through Abel as though he were mist.

"I am sorry, Dinah," he whispers. "I did not mean it."

I have been thinking of how Abel must pay, but there is no need. Dinah has put her own shun on him and she shows no sign of breaking it. I sit down next to Dinah. She hands me a potato and a knife.

"Let us ask Uncle if we may pick blackberries this afternoon," I say to her.

A moment of hesitation and then she nods. "Yes," she says.

I pluck the pastry from Abel's still-open palm. It crumbles sweet and buttery in my mouth. I have done His will and am rewarded.

* * *

Woken by weeping. Flickering light spills under the door. A candle in the corridor, held by a shaking hand.

"No," someone says. It is Nora or Alice but I cannot tell which. She breathes in shudders. "Don't."

"Come along," Uncle says. He sounds weary. "Come and rest, my dear."

"They are children," the woman says.

The sobbing recedes down the corridor. Uncle's door opens and closes. Behind it the voice becomes shrill and fierce. It is met by Uncle's low tones. Soothing.

A hand creeps into mine. Dinah is awake, too. I hold it tightly, grateful. Dinah lights the candle, even though that is not allowed. In the uncertain light she looks very young.

"Why are they fighting?" Dinah says, hushed. "Who would argue with Uncle?"

"I do not know."

Quiet steps approach our door.

"Someone is coming."

Dinah blows out the candle and we dive beneath the blanket. The door creaks open.

"I smell the wick," Nora says. "I know you've just had the candle lit." But she does not scold. "Light it again. We must talk." Her face leaps into view, hollows glowing. She sits on the end of our bed. She seems composed, her face smooth and unmarked, grey eyes large and clear. She does not look as though she has been weeping. But I can never be sure with Nora.

Nora says, "I have come to tell you about how the sea comes in, and your duty."

I listen in growing disbelief. "Like Sarah and Mr. MacRaith? Like the sheep!"

"It is our power and our purpose," Nora says. "To bring forth children from the sea. It is our honour to be His vessels. He will speak the hour. You will choose someone, as Alice and I chose your Uncle. Then you will bring a child from the ocean and the isle will be glad."

"How do we choose?" asks Dinah.

"The Adder will guide you," says Nora. "It is a serious choice. You cannot have just a handsome face!" Dinah giggles and Nora smiles. They are flushed and gossipy. I curl up into a ball.

After Nora goes we lie in silence.

"Dinah," I say after a time. "Do you think you can . . . do the duty?" Even the word lights a little cold flame of fear in my stomach.

"I suppose so," says Dinah. "You have to, so that the sea can bring you a baby. Just think, a nice baby! I have never met a baby, but I think I would know how to take care of one."

"Would you?" I hear the doubt in my voice.

"Yes," says Dinah softly. "I would."

"Why must the duty only make babies?" I say. "If it made porpoises or spider monkeys . . ."

"You are only a little slug," Dinah says. "You have not even had your time yet. You will understand one day."

In the forgiving dark, I slip my little knife out from my cuff. Blood, a few drops hidden in a dark corner. Warmth courses through me and I feel better after that.

* * *

The bad dream again; the darkness humming, her soft presence all about me. The sadness is unbearable.

Someone puts a finger across my lips, breathes *quiet* in my ear. Hands on me in the pitch-black. She has followed me out of the dream and into the world.

"Eve," Alice says. "Come, now."

"Come where?"

"We must go on a journey," Alice says. "It will be strange, but at the end of it you will have food to eat and other children to play with. Won't you like that?" She tries to pull me out of the bed. "Do hurry up."

"But," I say, practical, "it is night."

Dinah stirs sleepily. "Eve," she says. "Shh."

"I will keep you safe," Alice whispers. "Uncle wishes us to go. He needs us to do something special for him. It is very important." I feel her, alert, listening for approach. She strokes my head. "Please," she whispers, "I know that you are afraid, darling. I know it seems impossible. But trust me, we must go *now*. Take my hand. Out of the bed you come. Very good! We will take one step together. See? And now another. And faster, a little . . ."

Alice hurries me down the stairs. The coals of the fire in the hall bathe the walls in crimson. Alice has a lumpy bundle on her back. Things tied up in an old blanket. She has rolled everything up in a hurry. She is stealing me.

I tear my hand from hers and scream.

Uncle is here, a mountain against the darkness. His arm swings like a pendulum and his fist connects with Alice's jaw. It sounds like an axe hitting the block. She stumbles and falls. He draws back his arm again but she crawls away with surprising speed. Then she is up, and the air shivers with her passage. The front door crashes open. Uncle runs from the hall after her and then they are gone.

I bank the fire, shivering. I do not understand what is happening. Dinah comes, trailing her blanket. We huddle under it together. Then Elizabeth trots down, and Abel, their hair crazed, eyes weak with sleep. Nora arrives. She glowers, running to the door at every sound from outside.

"What is happening?" Abel asks.

"Alice has run away," I say. At the same time Nora says, "Alice is dead."

* * *

Uncle returns before dawn. There is something dark on his sleeve that smells of tin. Did Uncle shed blood? "She is gone," he says. "You did right to call for me, Eve."

"You hit her," I say.

Uncle puts his hand over his eyes. He sighs, sounding tired. "I could not think how else to stop her." He takes me in his familiar arms. "It is very dark out there, and I knew she might come to harm. I called for her to come back. I chased her for miles. But with my lame leg, I was no match for her. The further she ran the weaker the benison became. The beasts of the impure world ran after her on long, dark limbs, their eyes full of fire. I tried to protect her but it was too late. I found her at the bottom of a gully. Her neck was broken. The night beasts had driven her to her death."

It is not possible that Alice is no longer alive. Her assessing blue eyes, her slim hands, her voice.

Uncle says, "I am sorry, little Eve. But I am here with you."

I hit Uncle as hard as I can in the chest. I struggle in his arms. "I do not want you," I say. "I want Alice back." I am aghast at myself. But it must be someone's fault.

Uncle looms like a tower. "We are bound, you and I," he says. The traces of the Adder's voice are like scratches across glass. "You cannot undo it. Nor would I wish it, no matter how many times you hit me."

I cannot stop the sounds that are coming from me. Everything is bad.

"Evelyn," says Nora through her teeth, "we are all worn to a thread."

Uncle crouches and looks me in the eye. "I know," he says. "It is sad to lose a friend. But we who remain are here together. You are loved. We will not leave you." Uncle looks at Abel, Nora, Elizabeth. "Come, my pups. Come."

We hold one another. Dinah's heart beats hard against my shoulder. Abel's breath has a wet catch to it. They are sad too. That makes it better somehow.

"We will bid Alice farewell at dusk," Uncle says. "We will send her off with fire."

* * *

We burn Alice among the standing stones at sunset. Uncle brings the bowl and we eat sacred honey from his fingers. Dinah and I throw branches of alder and wych elm on the pyre. The benison spreads its golden tongues across the lines of the circle into me, and all of us. Atop the wood sits Alice's body, draped in white, with all her possessions. There are not many. Boots, comb, shawl. Uncle would not let us see the body. Too horrible, he said, what they did to her.

It smoulders. Damp, like everything at Altnaharra. We run fast about the fire, dizzy in the heavy smoke. It catches, roars up, the heat strange on our faces. Fragrant smoke, thick on the damp air. Alice will not see His return. She is simply ended. I cry. Why did she run from us, who loved her best? Next to me Abel cries too. His nose and eyes are sore pink in his pale face. Nora holds Dinah. Elizabeth will not leave Uncle's side. She makes a small yowling noise.

Nora and the Adder sing to the world and the benison comes. On the song Alice goes from the isle, drifts, windswept, out to sea.

* * *

Another cold dawn. The useless cry that begins the day. Knees on the cold pine, mind still half-shrouded in night. The draught strokes his forehead where it rests against the boards. So many crannies and draughts, this house. Was it ever warm? O Lord. Where are You? He is abandoned. Forgiveness is denied.

Before the mirror, his face is stippled with white beard. When did he grow old? Each day he comes closer to judgement. Even the cracks in the shaving soap seem cruel.

In Jamie's room the early light falls across his sleeping face. The familiar planes of it, his bones, the familiar mingling of love and horror. My son. This world is too perilous. Better that he should have remained unborn. *Or that he were already with God, safe from sin. Jamie's brown forelock lies over his nose, moves with his warm breath. His hair is far too long.*

He reaches to brush the hair from his son's face, but stays his hand. Tenderness is untruth. The strap is honest. Sinners, all. He is heartsick with shame. Guilt wraps around him, a pulsing cowl. He will never be free. Temptation came to him at around Jamie's age, marched beside him, as constant as God. Two companions—the Lord and his desires. The one began to rule him, now the other is gone. Spare Jamie that, *he prays.* Make him a better man than I. *If that cannot be done, well, he must beat the girl Dinah until she cannot recall Jamie's name.*

He eats in the kitchen, standing because he has never liked this room. It was always hers and everything in it still sings, Louisa, Louisa. *Her cold breath in the kettle. The sound of her skirts in the pantry. Dead hands reaching from the bread bin. He does not think she went to Him when she died. He always suspected she might not. She was a weak woman. Married less than seven years when the fever took her. He cannot summon her face, but he sees her each day—the sullen look in Jamie's eyes, his long silences full of something.*

They could afford to moon, the two of them, as long as he kept his hand on the tiller. She resented discipline, as Jamie does. But without it they would drift, then founder. The cow needs milking, the rent paying, the linen laundering, the gatepost mending, the lessons teaching, the potatoes digging, the church attending, the tithes finding, the prayers saying . . . All the labour and care of a Christian man for those who depend on him. There is never thanks for it in this life.

Well, there you are, and the cow needs milking this very moment.

He goes out into the sunrise. These early moments alone in His creation are a stolen solitary pleasure. He walks towards the pasture at the edge of the village where the cow is kept. At such times this thought often wanders through—perhaps I will not stop at the borders of Loyal. Perhaps I will walk on and on, down the sea path, on into the world, find some place where yellow-haired girls do not look at me with such eyes. But of course there are yellow-haired girls everywhere.

Morning is a gleam over the water. He stands to watch the miracle. No less a miracle because it happens each day. Everything is lit in splendour. He is blinded by His glory. Fear thou not: for I am with thee.

A voice speaks, as if from the heart of the sunrise. Now is the reckoning, *it says. A figure comes between him and the light.*

He starts back. God? You are returned to me? *The black figure raises both hands behind its head. Sunrise reflected on the blade makes it seem a flaming sword. It is only at the last minute that he sees: not God, not Him at all. But the blade is at his throat and a rough ripping sound spreads through the world. The dawn-lit earth spins before his dying eyes.*

*   *   *

I am upright in bed, my flesh crawling with horror. Dinah stares at me. "Eve," she says. "You were dreaming. You spoke in such a strange voice."

Hector MacRaith the schoolmaster is dead.

The letter was an act of power indeed. It was I who shed MacRaith's blood, though my hand did not wield the knife.

I find Uncle in his chair facing the morning sun. For a moment my eyes are dazzled by the sea behind him. It seems that he is floating an inch or so above the seat.

"Uncle," I say. "Something terrible has happened."

He turns his mild gaze on me. "Yes," he says. "I feel it too."

"Mr. MacRaith is dead," I say. "He was murdered at dawn."

Uncle puts his hand on my head. "My Eve," he says. "His will be done."

"But Uncle, he is *dead*. We did it. The letter—"

He takes my face in both hands. "Never speak of that. You will be blamed."

"I did not know what would happen," I say. "I only wanted him to be punished!"

Uncle sighs. "They will not believe that," he says. "It was full of foul words that a young girl should not know. If they discover that you wrote it they will take you away from here and I will be powerless to stop them."

"I only wrote what you told me to write," I say.

"Evelyn," he says gently.

Shadows swim over my memory. I cannot now recall how events unfolded. But I know I lay in Wane plotting Mr. MacRaith's destruction. I wanted something bad to happen. To him, and to Sarah. So perhaps I did wish for his death.

Uncle is watching me. "Yes," he says, "power has a price. If you travel in that world you will lose parts of this one. Something must always be surrendered." He takes my head in his warm hands and kisses it. His love warms me.

Nora brings the news from Loyal that afternoon. Enough to know that what I saw was true. The path out of the village, the paddock, the unmilked cow, Jamie asleep in his bed, waking to find that the world had changed and his father was no longer in it.

A policeman will come from Inverness, they said.

* * *

There is a murderer on the loose. We are not to wander.

The weather is strange, neither rain nor sun but a low, dull warmth that feels like decay. Tempers grow short. The cream will not churn to butter. The fish in the nets are full of white worms and Haystack the pony has poison in his hoof. He limps and bellows. Hercules will not eat. The frog kicks him as it scrambles about the tank, but still he does not move. The frog dies after two days and Uncle must throw it to the gulls. Some thread has been pulled and we are unravelling at a great rate.

But still someone must go to Loyal to fetch flour and wool and a bucket to replace the one that sprang a hole last week. There is debate about who to send. Dinah says that she will go and Uncle says that she will not, their reason being one and the same, which is Jamie MacRaith.

In the end I take the coins from the kitchen table as they argue and slip out of the castle, down the hill and across the causeway. Perhaps they will still be arguing when I return from Loyal. Perhaps I will be murdered and no one will notice.

*   *   *

I come back through the oak wood, the new bucket clanking painfully against my hip. The wool and the packet of flour rustle inside, whispering against the tin.

The oak wood has a different voice to the beech wood: it sings lovely and low. Beside me the burn rushes cold and above me the canopy is alive, birds shouting overhead. I have no heart for it all today.

A stag beetle stands in the path, his long horns waving. I take him in my hand and he touches my nose cautiously. *Lucanidae.* I wish I were him. Perhaps I could be. Perhaps I will go into him with the eye and not come out, live the rest of my life on the forest floor.

"And in the woods I met a sìdh," says someone. "A wee fairy girl who eats beetles." A shadow falls across the sunlit grass and I look up.

"Good God," he says. A man in a white suit. His eyes are green and tawny like the autumn land. His cream hat is jaunty. A dazzling array of feathered things clings to the band like beautiful insects. Pink, green, blue, gold.

"Apologies," he says. "You remind me of someone I once knew. I would put your friend down. He is about to disappear into the neck of your shirt."

The beetle crawls across my wrist and away, into the shadows.

"This will taste better than a beetle." He puts in my palm a soft black pellet resembling sheep dung. The scent of it is heady. I put it cautiously on my tongue and am caught by ropes of muddy sweetness.

"What is it?"

"Liquorice," he says. "What kind of childhood have you had, young woman, that you don't know the taste of liquorice?" He looks me up and down and his face changes. "That is quite the set of bruises. What is your name?"

"Eve. Evelyn."

"Well, Evelyn, would you like to see my hat?" He hands the hat to me. It is too clean to be real. The little insects made of delicate feathers, the riot of colour, the shining fish hooks within. The best one is iridescent blue and green; all the colours of a kingfisher's back. I stroke it. It gives me a feeling.

We sit on a fallen tree, alive with orange lichen. The man tells me which fish can be caught with each particular lure. *Perch. Trout. Tench. Lamprey. Salmon.* I tell him the proper names for the fish. *Perca, Salmo trutta*, and my favourite, *Tinca tinca*. Around us the woodland murmurs.

The man has very white, straight teeth. If he were an animal he would be a sheepdog, like the ones who pass through Loyal on Saturdays, slipping subtle among the woolly bodies.

"Now, Evelyn," he says. "Why should so knowledgeable a person, with every reason to be pleased with themselves, have a rain cloud above their head?"

"I do not."

"A thunderstorm."

I cannot tell him about Mr. MacRaith, of course. I should say nothing. Strangely I find myself telling him about Alice. Her straight back and her direct gaze. "She is dead," I say. "She fell into a gully and died. We fought and then she ran away. Perhaps if I had not been so angry with her she might still be alive. I could have prevented it."

"One always feels like that," he says.

"Uncle tried to stop her," I say. "He followed her all night. He held her as she died. He had her blood on him when he returned . . ." I shed that too, piece by piece.

"Who is your father, your mother?"

"We do not have such things. Family is impure."

"Who can blame you? Fathers—such a bother. So, your Uncle brought you here to live?"

"No!" I tell him that we are from the sea, then I tell him about the benison, and the Children, and how we are waiting for Him to come. The man listens in silence, bright eyes fixed on mine. No one has ever paid me such close attention.

"It sounds as though you are very peaceful at Altnaharra, in general," he says. "You must have been frightened when the schoolteacher was killed, and so soon after your Alice."

"I did not like Mr. MacRaith. He gave Dinah the tawse. One hundred strokes."

"One wouldn't like him after that," says the man.

"And he was in the cupboard with Sarah Buchanan," I say, gratified. "It gave me a bad feeling."

"You saw them?"

"No." I try to match his casual air. "I just know things. I see with the eye. Uncle is teaching me to use it."

For the first time since we met he takes his gaze from me. His eyes narrow. "Is he, indeed?"

I am frightened. "I do not usually talk so much."

He shakes himself and smiles. "Well," he says, "it is my job to talk to people and make them talk too. I am a policeman, you see. My name is Chief Inspector Black. But I feel that we know one another now, so you may call me Christopher."

"No!" He must have power. He has drawn me out as easily as water from the well.

"I'm afraid so," he says. "But there is no need for alarm. Will you not shake my hand?"

I take it. "You wish to find out who killed Mr. MacRaith," I say carefully. "Do you think that you will?"

"I think I already have," the man says. "There was a note. Well. What you said about the cupboard. It was the last piece of the puzzle."

"I did not say anything."

"Do you know what a microscope is? Perhaps not. I have a feeling that you would like it."

I am wary. I should run. But he is very interesting.

We walk together along the dashing stream. "There was a human hair found on the corpse," he says. "Inside one of the wounds. It is not Mr. MacRaith's hair, so it may belong to the murderer. Hair is unique. Each person's is a different thickness, and has distinguishing marks and characteristics. We are trying to encourage the courts to embrace fingerprinting, too, but it must be softly, softly all the way, with any advance, any innovation. It is so aggravating . . . What was I saying? Oh, yes. Hair is unique. So I am taking hair from everyone who lives nearby. I will compare them all under a microscope, and when I see a match—there we are! We will have someone who, if not guilty, must at least produce an excellent explanation!"

"Are you going to take my hair?"

The man smiles. "I have already taken it," he says, holding something almost invisible between finger and thumb. "This hair holds secrets. I'll show you, in exchange for that penny in your pocket."

"I do not have a penny!"

"Don't you now? Do look."

I put my hand in the pocket of my skirt. In my palm is a shining penny. I look at the man with new respect. He does indeed have power.

"It's settled," he says, plucking the penny from my hand. "I will show you the secret. Come."

* * *

The bothy is dark and filled with fishing clutter. The man's clothes are a riot of colour in the wardrobe in the corner. Mauve, cream, yellow, blue like a clear day.

"Reading a crime is like working out a magic trick," the man says. "You must look where you are not supposed to. The magician is trying to focus your attention *here*," he produces another penny from behind my ear, "while the real trick is happening elsewhere."

"Where is the real trick?" I ask.

"Sometimes you must wait," he says. "You don't know until later."

He leads me to a bare pine table set beneath the window. On it stands a contraption of golden metal.

"This is the microscope," the man says.

Clipped to pieces of bright card, held between two plates of glass, are locks of hair. Familiar names stare up, written in the policeman's elegant hand. MacRaith, Buchanan, Dromgoole.

"Who did you think I was?" I ask.

"I beg your pardon?"

"In the wood when you saw me you thought I was someone else. Who?"

He writes *Bearings, E.* on a piece of card. "Here is the secret," he says.

In the brightness of the microscope the hair looks thick and dead, covered with mysterious patterns like the skin of an adder.

"We can identify a person from a single strand of hair," says Christopher Black. "What is the thickness of the cuticle? How dense is the pigment in the cortex? What is the diameter of the medulla? Sometimes there are other secrets hidden there—whether someone has been ill, for instance, whether a woman has had a permanent wave, whether the hair was torn from the head."

It is another way of seeing, like the eye. "I like it," I tell him.

"I like it too," he says. "It is the beautiful evidence of God's logical hand." He sighs. "But I am reminded that I must use it to hang someone. *What makes a man do such a thing?* is a better question than *how shall we punish him for doing it?* And yet we only seem to ask the latter." He is not talking to me any more. He is arguing with memory, as old people do. He must be nearly thirty turns.

I hear my name called. *Eve.* I look through the window. Dinah stands knee-deep in grass looking at the old blackhouse. Her face is frightened. White clouds of dandelion clocks whirl about her on the breeze.

"I must go home now," I say to Black.

He nods, his eye still on the microscope.

"What are you doing here, Eve?" Dinah asks. Her hands fret, pulling each finger in turn.

"How did you find me?" But I know. She was not looking for me. She was looking for Jamie MacRaith. This is where they meet.

"Come," she says. She looks closely at me. "What have you done?"

"Nothing!" But my heart goes cold. "I talked too much," I whisper. "Please don't tell."

"I will not give an account, but you must come now."

A shadow falls between us. Chief Inspector Black. Dinah sees him and a smile comes over her face like light after a storm. I see everything slow inside her. Her heart, her muscles, her mind. So it is not just fear that does that.

He lifts a copper lock from her shoulders and separates a single burning strand, plucks it from her head.

Dinah turns towards him. He takes a step back, away from her.

"Go home," he says amiably, and vanishes into the dark house. Dinah's eyes follow him. She stands watching the bothy. Some feeling in her I do not know.

"Dinah," I say.

She turns without a word.

I follow her home, bewildered, calling, *wait, Dinah, wait*. I thrust my hands into my pockets and something brushes my finger there. I remove it. In my palm there lies a bright iridescent fly, fashioned of soft feathers the colours of a kingfisher's back.

* * *

A hen settles on my toe. I shove it off. It pecks my shin hard, fixing me with an outraged amber eye. Irish Dromgoole's henhouse has a slitted view of Loyal's cobbled street and one neat white cottage. Mr. Buchanan's nets are spread across the wall to dry in the sun. The smell of them reaches me even here. Salt, tar, death. They drip, pattering on the little flagged path, making the cobbles slick and shining in the sun.

I come here most days to watch. I have been waiting for it to happen. Today it does. There is a great roaring and clanking and a black van backs into view. I suppose the van is a strange sight. I have seen the village children chasing it. But it is not surprising to me. It is the sort of thing I expect to exist, made for capture. The road narrows by the Buchanan house and when the van can go no further, it comes to rest.

The door to the cab cannot open very wide. Two black-capped men with shiny buttons slide out, then Chief Inspector Black. They open the Buchanan gate and go up the little path to the door. All life is gone from the Chief Inspector's face. Mr. Buchanan answers the door, eyes still sewn up with sleep, hair stringy and stiff with brine. He has only just gone to bed, come in from night fishing.

Sarah is behind him, so is Mrs. Buchanan. Their faces are crumpled like balls of paper. They are startled, not ready for the gaze of others. Buchanan holds an arm across the door, as if to shield them from the policemen, the light.

The policemen do not want Sarah or Mrs. Buchanan. They want

him. "Hamish Buchanan," says Chief Inspector Black. "You are under arrest for the murder of Hector MacRaith."

They put manacles on Sarah's pa. The chains shine against his thin white wrists. Hamish Buchanan turns as if to say something to his daughter, his wife. They reach for him, arms stiff and longing. But he just shakes his head and then the two officers open the doors of the back of the black van. They put him in it, then get into the van and it roars into life and goes.

Sarah runs into the street. She turns and looks straight at me where I sit in the dim henhouse.

"I know what you did," she says. Her patent-leather shoe slips on the fish-wet cobbles. She falls, but does not get up. She lies, cheek to the wet stone, and cries. Her hand curls and uncurls as though if she could clutch some invisible thing, all would be well.

* * *

The coast path back home seems long. Sarah's hand grasps the air before me. I see again the gleam of black patent leather, catch the scent of salted rope.

But it is Jamie MacRaith who is suddenly before me on the path, brown forelock ruffled by the wind.

"Evelyn, is it?" he says. "You should not be out alone." His eyes are swollen as if he has just woken up. One of his bootlaces is untied and there is a sweet, rotten smell on his breath. Liquorice?

He sways and steadies himself on my shoulder. His hand brushes my ear. His fingers find my earlobe. He tugs it gently. It is not liquorice on his breath.

"Why would they name you after her?" he asks. "The old story, the *Eubha Muir*, my family calls her in Gàidhlig. In English you would say Little Eve."

"I do not know what you mean."

"Oh," he says sadly. "She lives in the water about the isle. She wants something. I do not recall what. She draws men out into the depths and drowns them."

"There is nothing like that on the isle," I say with scorn.

"You don't know everything," he says, squinting at me. "Though you think you do. Altnaharra belonged to the MacRaiths before the English took it. By rights it belongs to us still."

"That is not so." I try to put the sea in my voice as Uncle does. "It has always awaited us." Altnaharra's rock is our bones. Our blood runs through its earth.

Jamie's weight grows on my shoulder. "Pretty thing," he says to himself.

I am aware of his height, his arms, shoulders, the breadth of his chest. It does not seem a body but rather a building he lives in, made of bone and muscle. His long-fingered hand rests on my arm, its bitten, blackened nails. A sliver of pink on his jaw where the razor caught the skin.

"What do you want?" I say, shrugging him off.

"The world is against me." He shivers. "Will you deliver this?" A smudged envelope marked in his unsteady boy's hand. *Dinah.* "Tell her I am—no." He closes his eyes. "Forget that. Why should you, if I cannot face it myself?" There is a twitch in the side of his mouth. It makes something twist deep inside me. Perhaps he is right, and I am like the thing in the old story. I do send men to their deaths, after all.

He stumbles past me, heading for Loyal.

* * *

Supper. Bread, three mouthfuls. Cheese, three mouthfuls. Honey, one mouthful. I slip the letter under Dinah's plate. She takes it into her lap with a white face. She knows what it contains.

In bed I shield the candle flame with my hand and hold it for Dinah as she reads, tears streaming down her face. I whisper to her and stroke her but she stares straight ahead and does not seem to notice me at all. Jamie MacRaith is going to the War. He wishes her not to think of him again.

"Burn it," she says.

I hold the flaming letter. The flesh of my hand glows warm and rosy. In the web between finger and thumb I clearly see the outline of two narrow fangs. I drop the smoking remains into the water jug then hold her tight.

Tonight I dream Dinah's dream. I look down a tunnel into a dim burrow where white rabbits sleep peacefully, all curled about one another. Babies, adults, all asleep. Their ears flicker, their hind legs twitch, they are lost in dreams of clover. No creature comes with needle teeth to threaten them. Dinah has got that all wrong. I must remember to tell her that when I wake. *There is no reekling here.* Why does Dinah think that there is danger?

My body hugs the earth. My narrow tongue. My eyes unblinking.

Blackberry day. At the end we are sun-dazed, shoulders pink and sore. We suck blood from scratches and juice from our fingers. As we crest the last rise, the causeway comes into view, and the castle, grey against the shining sea. We stop.

On the causeway a figure ploughs determined through the shallows. Someone is going to the isle. Someone wearing dark clothes, who holds a white thing like a paper boat in their hand.

"Who is it?" asks Dinah.

"It is Nora returning from mission," says Abel, uncertain. He must be right, because no one sets foot on the isle except us. But the person is not shaped like Nora.

"It is the policeman," I say. We run down the hill, blackberries bouncing in our baskets.

The man is in the hall with Uncle and Nora. His voice is raised. We put down the baskets and press our ears to the great oak door.

I hear Alice's name but I cannot make out the rest. I press my ear so hard against the oak that it sings. The door is suddenly flung open.

"Come in," says Chief Inspector Christopher Black, white hat in hand. "All of you."

We stand before Uncle in order of age.

"Look," he says to Uncle. "How can you keep them like this? Do you not see their condition?"

I do not understand what he means. I try to look at us, the Children, as if I have never seen us before.

Abel wears a shirt made from a brown potato sack. Fading grocer's print runs across his chest. He has on a pair of men's cotton underthings, torn and rucked up with burrs. His yellow-white hair is caked with something that could be mud.

Dinah has tried to turn Nora's old nightgown into a dress. It was once white, is now yellowing and is composed mostly of darns, which are unravelling. Two of her teeth are missing, one near the back and a canine near the front. Her hair is nicely brushed as always, tied up in a tidy knot with butcher's string.

Elizabeth sucks her cracked wooden spoon. Her bony wrists and ankles protrude from her dress, a pillowcase. She has a raven's feather in her hair.

Nora's raiment was perhaps once white, but now it is torn at the knee, stained. Her arms are braided with red welts. Something in the water stung her as she was gathering kelp.

"They have lice," Black says to Uncle as if we are not there. "Not a pair of shoes between them. And they are starving." He says to Nora, "You're losing some of your hair, I see. In your condition, I would eat a little more. *You*, however," he says to Uncle, "seem to be in the pink of health."

Everyone knows that the Adder needs more food than we do. The benison saps his strength.

Black says, "You have filled all these children with nonsense and fear. Your cruelty to their minds is as great as that to their bodies."

Uncle says, "There is no crime being committed here, Mr.—"

"That would be Chief Inspector, Colonel. No crime? I wonder. What might I hear if I were to make enquiries about you with my colleagues at the Met?"

"We do not speak of the past," Uncle says. "And do not call me Colonel. That is no longer what I am."

"I speak of the present," says Black. "This is ungodly." His mouth narrows into a fine line. "It offends me; morally and in my heart. Where is the paperwork proving that these children have been handed to your care? Where are the birth certificates?"

Uncle goes from the hall. When he returns his hands hold papers: stamped, yellowing, curled.

"Birth certificates," he says. "They were taken from mothers who could not care for them. There is the agreement for Dinah. Born to Aisling Smith, addicted to spirituous liquors. She is of age and no longer subject to removal by the law. And here, for Abel. Mother a street-walker who gave birth to him in the Glasgow workhouse. Yes, what a crime I have committed, Chief Inspector! To take in these poor little souls, raise them as my own, love them as my own . . ." He thrusts the papers at Chief Inspector Black. His mouth trembles with feeling.

"You wanted to find your mother, Abel," I whisper. "Now you know."

"Shut up, Eve," he says. He weeps. Dinah begins to cry too.

"It changes nothing," says Uncle fiercely. "You are mine."

I do not think we have believed for years that we were lifted from the sea. Even so, there is something terrible about being a name on a piece of paper.

Inspector Black looks up. "The girls you call Evelyn and Elizabeth," he says. "There is nothing here, no documentation."

"We do not know their parentage."

"They did not emerge full grown from the waves."

"We found them," Uncle says. "On the rocks of Altnaharra after a storm. Evelyn is sixteen. You cannot compel her."

"She does not look sixteen," says Inspector Black. "You cannot expect me to believe it." Once again I curse my height. I am small even for my fourteen turns.

"It is the truth," says Uncle.

Baby Elizabeth takes my hand.

"She is sixteen, too," I say.

Elizabeth nods.

"This is our home," I say to Christopher Black. "You cannot make us come."

"Evelyn," Black says, "you owe this man nothing."

"It is well known in the village that Elizabeth and I were abandoned on the isle," I say. "This is where they used to bring the babies they did not want. If it were not for Uncle, Elizabeth and I would have died." It must be true; the rest is.

Christopher Black looks at me for a moment, head to one side. "Are you sure?" he asks.

I nod. I think of Jamie MacRaith's sad eyes, his drunken gait. I think of Sarah Buchanan lying in the road as her father was taken away. I do not want to be alone like them.

"Remove yourself," Uncle says.

"You have not heard the last from me," Black says to Uncle with his white smile. "I am the law. I will not simply stop."

We follow him to the causeway and stand in a line to watch him go. He wades, stumbling a little, seawater creeping up the legs of his fine trousers. He reaches land and walks away on the path. At length he is only a dark mark fading into the purple. The setting sun blazes behind us, casting our shadows long across the shingle.

"Uncle," I say. "Did I do well?"

He puts a warm hand on my head. Love pours through my body.

"Eve," he says gently. "He spoke of things that he should not have known, of our ways and the secrets of the isle. How did he learn such things? From you."

I cannot meet his eye.

"You are now a stranger to His grace. Go. May the night beasts deal with you as they will."

The words sink in slowly, like cold into the bone. Dinah told on me, after all.

"Eve is dead," Uncle says to the others. "The thing that wears her skin is outcast."

Uncle does not touch me. I am thrust forward, as if by a strong hand. I fall to my knees in the shallows. I rise and turn, coughing. I call to Uncle, to Dinah, but they have already turned, are walking away from me up the hill. There may as well be a wall between us. The isle is closed against me.

* * *

For a time I watch Altnaharra from the shore. Light flickers, delicate, in the windows, warm against the dusky air. Bats go by on their snapping wings, like something broken and mended again, broken and mended, faster than the eye can see.

The tide rises and the sea breathes out, creeps up the shore. The broad shape of a seal comes up the beach, scattering the shale before it. Another follows. Their pelts gleam under the night sky. They bark and rear up, dart their heads at me. More come out of the water, crowding the beach. Moonlight reflects off a hundred round black eyes, all fixed on me.

I am not permitted here.

The world is different at night. The forest is a tangle of imprisoning branches and I go slowly, hands outstretched. I thought I knew the paths, the sounds. But I do not know this hooting, chilly land where the undergrowth trembles and eyes shine at me from the tops of trees. I know how Alice felt, now, but Uncle will not try to save me as he did her. I am alone with the night and all that lives here.

Something tall walks just behind me. Its cold breath is on my neck, its long fingers trail down my back. Its eyes are red as an adder's. Its black tongue flickers. It dogs my footsteps but flees whenever I turn to look. I go faster to outpace it. However fast I go, its dead heart is there, beating just behind my own. It is the needle-toothed thing from Dinah's dreams. But this is not a dream. Here in this dark world it is real. Its breath is on me, its mouth, the barest graze of its fangs. My ankles are in its long fingers, the earth tips and I fall. A claw is drawn along my cheek. A wet mouth strokes mine. I think I am weeping; I cannot hear anything above the sound of my heart, my sawing breath. The blackness wraps about me, coils about my neck. The night grins widely, sharp teeth are everywhere: in the sky, the leaves, even the earth has jaws. My whimpers grow to screams. *Hush*, says the reekling. *Come to me.*

* * *

Someone is above me. His hat is tipped low over his face. Colourful feathers in the early light.

"Uncle does not want me any more," I say. "It is your fault." But I know the fault was mine.

"Come inside," he says.

Chief Inspector Black gives me his hand and helps me rise. Navy blue to the east. The claws on my skirts are bramble bushes, the fingers about my ankle ivy, the hand on my mouth young leaves, wet with rain. I hear the burn darting quick in its channel. The clearing is ahead. The bothy stands there, dark. Why would luck lead me here?

Inside Christopher Black gives me a cup of water and a bit of cloth to blow my nose on. That makes me feel better. Perhaps it will be all right. Then he puts an arm around me and it is all wrong. His shoulder smells like cloth and fresh grass, not like smoke and leather. No golden light springs from him. He is not Uncle. I push him away with a moan.

I do not want him to see me cry but I cannot help it. It all spills out. I will not see Altnaharra again; my Dinah. The stone turret room, the ocean. When I die I will not go to Him. I will just end, like Alice did, become grey ash or be eaten by worms. Uncle will never place his hand on my head again.

Black gives me a piece of liquorice. "We must go," he says. "He was angry. He will be regretting his haste. I think he will come after you."

I shake my head. He does not understand. The Adder's word is law. Uncle will not change his mind.

I sit stiffly in the unforgiving cage of metal of his automobile. It rattles and bounces along the track south towards Tongue. I feel it as we travel south, further and further from Altnaharra. The cord that binds me to the ocean stretches ever thinner.

* * *

We stop in Tongue at a place called *Hotel*. My hands leave dark prints on the creamy walls. The man at the shining desk has shining hair, sleek and flat like a seal's. But he is not a seal. He smells of sticky things. The vaulted lobby is empty but there is too much noise. Mechanical ticks and chimes, the rustle of paper, bells that pierce the air like needles.

"You're in luck," the man says, and even his voice shines. "Next week we close. Requisitioned. We're to be an officers' convalescent home."

"Ah, well," says Inspector Black. "It will be over soon."

"Everyone says so, sir," agrees the shining man.

Christopher Black murmurs something to him. He raises his eyebrows but looks me up and down and nods.

The linen tablecloth is whiter than any cloud. Lights overhead wink with ropes and pendants of glass, bright as blades about to drop. Glasses on the table, too, brittle as shells. On the plate before me is something glutinous and pink. "Meat is only for the Adder," I say.

"It hardly qualifies as meat. Can you stretch a point? You must eat something."

The shiny man appears at the table. He gives Black a brown paper parcel. The Chief Inspector gives him money.

"Here," he says to me. "Put these on."

In the parcel is a grey woollen coat. It is worn at the elbows and darned at the collar but it is thick and warm. There is also a pair of black leather boots, worn into the shape of someone else's feet.

I put them on. My feet feel very heavy in the boots. The coat smells of peppermint and tobacco. There is a farthing in the pocket.

"I am losing the benison," I say. "I can feel it."

"It was never there to lose," says Christopher Black. "He keeps you starved, half-dead with exhaustion, always vying for his attention. That place is the very edge of the world, Evelyn, and you have been taken to the edge of what a person can stand, or be."

"Do not talk about Uncle. You do not know anything about him." I try to drink some water but my teeth come together too hard. There is a crisp, high sound. In my mouth is a perfect half-moon of glass. Water leaks onto the white cloth from the broken rim.

I carefully remove the piece of glass from my mouth then push the chair back from the white table. The legs scrape through treacherous soft carpet. I run from the room across a wide hall that is red as fresh blood. The boots hobble me, unbalance me. I stumble and cry out. Men in white jackets turn. There are white, blank ovals where their faces should be. I push out through swinging walls of gold and glass, out towards the light.

The street hits me. Engines like the rattle of teeth, small hands in white kid gloves, a porridge-coloured dog with a crushed face, black railings, hard paving, pipe smoke, paper bags dancing on the wind, air like vinegar burning, the sky a mere tear in the dark stone. Everywhere the stench of unfamiliar matter. I cower back against the hotel's white wall, its shiny black railings. This world is all the horror Uncle promised.

"It is all a matter of degrees," says Chief Inspector Black. He stands before me, companionable in his cream suit. "You have been raised by your 'Uncle' to believe that there is a snake in the ocean waiting to take over the world. It is not so great a step for you as it might be for others, to believe you are connected to the world by some invisible energy. But that is wrong. A snake is not a magical thing. It is a reptile. It would be happier in the wild. The benison is just a feeling. Of ecstasy and oneness, created by strong suggestion acting on a weakened constitution. True happiness comes from God, and the fulfilment of duty. The benison, all of it, was not real, Eve. I know it seems as though it was."

"It is real," I say. "More real than you."

"Let us try." He reaches out and slips the knife from where it hides in my cuff. How did he know it was there?

"You wish for me to cut you?" I ask.

"Certainly. Do you need much?"

"A drop."

"So the amount does not matter? What about accidental wounds?" He stops. "I will ask my questions later."

I nick his thumb. A speck of blood rises, the size of a flea.

I wait for the eye, for the moment when my self ebbs away and I am washed on the shore of another mind.

Nothing happens. I stay where I am, trapped inside myself. "The eye is stretched too thin," I say. "We are too far from Altnaharra."

He looks at me with sympathy and says nothing.

"It must be real," I say reasonably. "Or this would be all there is."

"I am sorry," Black says. He takes off his cream jacket and hangs it carefully on the black railing. He regards the dirty step for a moment, then sighs and sits down next to me.

"There was a note delivered to Hamish Buchanan," he says. "It told him in bald terms what Hector MacRaith was doing to his daughter, Sarah. Buchanan confessed that it sent him out of his mind. He killed Hector MacRaith on account of that note. Now he will go to the scaffold for it. Have you seen a man's face when he knows he will be hanged? I have, too many times. Hamish Buchanan's was no different. When he confessed, his eyes had already died. Whoever wrote that letter has taken two lives. Do you understand me? And that may not be the end of it. He is not wrong on every count, that man you call your Uncle. To shed blood, to take a life, these are acts that confer power. It can become something a man or woman cannot live without. Did you write that note to Hamish Buchanan?"

After a moment I nod.

He says, "It was a very . . . adult letter."

"I did not mean him to die." I wipe my tears away angrily. I will not betray Uncle.

"Perhaps not. Our actions often change us and the world in ways we cannot anticipate. I will tell you a story. There was once a little boy who was very angry, and he had cause to be. He had two fathers. One was a very good man who whittled animals from reeds, taught his son to fish and worked as a tailor. At night, however, the other man came into him. This man drank until he could no longer place one foot in front of the other. This man burnt his son's skin with matches, broke his bones, cut him with a knife. He did other things, worse things, to the boy's sister. She was small and dark and quick. She could play anything you sang to her on the piano. Brother and sister were best friends. But the sister couldn't stand what was being done to her, so in the end she ate rat poison." He draws a long breath that seems to go through all of him, from his head to his toes. "It was the worst day," he says.

"That same night the man beat the boy about the head until the world was one great ringing bell. He broke each of his wife's fingers one by one and knocked her unconscious. He burnt the boy's arms and wrists with the glowing tip of a poker. At last he fell down, insensible, before the hearth." Christopher Black unbuttons his pearl-fastened cuffs.

"The boy looked at him as he lay there. He took up the poker and stood over him in the dark room. There was only the sound of the fire. He thought how easy it would be to strike him, and then push his father's head into the flames. It would seem natural, like an accident, for everyone knew that his father drank. No one would enquire too closely. But the boy knew that his heart would bear the mark of it, always. He would never be free of that act. It would be a milestone on a blasted road, down which he would travel further, further . . . Right and wrong—they are just words. When we are standing in the dark, holding a flaming poker, there is only one thing to consider and that is ourselves. Can we hold such an act within us, without being irrevocably changed?"

Black strokes the bracelets of charred flesh that circle his wrists. The old burns are shiny, with livid red ridges. "He fell down the stairs a month later," he says. "Broke his neck. I think of him every day, whenever I see these. But I am always relieved that I did not do it. That he could not change me utterly."

"Why are you telling me this?" I ask.

"You left that place," says Inspector Black. "You decided."

"I did not decide! I would be there now if I could." The thought makes tears well.

"You can choose another way. You have already taken the first step."

"I look like her, do I not?" I say. "Your sister. That is who you thought I was, when we met. That is why you are trying to help me."

"She was your age when it happened." He looks down. "Perhaps you remind me of her, somewhat."

"But I am not her," I say. "And I do not want your help."

"You came to me," he says, "so I have no choice."

I look at him. A man who does not eat sweet things but carries them in his pockets, as if a long-dead hand might reach from the grave at any moment to beg for a piece of liquorice.

* * *

The platform at Tongue whistles with wind and sunshine. The trains are not for us; the trains are for the soldiers. Chief Inspector Black is told this, many times. But he persists, holding out his battered badge. "Official business," he says, again and again. "She's a witness." This said with a thumb cocked at me.

We wait for hours on the platform. I lie down on the cold stone and drift half into sleep. I hear Christopher Black speaking to someone. There are replies but they come through crackles in a tiny voice. I look through my eyelashes. He is in a little glass room at the station wall, talking into a black thing like a handbell on a cord. He speaks quietly.

At length we are loaded onto a third-class carriage with a crowd of shouting boys dressed in green. The boys whistle and cast eyes at me like the boys in the schoolyard do at Dinah. It is not because I am pretty, I understand, it is simply because I am there. They soon settle, sleeping with practised ease on their kitbags, caps shading their eyes. Some of their faces remind me of the does in the forest, their thin necks and long eyelashes. Some of them are afraid. I don't need the eye to see that. Others have gone beyond fear into nothing. An older man in the corner shakes. He has no ears. Red and purple burns cover him.

"Where are they going?" I ask.

"France," Christopher Black says, "to fight in the War."

Uncle told us. *War is a hungry beast. It must be fed boys.*

"What will happen when we reach Inverness?" I ask.

"I will report to my superiors," he says. "We will go to Inverness Police Station."

"Will you arrest me for killing Mr. MacRaith?"

"No," he says. "That was not your fault."

"And after that?" I ask.

"I expect we will find a family to take you in. They will teach you Christian thought. School, a home, family. How does that sound to you?"

It sounds bad.

The train roars, rattles my teeth and bones. Christopher Black asks me question after question. He asks about the benison and the eye. He asks about the Tale, and about Alice. He seems particularly interested in the two men who tried to kill Uncle, who were taken into the isle and never seen again. Who were they? Where are they now? What were their names? I shrug. I have never thought them important. I do not wish to tell him anything but his tone is so quiet and gentle. He circles around again and again to the things he wishes to know, so that in the end the words seem to crowd my mouth, eager to be said.

"I am tired," I say, to make it stop. I roll my coat up under my head and pretend to sleep. Every so often I open my eyes a fraction to see what he is doing. Christopher Black is reading a book. The cover is very bright and has a sun on it and a man. It is about a word I do not know, a *Tarzan* and it is by Edgar Rice Burroughs. Black laughs to himself as he reads. Every so often he turns his bright gaze on me, considering.

I think Black wants Uncle and the others. He will take me to a police station and they will make me tell them things. Then perhaps they will go across the causeway in a black lorry and take Dinah and Abel and Elizabeth and Nora and Uncle.

* * *

It happens as we pull into Inverness. The cord that binds me to Alt-naharra breaks. Again and again I ask for benison, but I am alone. It is like a knife-thrust. But there is no time to feel it. From the train I am spewed forth into a nightmare world. Buildings of tall grey stone lean across the sky, cutting out the light. There is no quiet, no inch of the world not filled with din and stink. The people mill and bray like unsettled cows before a storm. Bad rain. Black air. A giant dirty hand has been clapped down over everything.

Christopher Black weaves through crowds of dark shoulders, whiskers, silk skirts, piles of litter blowing everywhere in the wind; through market stalls, by carts of apples, the scent of their skin green in the hot air. *Pencil portraits, done while you wait.* Dying oysters shrink on ice barrels in the warm afternoon. Fish heads are trampled to liquid underfoot.

On a table books rear in piles, their leather bindings frayed. I think I see familiar words etched in gold. *Kingdom Animalia et Plantae.* I have a rush of horror thinking of impure hands on it. My secret. But when I look closer the book is something quite different, about armies. I shiver. I think of the stars in the cold northern sky. I think of the call of the seals and the clean scent of the sea. Do they exist? Have they ever? I will die here.

He keeps a hand on my shoulder. A light, constant grip.

Sweet smoke drifts from the mouth of a crimson tent. The sign above reads, *The Amazing Elsie! Fortunes told, Minds Read, Your Future Divined. All 2d.*

"Do people pay to have their minds read?" I ask.

"People pay for the pretence," Black says. "For the illusion of a world beyond God's creation. It is not illegal. Some people seem to think it harmless. I cannot agree."

A freckled boy bumps into me. He carries a stack of newspapers under one arm and is wearing a sandwich board with words on it, a familiar name. Christopher Black pulls me away, but I see the headline. Hamish Buchanan was hanged today.

"An eye for an eye," Black says. "Of all God's teachings, it is the one I wrestle with the most. It is from the Bible. You will come to know it."

"An eye for an eye," I repeat. There is always a price. I think of Sarah lying in the mud crying for her pa. The wheels of the black van retreating. The fishing nets spread to dry on the garden wall. Maybe the nets are still there, stiff in the sun. Hamish Buchanan will not come back for them. He paid the price for my power. Sarah paid. Jamie paid. Only I have not paid.

"We will go to the station," Black says. "You need to make a statement." He leads me towards a road where people are standing in a line. We join it.

A girl carrying a wicker basket brushes against Christopher Black's shoulder and he recoils. The girl shrugs and slips in behind us. Someone groans, a thin woman makes a *tsk, tsk* sound. "There is a queue here, you'll notice," she says to the girl.

I turn round and stare. The girl grins at me as though we are together in a good joke. One crooked front tooth overlaps the others. She has a face like a clever deer. Her skin and hair and eyes are different shades of gold.

I recognise her. "Hello," I say with a leap of pleasure. It is like the first sight of Altnaharra after school, or when Dinah teases me.

The girl raises her eyebrows. Her green-gold gaze is curious. She spits neatly into the street. Of course I do not know her. I wish I had not said anything.

A monstrous engine comes to rest beside us. The line of people shuffles towards it. Beneath the shrieking and grinding I hear a familiar sound, the long drag of scale and muscle.

I peer into the basket under the girl's arm and my heart begins to gallop. A thick body poured into coils. A cunning, narrow head, a dark tongue. He is not like Hercules. He is larger, far from home. Mites crawl on his skin. The shining olive, cream and brown of him is dulled in places. He lifts his striped head. His eyes are dark, soft-looking. No wonder I recognised the girl. What would a real girl with a real snake be doing in this forsaken place? It can only be a sign. I thought I was alone, but I am never alone. He is with me.

You wish to be the Adder, a voice says, within me or without, I cannot tell. *So be the* Adder.

I gasp.

"It is merely an omnibus," Black says. "Very well. We will walk." He turns away, beckoning for the queue to pass us. His hand leaves my shoulder and for a moment his attention is elsewhere.

I step back into the crowd of bustling bodies. The girl with the snake watches, impassive. As Christopher Black turns towards me she steps neatly into his path, shielding me from view. I turn and run.

I steal a sack from the oyster stall and drape it about my shoulders. The city roars. I understand that one can be lost in it. Sinuous, toothy things live beneath its surface. Light flares in doorways, faces are disassembled into mysterious planes, eyes glint from cavernous shadows. Stone above me, stone beneath me, stone towers to either side, shutting out the sky.

Rain falls; it tastes of ash. I trip on something, a foot perhaps, and shrill curses follow me. I do not understand how it all connects. Does it ever end?

I am seized by the scruff of my neck and pulled up short, gasping for breath. Something looms. A policeman, face shadowed under a cap, the high collar of his tunic pushing his chin into plump lines.

"Only pickpockets run that fast," he says, and his fingers are everywhere, patting, feeling. I asks for benison but again, nothing comes. He shakes me. "You come along." His hand is thickly furred with dark hair, like the moss that grows on the cliffs at Altnaharra. I drag my nails hard across the wrist, I bite his hand, the blood rises like the juice of a pear and he lets go.

* * *

I do not stop running until Inverness has given way once more to pasture, and then to heath and hills. I leave the boots at the foot of a young willow and hang the coat on its branches. It dances, filled with breeze. The ghost of who I might have been.

I head north. I do not sleep. There is no need. I drink from deep black lochs. On the first day I find a nest containing pigeon eggs and eat them. I take no more food after that. Uncle is right. Hunger brings gifts. I go through ancient mossy twisted woods by night. I do not fear the dark. In a clearing open to the moon I hear low voices singing. There is the peal of mellow bells. I turn aside and give them a wide berth. Many old powers reside in this world. Not all may be named, not all should be trusted. But I have nothing to fear. I am under His protection.

In the bright morning I find a sunny, sandy track that meanders through the heather. I follow it. The wind is up and white clouds scud across the sky. Altnaharra is like a star inside me, growing brighter. The stink of the world, its rotten, impure heart, falls away.

I was wrong. It is not possible for two things to be true at once. I must choose. There can be no more impurity, no more *Kingdom Animalia*. I understand that faith is not rest but action. I give myself anew each day.

First, I will pay for the gift of the eye.

* * *

Before dawn on the third day the isle is there, dark on the horizon. Home. My heart seems to burst. The tide is low and the causeway glimmers, a mirage. The water feels fresh and cold about my ankles.

There is nothing like the touch of the sea on a young morning. Will the isle close against me like a door?

I set foot on the shingle. It is quiet, or what passes for it on Altnaharra. The plaintive cry of the seals; the wind filling my ears. It is the sound of being.

I know where I will find them. Today is the seeing.

* * *

The Children are among the stones, heads bowed. Uncle stands before Cold Ben holding Abel. His lips move. Abel weeps and nods. It should be me in Uncle's arms.

I go to the bowl of honey where it sits on the grass. I take it on my fingers. The golden thickness on my tongue.

When they see me, everything goes still. Uncle pushes Abel gently from him.

"Get you gone," he says to me. "Impure thing who walks in Eve's skin. You have no name. You are not of Altnaharra. *Go.*" The pressure of his will builds in my head.

I shiver with his power. But I stand firm. I swallow my hurt, hard as a pebble. *Be the* Adder. I come close to Uncle. His beard brushes my cheek. I put my lips to his ear. "I know the true nature of the trying, Uncle. It does not end with Hercules. It does not end when you become the Adder. It never ends. All of life is the trying."

"Your words mean no more than the call of the gulls," he says.

"John, do not allow her back here," Nora says. Her grey eyes are fixed on me. "I do not want corruption near my unborn child."

I go to Nora, take her head in my hands. "Your first was a baby named Amy," I whisper. "You loved her and sang to her but she died, leaving you with nothing but a pink ribbon. That first loss was the one that twisted you, made you the bitter old thing you are today."

Nora pushes me away, hand to her mouth. She looks as if she might be sick.

"You are seen," I say. I step back from her, heart hammering. I speak aloud to the isle. "I will be the Adder. I will pay for what the isle gave me. An eye for the eye." I kneel. I am afraid. I draw my dagger from my cuff. I give it to Uncle.

He speaks quietly to Nora. She demurs, but the Adder says, "Bring me what I need."

Nora brings a bucket and a lit torch. The scent of pine tar rises. Uncle takes the torch. The flame licks the blade of the knife.

I kneel and stare up at the new sun. "The right," I say. I am shaking. With her thumb Nora parts my eyelids, holding my right eye open. Uncle holds my head still with one hand. He takes aim with the other.

It seems to happen very slowly. The blade is small, held high above his head, and then it comes down and fills everything. The world is made of it. There is no pain yet. A plunging sensation deep in my eye socket and a deafening hiss. One side of the world goes dark. A warm scent. Flesh cooking. A slight sound, a fish jumping in a stream. Something falls onto the grass before me. A jellyfish with fine, red, streaming tendrils. There is a terrible noise. Raw, broken. It is my screaming. My body wants to run but it cannot. Everything is shaking. The grass, the air.

"It is nearly done." Uncle's voice comes as if through water. He steadies my head and pours something warm into the void, filling the raw space. Pine sap mixed with honey. The sap begins to cool. There are the first stirrings of pain, its promise. It will be the worst I have ever known. The dark half of the world spreads, consuming the light. Someone has been sick, I smell it. I think it was me. Half my head is empty, half the world is gone for ever.

"Is it done?" I ask. "Have I paid, Uncle?"

Uncle's hands are on me. He says, "You have paid." He takes me in his arms. I feel his tears in my hair.

The pain descends, beating great red wings. I am grateful to fade into the dark.

* * *

I am held by thick coils. A black snake. Its head weaves before me in the dark, burning eyes fixed on mine. It opens its jaws. Fangs, long, curved blades, strike quicker than thought, piercing my skull. My blood pours forth. I plead for mercy, I struggle, but the coils hold me easily. Again and again it strikes, plunging fangs into my eye socket. Years pass. I die and die again.

* * *

The sound of the sea. Dinah is here, I feel her.

I open my eye. I am in our room. Autumn light pours through the window. Dinah holds a tin cup at my lips, cool to the brim with water. My head is bound with clean linen. It aches but it is the memory of pain, not pain itself.

"We are supposed to take turns sitting with you," Dinah says. "Nora will not. She is afraid of you. I am not afraid. Need I be?"

I shake my head. I wish I had not. The room tips. There is too much space in my skull.

"Why did you do that, Eve? Why did Uncle do it?" Dinah shivers.

"It was the price," I say. "There was no choice."

"You may well say that." Her mouth twists. "You did not have to watch it."

"Uncle sent me away because you told."

"He knew I had gone to find Jamie," Dinah says. "I had to give him something else to be angry about. Do not hate me, Eve."

I shake my head. It does not matter. I am no longer the same girl. "Help me up." I am weak as a new lamb. Dinah holds me firmly about the waist.

We go down through the quiet castle to the shore. We weave and sway like old people. Even so I am soon breathless. I slip, and one leg plunges into a rock pool, knee-deep. Dinah gives a surprised stutter of laughter and helps me out.

We go to the east of the isle where the blue pebble shore curves into two protecting arms. The seals watch us, tucked into the crevices of the rock. In their round eyes is the deep mystery of the world. Dinah wades out into the shallows. She is changed, too, this summer. She is not the Dinah who met Jamie MacRaith in the meadow. Puzzlement and sorrow hang about her. She turns her face up to the sky and closes her eyes.

I shiver. The first sign of the season's turning. Dinah always mourns autumn's passing like a death.

We will begin to lay in food and wood for winter, soon. We will board up the doors and windows, stack the walls of the hall high with logs and stores from the cellar. We will lie down before the fire and for the deepest part of winter we will sleep, waking only for food and water. It is a time of long dreaming, as outside snow drifts high against the walls. We will awake, gaunt, in the spring. Once the castle was buried in snow and we had to dig our way out into the light.

My fingers find something in my pocket. Paper, tightly folded into a small wad the size of a button. It ripples in the breeze as I unfold it. Newspaper. The *Inverness Argus*, dated two months ago.

I see the photograph first. It is of me. I wear a strange, puffy dress that spills out with lace. My hair is dressed in loose rolls, piled high on my head. Some evil power has split me in two. This shadow version of me lives among the Impure, wearing a dress made of beaten egg white.

But no. She is fairer, taller. This girl's skin is as smooth as fresh milk. I would guess that she has never been on Wane. The long, dark brows are the same, the triangular face, the jaw. But the angle of her head is playful, the brows slightly raised. The eyes are deep-set like mine, but larger. The lashes are dark and thick. Her thin lips are softly parted. My face has never worn such an expression. And then I know who it is.

The photograph must have been taken many turns ago, before Alice fled the corrupt world and came to Altnaharra. She looks young.

I touch my lips with a trembling finger. I trace the line of my brow. I feel the shape of my jaw. Alice looks back at me through the newsprint, through time.

The headline reads, "Missing Peer's Daughter Found Alive." "The Hon. Alice Seddington," it says, "the object of a nationwide manhunt fifteen years ago, has been found in the luggage hall of Aberdeen station. Miss Seddington claims no memory of the years since she went missing from her home that fateful day."

These words are wrong. Alice is dead. We put her to the flame. Uncle would not lie about such a thing.

"Eve," calls Dinah. I look at her where she stands, calf-deep in shining water. She needs me.

Any one of us can be corrupted. I narrowly escaped it. There must be no more school, no more traffic with Loyal. Duty settles about my shoulders.

The wind takes the paper from my fingers. I let it fly.

DINAH

1931

DID you think you had heard the last from me? No, I have more gifts for you; more days I do not need. It has been ten years but the memories are still bright.

* * *

The inquest took place at the Jugged Hare on 2 January 1921. I sat in the front row. The guest of honour, I suppose. The room was hot and smelt of tar. The shingles were melting in the heat from the chimney.

Word had spread about the district and people came from miles around. The London papers were in attendance, as was every Scots periodical. The more agile members of the crowd piled onto windowsills and climbed into the beams. The Procurator Fiscal, Justice Abernathy, was forced to order the bars be put down on the doors to prevent more people crowding in. One woman fainted and was half-carried out into the air to be revived.

The bodies were presented. They were brought to the platform, bound tightly on wooden stretchers, then set upright against the wall behind Mr. Abernathy to be displayed to the crowd. I am told that the usual practice at inquests is to seal the corpse in a lead coffin with a glass window over the face, for identification. None of the materials for such a coffin were at hand in Loyal. Instead the dead were tightly swaddled in cheesecloth soaked with quicklime, leaving only their faces uncovered.

They lay peaceful in their white cocoons, as if awaiting a great change. Each eye was sewed closed by a single stitch so you could not see which ones were missing. The odour of decay was oppressive. Many of the crowd pressed handkerchiefs to their mouths. The landlord of the Jugged Hare was later forced to refinish his wall and floor, as the bodies leaked fluid into the plaster and boards.

They were going further into death. They were leaving me behind.

Jamie MacRaith identified the bodies with a murmur and did not look at them. The Procurator let him go, acknowledging that "Mr. MacRaith has indeed seen enough."

When I was called there was an audible gasp, and the assembled crowd tutted as I took the stand. Many of those present had known me as a girl, though I had not been seen in the village for some years. I was sadly bruised and my head bound. My eye ached with its absence. I was wrapped in a cloak and shivered all the while. But people are kind. The *Dundee Herald* observed that I had "lost nothing in beauty or dignity," though what the *Dundee Herald* knew of my beauty or dignity I could not tell. I recited quietly the names of my family. Yes, that was Uncle and that Nora, and Elizabeth, who had been but fourteen. Then there was Sarah. My voice caught and I pressed a hand to my mouth. Did I go pale? I believe that I did.

"Miss Bearings," said the Procurator, "I understand that this causes you grief. But the law must be served."

I said, "When a loved one dies, a pact is broken. I feel this fivefold, for I have lost all my family in one swoop." Here I gave way to tears. There was a murmur of sympathy for my plight.

Abernathy asked me, "Do you know who has done this?"

"Eve did it," I answered in a very dull voice. "Evelyn." I leant forward towards the front row of the spectators. "She and I were close as sisters once. We protected one another, helped one another, comforted one another as sisters would. But three summers ago she changed. She began to write letters . . ." I paused. "I do not know how to say it. They were obscene. She would deliver them by hand. After that she would be well, for a time. It was as if this act gave her some peace. But whatever it was built up in her again, and she had to write another. Perhaps you recall the sad result of one of these letters? It provoked Hamish Buchanan to defend his daughter's virtue in the most final way." I had thought there were no more tears in me, but I was wrong.

Beside me, Jamie MacRaith stirred, uneasy.

"She began to shed her own blood in rituals. And then she put her eye out with a knife. I watched it happen. What girl of fourteen would do such a thing?

"After that summer we became her prisoners on the isle. She kept the key to the gate about her neck. She starved us, and locked us up in the dark for days on end, cut us for her blood worship. For three years I have been her captive.

"As time passed her madness grew. She desired more power, and blood was no longer enough. An eye was no longer enough. So at the death of the old year she half-blinded us, then slaughtered us on her altar. Do you understand? We were an offering."

The air in a room changes when truth is spoken. Have you noticed? Everything goes still. I trembled. I was there again, among the stones and the mist.

A woman in the front row began to cry. "What an *evil*, wicked thing," she said. "I hope they catch her and hang her." Some gentlemen took off their caps.

"Please, Miss Bearings," said the Procurator, "if you could take us through the events of that day."

"She put something in our food in the evening," I said. "I do not know what. It made us all very sleepy. Sarah Buchanan was to deliver white wool to us for the ritual. The last thing I recall is going to the gate with Evelyn to collect it. I remember her taking out the key she kept about her neck and opening the lock. After that . . . nothing.

"When I awoke I was in the circle of stones, with my family about me. I saw the faces of my loved ones, white against the grass. Sarah's face was close to mine. She was dead.

"A torch burned in the centre of the circle. Evelyn stood there. She was wearing her shift, and was covered in blood. She held something metal, shining and thin.

"She did something to Uncle's corpse, I could not see what. Then she proceeded around the circle, pausing by each one of us. There was a soft noise and I saw that it was made by the needle going in. She took the eyes . . . I hope that they were all dead. Oh, I hope so . . .

"I lay still so that she would think me asleep and I waited. I could not hope to outrun her. I was sluggish with the drug. She came to me last. I had to let her do it—had to—so that I might perhaps live. I saw it come down, the needle. Then the pain came, and one eye went dark.

"Sometimes pain takes you beyond it into another place. I think I fainted. It was a blessed relief. When I came to Eve had turned away to greet the dawn. She thought that she had killed me. Her legs were bare and streaked with blood. I hated her so much, it gave me strength. I leapt up with all that was left to me and knocked her to the ground. We struggled. I took the needle from her and struck at her with it here and here—" I showed the areas on my midriff. "She bled. I think I might have stabbed her in a vital place. She staggered away, I do not know where. In the distance I heard a sound, like something coughing or grinding."

"Could this have been an automobile engine?" asked the Procurator. "A green AC was seen on the coast path on the evening of the murders, driving towards the isle. A little girl saw it. She thought it was a Weller engine. It was remarkable, as motorcars are not common in these parts."

I said uncertainly that I supposed it could have been an automobile. I was not very accustomed to them. Or to seeing so many people, or to being questioned . . .

"In which direction did the car go, Miss Bearings? It is most urgent that you think."

"I do not know," I said simply, and began to weep. One person cried out loudly, "For shame!" Proceedings were suspended for some minutes while I was revived with a nip of whisky.

According to the *Inverness Argus*, "There was not a soul in the place that did not wish to help," for I was "so lovely and so sad."

"You cannot simply turn off feelings," I said through my tears. "I know that she is an abomination, but she was my friend, too, for many turns. Who do I have, now?" Shining tears seeped from the slit of my dead eye. "We were not very kind to her sometimes. She was so little and odd. Poor Eve. No, let me be." I pushed away the ministering hands. "You did not know her. You will say things about her now, as though you did—but you did not."

The Procurator continued, but hereupon I could not make sense of it all, and I could see that my answers did not satisfy. The world was too large and I too small in it. He asked me what poison had been administered to the Children. I told him that "it was done by the Adder." He asked me of our lives on the isle. How could I find the words I did not know—for the benison, for the net of gold that encircled us all? For what was gone, which was my world. I wept until I could not breathe and they were forced to remove me from the stand.

Constable Firth of the Tongue police appeared next and stated that a description of the mysterious car was being circulated to all forces and that there were roadblocks in place in all directions. Constabulary from five towns were searching the sea, the coastline and the moors for the body or person of Evelyn Bearings, but so far they had found no trace. As the constable told the Procurator, "It is very wild out there, and there is much country."

"Make no mistake," said the Procurator, "you must not rest until she is caught. There has never been a more dangerous criminal."

The old doctor then took to his feet.

He said he thought that the bodies had spent some time in the warmth, as there was some blowfly growth in the orifices, which could not have advanced so far in the freezing temperatures in which the bodies were found. From the growth of these *Calliphoridae* maggots he could determine the order in which the victims were killed, and how far apart their deaths were. The first to die had been the girl Sarah Buchanan, some time on New Year's Eve. Some five or six hours later, in the early hours of 1921, Elizabeth Bearings and John Bearings had met their end. Last, a bare two hours before Jamie MacRaith had come upon the grisly scene, Nora Bearings had died.

The doctor paused here, for I had begun to scream. The Procurator instructed that I be taken upstairs to rest. A kindly-looking constable with large moustaches tried to do this.

But I fought him. "I will hear every word of it," I said. "It is my right."

"Very well," said the Procurator. "As long as you recall that these are legal proceedings. There cannot be disruption."

On being asked to pronounce on the manner of death, Dr. Mc-Clintock declared himself puzzled. There were marks on the bodies, he said, puncture wounds.

"I concur with Miss Bearings' account," he said. "Two poisons were employed—one taken orally, the other intravenously. I conducted two tests in accordance with standard procedure. First, I injected the stomach contents of each victim into five dogs. I then injected a small amount of serum, made from the blood of each corpse, into five different dogs. The animals which were injected with the stomach contents displayed symptoms of delirium, frothed at the mouth and fitted over the course of three days—but they did not die. This indicates a fast-acting toxin, administered by mouth, which was not fatal, and whose onset, duration and severity is uncertain. The substance disorientated the dogs and excited them. Some slept but some were in a frenzy." McClintock's unease was written on his face. "That substance would not have killed alone. In fact, were it not for the second test I would have asked the court, was this not some terrible accident?" The crowd shuffled, mutinous. What were they all here for, if not a murder?

"And the dogs who were injected with the victims' blood?" asked the Procurator.

"All dead within the hour, Your Honour, and in agony. The injection site inflamed and necrotic. I would not wish such a death on anyone."

There was a murmur of outrage and approval. This was much better.

"I recommend," said the Procurator, "that the stomach contents and the blood be further tested."

"Let the record show," said McClintock, sounding surly, "that none of this solution remains, as I have used it all in my own testing. But I can assure you that my findings are correct." It was some time before the Procurator could make himself heard. He instructed that the corpses be removed and put back in the cold of Jamie MacRaith's cellar.

The next piece of evidence was a letter. This letter had been delivered by hand to the police station in Tongue on 20 December. After comparing the handwriting, the authorities were satisfied that the letter was in the hand of Nora Marr. Portions of this letter were read aloud by the Procurator.

I am afraid of Eve. She has always liked to hurt things. When she was young she would cut herself for sport. Now she does *not sleep. She walks the halls in the night. She traffics with darkness. She converses with invisible things. She says they demand our lives. We cannot get off the isle. I am afraid.*

There was silence after he had finished. The *Highland Enquirer* wrote, "It was as if the voice of the poor dead woman was for a moment heard again, ringing about the room."

"It seems to me," the Procurator said heavily, "that a great evil has come upon our good village. I am sorry that we did not heed the warnings."

"A question, Your Honour." A man stood in the assembled crowd. He was dark, dressed in a seersucker suit of excellent cut. He held a homburg in his hands. "I am Christopher Black, formerly a Chief Inspector of the Inverness Police," he said. "I urgently submit my request to the Procurator to interview Miss Dinah Bearings."

I had never liked this man and I liked his intrusion here even less. What business did he have to interview me?

The Procurator Justice Abernathy seemed to agree, for he frowned. "You have no authority here, Mr. Black," he said. It is not for you to interfere with these proceedings. I know who you are. I have heard."

"All the same," said Christopher Black. "I would know of Dinah Bearings: where is her silver locket? It was not found on the isle."

"Sit down," said the Justice.

"As a concerned member of the public, Your Honour, I have asked a question. Will Miss Bearings be permitted to answer it?"

The Procurator looked at Mr. Black over his half-moon spectacles. "Very well," he said. "You may answer, Miss Bearings, if you wish."

"I do not know," I said. "The locket was lost at some time during those dark days. It is all quite a blur to me. You look well, Chief Inspector," I added. "Quite unchanged, in fact."

Some Loyalers in the audience smiled behind their hands. Perhaps they recalled me from my schooldays. I suppose they were thinking, "Well, she is still a flirt."

"Was it not your most precious possession?" asked Black.

"I have lost more than that in recent days," I said.

"The locket held hair cut from your sister Evelyn's head, did it not? Microscopic examination of that hair could be used to identify her when she is captured. I believe that the police—unwisely—did not retain the hair samples I took during the MacRaith murder investigation."

I raised my battered face and looked directly at him with my one remaining eye. "No," I said. "It was hair cut from my own head."

"That is no use, then," he said cheerfully.

"And I believe that you have asked your question, Mr. Black," said the Procurator. "We do not harass grieving women on the stand. This is not Inverness." He concluded the session by instructing the police to find the woman known as Evelyn Bearings and present her to the court to answer charges of four counts of murder and one count of attempted murder.

* * *

Mothers kept their children close. A night watch was put in place in Loyal. Those who must travel for their trade were encouraged to seek companions for the road. Families in outlying cottages were brought in. Women whose husbands were out on the boats were taken into households. It was very like that other time, I heard Mrs. Nettle remark. She saw that Jamie MacRaith was near, and stopped her mouth. The "other time" had been the murder of his father, three years before.

I kept to my room. I had never slept on ticking before and I found the bed dreadful, so I made a nest for myself on the boards and lay there to watch the darkening sky. Through the floor under my back

I heard the noise of the inn. There was much traffic and much business. The newspapermen liked drink and food and there was a great deal to discuss.

"She does look awful sad, that Dinah, aye," said someone. "I could give her some good cheer!"

"Someone would have to take her other eye before she looked at you," said another voice.

Laughter.

I slipped my locket from the collar of my shirt and warmed it in my hand.

* * *

I awoke to a clamour below in the yard. Morning, and she had been found.

Divers came across a wreck on the ocean floor fifty feet from the causeway. It was the remains of an AC motorcar with a Weller engine. A winch and pulley were set up and the car was pulled from the deep.

Sergeant Hackles of Inverness watched as the vehicle was brought out of the sea. "As the motor broke the surface," he reported, "I saw that the chassis was bright green. There was something behind the windscreen. A white face. The boys started shouting, and the lad manning the winch fell into the sea. The face moved, as if it was looking about, but it was merely the effect of the water that filled the interior of the car.

"In the driver's seat was the corpse of a woman. Water streamed out through the windows, the gaps in the chassis and the undercarriage. As the cabin emptied and the body was exposed to the air, we saw that the skull had been partially picked clean. Shore crabs and brown crabs poured out of the eye sockets, running down the chest and legs, seeking to hide in the water that pooled in the footwells and engine. There was not yet any smell except that of the sea. But I was unwell and I was not alone in that."

The hunt was over. Evelyn had travelled no further than two hundred feet from Altnaharra.

* * *

In the depths of Jamie MacRaith's butcher shop, I came face-to-face with Eve again. But she was not there. I saw that straight away. She had gone back to the sea. I leant in close and whispered my words into the ragged thing that had been an ear.

All that could be done had been done. I ordered cremation. I flung the ashes into the sea. But Evelyn's ashes I took charge of. I did not want her tossed on the wind. I put her in an old tea tin, rusted with age. She could not hurt me. So I thought then.

I petitioned the Procurator for leave to depart. "Altnaharra is where I should have died," I said. "Some depths cannot be bridged. I must get right away." He looked at my drawn face and granted it.

When the will was executed, I found I was the sole heir. I made Jamie MacRaith a gift of Altnaharra for life and he took up residence. Jamie was always somewhat lacking in imagination. He asked that I never come to the isle again while he lived.

"When I die," he said, "the very next day you may return. But I must live free of you and the past."

I agreed. I have done enough to Jamie. And I could not bear the sight of Altnaharra.

I give these days to you. I cast them off.

I know you. You are trying to find me. There is no chase without a quarry.

* * *

D

EVELYN

1920

TODAY is mission, and we go to the gate before dawn.

They stand before me in order of age. Nora, Dinah, Abel, Elizabeth.

I ask, "Who do you watch for corruption while I am away in the impure world?"

"I watch Dinah for signs of corruption," Nora says.

"I watch Abel for signs of corruption," Dinah says.

"I watch Nora," Abel says. He has become a silent young man. His white hair has darkened to straw. But some part of him is left behind; his body flickers between boy and man.

Dinah and I lift the three iron bars. We shoot the two bolts. Metal screams. I take the black key that hangs on a cord about my neck. I use two hands to turn it. The gate yawns open.

I slip the key back under my collar. It sits cold against my breastbone. My flesh never seems to warm it.

"Get things for the baby," Dinah says. "Nora is nearly due."

I give her a rueful look.

"Perhaps this one will live." Dinah always says that.

Elizabeth hugs Haystack and then me. She breathes, excited, into my ear.

"I know." I hold her tightly. "I will not forget." I have promised her a present from Inverness.

Elizabeth has been eating something—earth, perhaps. It is on her face, under her nails, in her hair, between the toes of her bare feet.

"I bathed you just yesterday," I say, exasperation rising. "Why should I buy you stout leather boots and socks if you will not wear them?" Elizabeth would be happy to return to the days of bare feet and grocery sacks.

"I wish today was over," I say to Dinah. "I hate going among them."

She smiles. "You will soon be back." Dinah has taken the white. Her veil flutters in the high breeze. She pulls it aside so that I may kiss her. Only I leave the isle, now. Uncle and I decided it was best. Three years have changed us all. We learned the lessons of that bad summer.

I lead Haystack through the shallows. He pricks up his ears at the wind whistling through the gate, his eyes are wide. I quiet him gently with my mind. The feathering on his legs is as thick as ostrich plumage and he hates getting his feet wet. I put two shillings in the wire basket then shut the lid fast. The crows like to steal coins. Jamie MacRaith is coming with Uncle's mutton later.

The clouds are low, heavy-bellied with rain. I ride hard for Tongue. Haystack grunts. He is lazy.

I am no longer welcome in Loyal—as they say, I have killed two good men. Sometimes I wonder how Sarah Buchanan is. She has her own troubles, I know. I hear things. She has a child. I leave Haystack at the inn in Tongue. They do not know me here. I am just a girl with a pony.

The train is very crowded and there is market day levity among the passengers. Best hats are carefully stored on the overhead racks. Pressed dresses smelling of verbena, lavender. Pockets full of coins.

Eyes bright with the thought of ribbons, beer and talk. I feel the old painful stretch, as I draw further from home. I close my eyes and see water. Uncle taught me this. Take the sea with you wherever you go. Make His blood your blood. Your bones His coral. Your flesh the yielding sand of His oceans. *Always with thee.*

It is just light when I reach Inverness, but the streets are already alive. There is the usual shock as I join their current. Ordure, corruption, all washing about me in dirty waves. I fight the urge to hold my breath, or clean myself like a cat. Out of the station. Across the road. Left, left, right. At the end of the street the market square is beginning to hum like an engine.

I find a good place for my small white tent. I am at the very limit of my power, here. It flickers in and out like a flame in the wind, but it will be enough. Beside me a plump woman sells oranges. On the other side a father and son display leatherwork: harnesses, saddles, belts. Four stalls over is an ornate yellow sign, with *Lady Spiritualist* spelled out in green. *Speciality, Reaching Those Fallen in Combat.* A tired woman stands by it. She wears a red turban and her eyes are painted like peacock feathers.

I have no sign. I wear dark, unremarkable clothes. I am not a *Lady Spiritualist* but something quite different.

It was my idea to use the eye in the market. Uncle said no, at first. I pleaded.

"Why not use their own impurity against them? Let me do this for us." When I returned with handfuls of coins he began to see the sense of it.

I see the first customer shortly after nine. A quick, furtive look in her, all sharp angles. She has seen fifty turns or so. Very thin. Mouth the merest kiss of red in her powdered face. Black fur clinging at her throat. They have left the head on and the animal snarls, caught in the act of dying. Her dress is silk, broad stripes of rich brown. Well pressed with pleats like knives. Red and white stones gleam at her wrist and in her ears are tiny flowers, more white jewels. Her shoes are snakeskin. That is expensive. One delicate buckle is undone.

These things are like signs and I have learned to read them.

I gaze at the cobbles. She must not feel observed. That would be fatal. They come here for answers but they do not like it known. I feel her approach in my skin. Closer, closer, until she stands over me. I look up slowly. I show her the things I want her to see. My face, pale and pointed. The black patch, covering the place where my right eye was.

"I am looking for someone," the woman says. "My friend, Mrs. . . . well, never mind. She said that a woman who knows things comes to market some days. But perhaps . . . perhaps that is not you."

"Come." Inside the tent the noise seems to drop away. There are two plain stools facing one another. I sit and take her chilly hand. "Mrs. . . . ?"

"De Vere," the woman says.

"That is not your name. But names do not matter here." It is good to be stern with the rich ones. They like it. I tighten my grasp, allow the barest hint of benison between our palms. Mrs. de Vere's eyes are fuddled by the touch. A powerful waft of cologne. A deep, brassy scent. So far it is the only surprising thing about her.

"I am Evelyn Black. I am not like the others. A medium, or a palm reader. You will not see the dead here. I come from the ocean and I bring with me its truth." I let the scent of ocean touch the air.

Wonder in her eyes. Their lives are drab, the Impure. They are impressed by the slightest act of power.

Her hands pluck at her wedding ring. A habit. Around the gold band the skin is raw. She does it for comfort. The husband is good, or at least Mrs. de Vere thinks he is.

"You are wishing he was here," I say. "But it is better that we are alone. Some matters are only for women." A useful remark, meaning nothing. "Let us begin."

I slip my knife from my cuff. I take her hand and raise a dark bubble of blood on her thumb.

Mrs. de Vere gasps and tries to tear her hand away. I keep her in a strong grip. "There is trouble," I say. "Tell me."

"It is my daughter," Mrs. de Vere says. Her eyes are glassy with un-spilled tears. "She's a dirty little cat. She has disgraced us, but she will not admit it. She is wilful and will not take her punishment. I do not know what to do with her!" Mrs. de Vere's fingers worry her beautiful shoes, pulling the snakeskin. She sniffs and takes a tiny scrap of lace handkerchief from her muff. The air is filled with that musky scent.

I must damp her down a little. It is too soon. "Mrs. de Vere. You wish to speak of your daughter. Very well. We will. But let us think of you, first of all." I breathe and half-close my good eye, watching Mrs. de Vere through the fringe of lashes. She is looking at my eye-patch and wondering. Let her.

"You were not born in Scotland," I say. Her hand stills in the act of twisting the ring. "Europe, I think. A name is coming—it is con-nected with the letter P. Does that mean something to you?"

"I was born in London," Mrs. de Vere says.

"P does not refer to a city." I am kind and reproving now, like Uncle. "A place or a person, I think."

Mrs. de Vere looks at me, expectant.

"A place . . ." I say.

She tenses her knees slightly. The merest rustle of silk.

"No," I say. "It is a person. Someone important to you when you were younger. I see the letter S, no, L, no, E. Yes, I see it clearly. P and E. A woman . . ." I rock gently from side to side, eye half-closed, watching Mrs. de Vere. "An older woman," I say.

"She was," says Mrs. de Vere.

"Whom you cared for, and who cared for you. You were a child." I feel it now, the line taut in my hands. "Her name was not Prudence—"

Silk rustles.

"But something much prettier."

"Paul . . ."

"It must be Pauline," I say.

Mrs. de Vere gives a tearful nod. She does not want to show she is stirred. "Can you see her?" she asks.

"I do not deal with the dead," I say. "I see you as a person of standing. You prepare yourself like this each day to face the world." I nod at her fur, her dress, her hair. "You spend time on it. It is an art. But there is something nearby that spoils your pleasure. It causes you shame." This usually brings results.

Mrs. de Vere's eyes are wide. "How could you know that?"

"It is in a chest," I say.

"Well, yes, a box. His letters. My first husband's papers. They are in the cupboard by the dressing table. Each time I sit down before the glass I think of that box. I promise myself that I will go through it and burn what must be burnt, but I cannot bear the thought." Mrs. de Vere laughs a little. Some feeling in her eyes. Fear. Of what?

"Miss Black," Mrs. de Vere begins and I silence her with a finger.

"The sea is speaking." I let the focus of my good eye drift, go past Mrs. de Vere, through her. That perfume—I know little about such things but I know it does not go with Mrs. de Vere.

"He gave you that scent," I say. "Your lover. He came back as he promised he would and then you married, at long last."

Mrs. de Vere sighs as though she has been waiting a long time for someone to say these things. "I fell in love with Alexander at first sight," she says. But George wouldn't divorce me, horrid man. He didn't have the decency to die until the *very* end of the War—not until Picardy! We began to think he *never* would. And I was glad, d'you hear? All the while I had hoped and hoped that the right one would come back from France, and he did. Alexander."

"And he came for you," I say, "in the most romantic way . . ."

"I suppose he did, yes! The moment he heard that George was dead, there he was on the front step, French mud still on his boots. The maid wouldn't let him in, he was in such a state. He brought me this scent. Vulgar, isn't it—men can never choose scent—but I wear it anyhow. Because he bought it for me. In the end I've grown rather fond of it." A tear falls from the end of her sharp nose.

"He was cruel, your first husband," I say. People always believe their former lovers cruel. "He did you harm. Not to your body but to your spirit." Mrs. de Vere is already nodding and pressing the scrap of lace to her eyes.

"Now you are free of him," I say. "Yet you are still afraid." I watch Mrs. de Vere carefully. "Not of him. You are afraid of yourself."

Most women are. Once I understood this, seeing them became easy. Men are not the same.

"You think that you have failed your daughter by not remaining steadfast in your marriage. You think that perhaps she is tainted by your example . . ."

"She saw us." Mrs. de Vere cries openly now, in the manner of one not used to it. Tears form tributaries on her powdered face. "She was meant to be at a party. But she came home early—she hated parties, really, and London."

"You think you ruined her."

The sound that comes from Mrs. de Vere is like a saw drawn across metal. "Did I?" she says.

I tip my head to one side, considering. "Perhaps," I say. "Perhaps not."

Mrs. de Vere nods and gulps, a little girl trying to be brave. "We could not return to London after her disgrace was revealed. But oh, how I hate it here." We have reached the crisis. Now I make her feel pure.

For the rest of the hour I draw memories and secrets from her like shining fish from the shallows. Mrs. de Vere laughs and cries again as I cast her life across the dim air. We lean together and whisper and laugh like girls plaiting one another's hair before bed. Mrs. de Vere thought she had come to find out her daughter's secrets, but she came for herself.

At the end, I help Mrs. de Vere to rise. She is emptied. Later she will recall no prompting or errors. Even now her mind is at work, making our time together perfect.

Mrs. de Vere says, "Would you accept . . . ?" I take the proffered pound.

"What now?" Mrs. de Vere says. She does not want to leave the cosy space where I tell her what to think and soothe her fears.

"We may meet again," I say. "Or we may not. I go where the tides take me. But I am often here on market days. You may tell your friends so."

I help her with her peculiar little feathered hat.

"She has not been discreet," says Mrs. de Vere. "My daughter was a fool and her absence was public. One can get away with so much if one is discreet, but she will not understand that. If only she really *would* go away, for ever."

I see then, as if it were written on the air, that Mrs. de Vere is thinking of having her daughter killed.

Mrs. de Vere shrieks.

"Hatpins," I say. "I am clumsy with them, you know. I do not wear hats." I push Mrs. de Vere out into the roaring market.

She turns. "Who are you really, Miss Black?" This happens sometimes. They have been deeply mined and they do not like it.

I give her another push and Mrs. de Vere staggers away, one snakeskin shoe still undone.

* * *

The money is for buying stores. There is no telling how long we will need to shelter at Altnaharra while He cleanses the world. We must be prepared to survive seasons, perhaps turns, as His floods wash away all impurity. Then we will be released into a fresh world where there is only the ocean.

I long for the day of His coming. I find each foray into the impure world more tiring than the last.

"Miss Black, indeed," says a voice.

I look up slowly. Chief Inspector Black stands before me. He is somewhat changed. Thinner. His sleek dark head is now touched with grey. His suit is a beautiful blue tweed. It seems a part of him, as his clothes always do.

He smiles. "I wondered if perhaps it might be you." He sits stiffly on the low stool. "It has been three years," he says. "It feels like longer. Much has happened in that time. To both of us, I think. And yet I have not forgotten you. You and that island and your uncle have become something of a hobby horse of mine, you know. I cannot quite leave it alone. Some might call it an obsession. And here you are and you have not forgotten me either, it seems. Wearing my name about the market like a stole about the shoulders."

"Black is a word like any other," I say. "I cannot think why I chose it."

"I think that you wished me to find you. Perhaps I am *your* obsession."

"No," I say. "Are you going to arrest me?" I do not know the rules about people who have run away from policemen.

"No. You still misunderstand. Believe it or not, I meant to help you."

"It is you who needs help," I say. "You and your impure God." He has power and I must remember that. I must not like him.

Something passes behind his eyes. "It is difficult to believe in a loving God," he says, "after Passchendaele."

"I will read you," I say. "No charge."

"I couldn't possibly accept," he says politely. "Save your energy for business."

There is a hum in him, a disruption. Pain. "You have lost something," I say.

"Everyone has lost something. It is the nature of these times."

I lean forward and lift his trouser cuff above his ankle, or where his ankle should be. His shin is made of smooth wood. "Loss."

"As for that, you would have seen it in my gait."

"I saw it in your mind."

He snaps his fingers before my face and says, "No, you did not."

I open my hand. In my palm is something small and black. The sweet muddy scent of liquorice.

I laugh before I recall myself. "I cannot take it," I say.

"It is bad luck to return a gift. Throw it away if you do not want it."

A small plump child is walking by with a fishing rod taller than himself. I take his hand. "Here," I say. "For you." He looks at the liquorice for a moment, closes his palm then hurries on in case I change my mind.

"Still baffling children with your magic tricks," I say.

"It is not so different to what you do. Observation, misdirection."

"What I do is nothing like that," I say, glad that I did not take the liquorice. "It is His gift." And I paid for it.

"You think you are unique, yet there are societies devoted to what you do, books written about it. And just as many devoted to disproving it."

"Not to what *I* do," I say. I nod at the Lady Spiritualist with her peacock eyes. "Her, perhaps."

"What difference is there? You both claim to provide answers in these sad days. You feed off grief and uncertainty, profit on sorrow."

"I am glad the War did not eat you, Chief Inspector Black," I say, "but I wish you would go now. I have much to do."

Christopher Black says, "Did you find something in your pocket, after we last met?"

"*Stop*," I say, with all the power I can summon.

"Only you can free yourself." He stands.

"I met a woman today," I say. "She said she was called de Vere. She came from somewhere nearby, I think—she had taken off her shoes for driving, but her dress was only a little creased. Her first husband was called George and was killed at Picardy in 1918. She remarried—a man named Alexander. Mrs. de Vere is going to kill her daughter," I say. "Or at least, she wants to."

I think of the unknown girl whom Mrs. de Vere would like to kill. Who is she? Perhaps she likes to swim, as I do. Perhaps she likes mushrooms or hates cabbage. All these things that will be ended by death. I know that I should not care. The Impure will all be washed away when He comes.

Christopher Black looks at me seriously. "What game is this?"

"No game at all," I say. "Only to show you the kind of *innocents* I *profit* from."

"What happened to your eye?"

I do not reply. He would not understand.

"The price for your return," he says. "Wasn't it?" He sounds sad.

I shake my head.

He goes with no word of farewell, limping across the crowded market.

I tie up Mrs. de Vere's money safely in my handkerchief and stow it in my apron pocket. It has been a good day already. I have done well. Uncle will be pleased.

I feel as though I might cry.

* * *

On my return, Dinah meets me at the gate.

"Welcome home, Eve of the Isle," she says, cheerful. "What an amount of parcels! Oh, the mutton is here." She takes it from the wire basket. A crimson line of blood runs down the white wax paper. "I will take it in to Nora."

With Mrs. de Vere's pound I bought warm woollens for winter. I bought tins of tongue and bully beef. I bought string and needles and candles, iodine and bandages, all to add to the stores in the cellar. Even so, I did not spend it all.

"Come, pony." Dinah stumbles on the shingle as Haystack shoves her hard in the small of her back with his nose. "Yes, you are hungry, I know."

I slip the key under my blouse, shivering at its touch.

Uncle gazes into the fire. Flames are reflected in his eyes. What does he see? The hall is filled with sweetness. Last autumn's apples make good fuel. Uncle seldom leaves his chair now; his limp is very bad these days. It's the cost of power. Hercules' tank is at his feet.

"Adder." I kneel and offer Uncle the remaining shillings.

He touches my head. "Eve. Give me the box."

I take the little box from where it sits by Hercules' tank. Heavy, bound with iron. Uncle unlocks it and tosses the coins in with a dull chink. Three years of taking money from the Impure in the marketplace. There must be a good amount. Uncle locks the box and I return it to its place.

He gives me honey from his fingers. The benison races through me and my empty eye socket burns with fire. Outside the window, the ocean rejoices, licks the isle with tongues of flame. The Adder's love warms me after the coldness of the world.

*   *   *

I leave the steaming pitcher and the iron bath in the passage.

Elizabeth's room is a bird hospital. Old fishing cages line the walls. In them, the soft shift of feathers, the beat of tiny hearts. Wrens, robins, gulls, an angry crow with a shining jet eye. They have sardine tins full of water and crusts of bread. They have dirty pink ribbons tied about their necks in bows. A dove makes a mournful coo. Some have splints on their legs, some on their wings. The room is filled with the odour of bird droppings. Birds are often dashed against the stone of the castle in high winds. In the past I would have taken them to the mainland to die. Now Uncle permits Elizabeth to mend the ones that can be mended.

"How do you do, Baby?" I ask. "You are making everyone better, I see."

Elizabeth comes to me, dancing. I hold her present above my head: a wooden bird carved from cedar. It has a suspicious, judgemental eye. She jumps for it and her golden hair flies. She makes little grunts of pleasure.

Then she catches sight of the tub in the passage, the warm steam rising from the pitcher. She turns to run, making a screaming noise in her throat.

I catch her with one arm and bring the bird down to eye level. "You may have it afterwards," I say.

She looks at me with longing and hatred. She knows that it is not bath day. But Christopher Black's disdain has followed me home from the market. "He will not have cause to despise us again," I tell Elizabeth as she struggles.

I wash her with soap, rub her hair with salt, vinegar and oil to kill any lice. I clean under her nails with my knife. I dry her thoroughly and dress her cuts and scrapes with iodine, then clothe her in a blue woollen frock. She weeps throughout, tragic and betrayed.

"There," I tell Elizabeth. "You look very fine!"

She will not look up. I offer her the wooden bird. She snatches it from my hand, kisses it and holds it close, turning away from me. It will be days before I am forgiven.

Something writhes in my stomach. Why can she not see that everything I do is for her own good?

I pry the wooden bird from her strong little hands. "You shall not have it," I say. "Until you know how to be grateful."

Her screams follow me down the passage, the stairs. Heat rises in me. Sometimes I long for the old days, before I had care of them all, when I was just Eve. My steps quicken.

I run through the hall and fly out of the seaward door. The sloping turf is good beneath my feet. In the white sky above, a sea hawk hangs, still as the stones below. I run until my breath becomes one with the wind. If I go any faster I will leave the earth altogether. The cliff approaches. As I reach the edge I cast myself upwards, out, through the cold sky. I find the hawk through the roaring wind. I am in him, washed clean of my own thoughts, desires. I blink with his fierce eye. I angle his spread wings against the delicate pressure of the wind. Water shines below like molten lead. The isle retreats. The small pile of mortal remains lies heaped upon the clifftop, in the circle of stones. We turn on the columns of air and go up, up and out to sea.

* * *

I call Nora to us in the hall, as I do each day before supper. She comes, eyes lowered. I raise blood on my finger and listen for the baby. It is curled up like a fern frond.

"It is alive, still," I tell Uncle.

He nods at Nora. "You may go and eat."

Nora smiles, tremulous. Usually the babies are dead by now.

When she is gone I say to Uncle, "Only a little more food, and only when she has a child in her. It may help her keep them."

"I will consider it," he says, smiling. "Always thinking of us, Eve!"

Supper: boiled rice with whey. *We do not speak of the past.* Eight mouthfuls. I am glad of it. The impure world leaves me tired and hungry. Nora sits down with a grunt, holding her belly. Abel eats standing, facing the wall.

"Abel is shunned," Dinah says. "He was disrespectful to Uncle today." Dinah passes Hercules from hand to hand. His diamond head caresses her thumb. She no longer fears him. His fangs have not grown back; perhaps they never will. They sit in my hand like ghosts. Dinah feeds him dead mice. We catch them in the cellar.

Uncle's mutton gives out a fatty scent.

*　*　*

Dinah removes my eyepatch. She smooths honey into the empty place and packs it with clean gauze. "There," she says.

The candle burns straight and tall, the wind taps at the shutters. The locket gleams silver on Dinah's white skin. She hides it under a loose flag. At night she takes it out and wears it. I do not tell. We each have our secrets.

I make sure that Dinah has turned away, then I slip the yellowed envelope from beneath the mattress. I carefully slide out the torn piece of newspaper; fine as cobweb now, faded with handling, one corner dark where the sea took it before I could snatch it clear of the water. Alice's gaze is still direct, her mouth still resolute beneath her strong nose. She looks into me and I look back. I touch Alice's face, once. I think the word without thinking it, allow it to form a space in my mind. When it has filled me, I slip the paper back into the mattress.

Dinah stares into the candle flame, stroking the locket with a finger. "You like this," she says presently. "Do you not, Eve? The locket."

"It is impure, as well you know." But I do like it.

"Would you like to wear it tonight?" There is a little shiver in Dinah's voice. "We could exchange. I could wear the key. Perhaps that is the sort of thing that impure girls do for fun—swap necklaces!" Dinah likes to imagine what impure girls do for fun. It means that she can be disapproving and thrilled all at once.

I shake my head. The key is my cold burden.

"Well," says Dinah. "Perhaps another day." She strokes my head. Her fingers have thoughts in them. She says, "Have you had your time yet, Eve?"

I shrug. "No."

"You are seventeen turns. You should have had it."

I tug her hair. "Fuss, fuss! Give me three things of the day."

"Oh," she says, pleased. Dinah's favourite game. "One. Rain pooled in the tops of the stones in the morning. In the afternoon they were crowned with sky. Two, when I held my mending up to the window, all the stitches were *exactly* the same size. And three—the memory of the oyster was in my mouth for an hour after it was swallowed. Now you give me three."

"I will give you one, for it is a big one. Someone in Inverness. Guess."

"Do the face," she says.

I think myself into him, which is the only way to make a good face. I feel his expression steal over me. Wide-eyed, calculating.

"Oh," Dinah says. She casts her eyes down. One finger twisting in a rivulet of copper. "Him."

"Dinah, you only saw him twice. You cannot have *thoughts* about him."

"Why not?" she says.

"He did look very bad," I say to myself. "As if he were pining for someone with dark red hair and skin like cream. He was muttering under his breath, a girl's name. *Dinah*, perhaps? Yes, I think it was. *Dinah, I miss you so . . .*"

Dinah stifles my words with her hand. I shriek into her muffling palm. She is pushing a handful of nightgown into my mouth when the door creaks its warning. We sit up quickly and straighten ourselves. Dinah slips the locket beneath her collar.

"Candle out," says Nora. Her face is swollen and glistening. She keeps a hand on the small of her back as if it hurts. "The Adder does not call for you tonight," she says formally. "Get into bed now." When we are beneath the blanket she bends with an audible grunt and blows out the candle.

After Nora is gone, Dinah whispers, "Eve!"

"I am doing it, Dinah!" I slip from the bed. My bare feet shrink on the cold stone. I open the window and wedge open the door.

I lie in Dinah's familiar warmth and my pounding heart slows. Dinah makes a sleepy, upset sound because I am holding her too tight. I hug her harder through her protests.

We have not yet been called to the Adder for the duty but there is no telling when he will say it is time. Each evening when Nora comes, I think: *it will be tonight.*

* * *

It is not sounds that wake one, but the edges of sounds, where they begin and end.

"They are only rabbits, Dinah." I take in the darkness. Something is missing. What is it? Dinah is not breathing. The mattress bears a cold dent where she should be. Dinah always sleeps through the night. Her slumber is as deep as death. Has she gone into her dream? Is she a white rabbit now? I tear myself from the bed.

As I run down the stairs, startled noises come from the rooms.

In the hall I stir the embers to flame and then grasp a pitch torch. I throw open the great door and run through ribbons of cold sea mist. Behind me, Uncle and the others shuffle, drowsy-footed.

I listen with my body. Then I run towards the causeway.

The sea is rough tonight. Dark waves rear to the height of a man, breaking in a rush of white foam. Dinah clings to the great metal gate. One pale leg is already thrown over.

I run through the shallows, waves slapping at my thighs. Salt spray fills my mouth. I grasp Dinah's thin ankle just before it is pulled beyond my reach.

"Dinah," I say. "It is all right. Come back."

Dinah's face gleams with mist and tears. "No," she says.

"What are you doing?" I shout at her. "Do you not recall what happened to Alice?"

"Oh, Evelyn," says Dinah. "Just let me go."

"Come down where it is safe!"

"Say that you were too late, that I was already gone, just let me go . . ." Dinah kicks me in the face.

I hold her until Abel is there. "Do not hurt her," I tell him. Abel pries Dinah's thin hands away, pulls her free with a grunt. She falls into the shallows, weeping. Abel picks Dinah up gently. She kicks, screams. I hold her legs. We carry her through the night. Dinah writhes and fights the whole way. The sounds she makes are eerie, like something dying or returned from the dead. We go to the Hall, where Uncle sits before the glowing coals.

"Dinah," he says. "Thank Him that Evelyn caught you in time."

"We are not safe," she says.

"We are behind walls of water and steel," Uncle says gently. "Dearest Dinah, we are safe."

"No," Dinah says. "The reekling is coming with its fangs."

"Dinah," says Uncle.

"We *must* go," she says. "All of us!"

"You are frightening the others," Uncle says. "Stop."

Dinah looks at him with eyes like holes. Then she screams, long and high. "It is coming. It is coming."

"Very well," says Uncle. He puts the cauldron of pitch on the red embers. The scent rises acrid and green.

Dinah weeps. "Please," she says. "Not Wane."

"Five days," Uncle says. "Five nights."

"I love you, Dinah," I whisper, squeezing her hand. "It will be all right. You will see."

* * *

I sit above the trapdoor each night. I talk to Dinah and tell her about the day. How the ocean was, and the sky. What birds are in Elizabeth's hospital. I pick three stems from the crawler, crowned with purple flowers the shade of vivid dusk, and feed them one by one through the gap between the rock and the trapdoor.

I come back the next morning. Torn purple petals and broken stems litter the floor. Dinah has forced the ruins of the flowers back up through the crack. I am glad to see it. Bad thoughts had been swimming in my mind, leeches in water. I take a petal gently between two fingers. Easily crushed; a flower, a life.

* * *

Uncle releases Dinah from Wane at dawn on the sixth day. We are waiting for her.

The trapdoor swings open and Dinah comes up the ladder. She is weak but her eyes are clear. She kneels before Uncle. "I have seen Him, Adder, and He has spoken. I see my error. Forgive me."

Uncle's eyes fill with tears. "Of course, my Dinah," he says. "Always and for ever." She flings her arms about him and they cling to one another. Abel and Elizabeth and I run to join the embrace. Nora smiles and strokes her tight stomach. *Uncle* is the name for *home* in our minds and hearts.

"Come," Uncle says.

The stones rear in the coming light, kindly and ancient. The sun blossoms through gauzy cloud, a cool pink dawn. The sea below shifts like cloth on a loom; it is the fabric of everything. We are in the very beating heart of the world.

We pass the bowl of honey round the circle. Dinah is still shaking.

"Should she not eat something more?" I ask.

"She is five days purified," Uncle says. "Her spirit will mingle with His like a comet striking the earth."

We join hands. I take Dinah's tightly. Dinah squeezes it back and relief floods me. I hate fighting with her. We are all together now, connected to the ocean.

"Nothing out there in the world compares with this," I whisper to Dinah. "I swear it."

Dinah nods. For a moment her smile looks uneven, a badly drawn line across her face.

"It is coming," Abel whispers. He races towards us over the sea; He hits like a breaker and we are gone, tossed in His golden mind.

* * *

When we come to it is afternoon. Our time with Him has sapped us greatly. Abel vomits and clings to me.

"We will drink peppermint," says Nora. She retches. She is quite green. "And then we will go to bed." I help her to climb the hill. She boils water in the great kettle and throws the dried leaves in. Scent fills the air. She makes tea with shaking hands.

I give Dinah broth, one sip at a time. She tries to take the cup from me.

"No. You will make yourself ill."

I soak bread in the broth and feed it to her, pinch by pinch.

"Your care for us is constant, Eve." For a moment Uncle's hand rests on me, warming the empty socket of my eye.

"Of course," I say simply.

* * *

Nora comes to douse the candle.

She stands in the doorway, looking at us in silence. I cannot breathe, the air is like cotton in my lungs.

"The Adder does not call for you tonight," Nora says, and goes. Relief courses through me, so strong that it resembles a different feeling. Grief, perhaps. Surely not hatred.

As I drift on the black tide towards sleep it comes to me that I forgot to tell Uncle about meeting Christopher Black in the market.

* * *

Breakfast. One piece of bread with honey. Four mouthfuls. *We do not speak of the past.* Abel is shunned for not finishing his tasks before dark the previous night. He was shunned last week, too. It has begun to seem like the natural way of things.

The report sings out all over the isle like gunshot. It is the peal of an old iron bell or someone beating an anvil. *Clang, clang.* We stare at one another.

"What is it?" asks Dinah.

"Someone is at the gate," I say. Has the black van come for us at last? I am cold all over.

"Who could it be?" asks Dinah.

"Perhaps they will go away," Nora says.

The hammering increases in pace and ferocity. Each blow feels as if it is striking directly inside my skull.

"I will make them go away," I say.

I walk down the sandy path that leads to the gate. I am still holding my breakfast. The hammering goes on.

I cannot see who is standing on the causeway behind the gate. As I approach the sound becomes deafening. The visitor is using a stick or a club to rain down blows upon the metal.

"Enough," I shout. "I am here." The hammering stops abruptly.

I kick off my shoes, hoist my skirts with one hand and wade into the water. I call through the dark steel, "What do you want?"

"Open up," says a voice. I don't know it.

"No. What is your business?"

"Do you have walnuts or a cucumber? I can pay."

"No. Go away."

The blow to the gate shakes it from top to bottom. The noise seems to last minutes, hours. After it fades I can still hear its ghost whining in my ear.

"Stop that," I say.

"I will, when you open up. I can go on all day." Another deafening blow.

"All right! Step away from the gate, do you hear? Ten paces back. Shout when you have done it."

The sound of splashing, retreat. "I have taken ten paces," the voice calls.

I unlock the gate slowly, my heart beating fast. It could be a trick. I listen for the bright click of handcuffs, the rumble of an engine. I open the gate a few inches, bracing myself. Nothing happens. The sea laps in the sunshine. Seals hoot. All seems as usual. I send up a little prayer to Him and push the gate wide. It swings open with a high sound.

A girl stands on the causeway. She holds a boy's cap in her hands which she kneads and crushes. In her other hand she holds the metal strut that she has been using to beat the gate.

Time slows. It is the sign, the girl who carried the snake in the basket. There is a crimson graze on her cheek, half-healed. Her nails are dirty and bitten and an amber beech leaf is caught in her loosely plaited hair. She is real. Once again a feeling of welcome washes through me as if I know her.

"Hello," I say again, stupidly.

She regards me. "Hello."

"We have met," I say.

"I am Rose. I don't remember . . ." Why should she recall it? Red shame creeps up my cheeks.

"Evelyn," I say.

"Please," Rose says. "I need help. When Betty stops she stops for good. She will not move and I must get her home."

"Who is Betty?"

She points and then I see it, standing in the sea at the end of the causeway. Its feet are granite, its vast hide is cracked glaze. Wide ears like sails, delicate and veined. A long grey nose like an arm. It dips this disapprovingly into the salty sea and blows water out in a spray. It is wearing a red blanket and a bonnet of red wool. Gold letters are stitched on the blanket: *Orde's Circus*.

The animal is like something from a dream, but I know what it is. Of course I do.

"Elephant," I say softly. The word sits soft and good on my tongue. The elephant has benison in her; I can feel it, even at this distance.

"Sometimes she can be tempted with nuts," Rose says. "I have money." She shows me a shilling.

"We do not have nuts."

"Well," Rose says, "something sweet, perhaps? Please." She puts out both hands, curls her fingers, as if beckoning me to do her will. It is a strange gesture, both desperate and appealing.

Honey drips golden on my thumb. Three mouthfuls, at least.

I draw the gate closed behind me. I lock it and slip the key beneath my shirt. We walk together across the causeway.

The elephant turns her cracked face towards me and watches us approach with an onyx eye. Close to, she is cross-hatched with wrinkles, the map of an arid land.

Rose hugs the elephant, thin arms spread wide about the base of the great, corrugated neck. She whispers something in one waving ear. The elephant knocks her cap off her head with her trunk. Rose presses her face harder to the elephant's chest. I wonder what it feels like, cheek against that hide, the pulse of that vast heart. I want to know so badly I can taste it at the back of my throat.

"If you do not come," Rose says to the elephant, "I will have to get the others." She chirrups and taps the elephant's leg.

Betty stands like a rock, puts her trunk gently about Rose's neck and sighs.

"*Come on*," hisses the girl. She prods the wrinkled leg again. "The others will bring the wire and the hook. Even if you can bear it, I can't. Not again. Just *move*." There are tears in her voice.

"Here." I proffer the bread. The honey oozes golden in the sun. The elephant puts out her trunk, delicate, questing. I move back a step, and the elephant follows.

"She likes it." Laughter bubbles in me, unexpected. "Look! She likes honey!"

I draw the elephant along the rocky shore, keeping just out of her reach. Rose guides me with a light hand on my elbow. After half a mile she says, "Here," and we turn inland. We walk in procession through the autumn woods. Now we are out of the wind, I can hear the sounds of the elephant: her breath like a waterfall, her footfalls, the dry creak of her skin. Her paintbrush tail whisks at the midges.

The big top is pitched at the foot of the hill they call Ardentinny. *Orde's Circus*, it reads. It is surrounded by wagons and small tents straining in the breeze. Each tent has a bright sign above it, describing magical people: *Strong Man, Fire Eater*, and, of course, *Lady Spiritualist*. The circus is passing through again.

The camp seems empty. They are still sleeping, here. They do not keep Altnaharra hours. But I cannot banish the thought of unseen eyes watching.

"Where?" I whisper.

"There," Rose says. "Third on the left." A bright yellow tent, *Betty* displayed in curling red letters. I lead us there.

"Take that off," the girl says, pointing at my scarf, which was knitted by Nora in rich green wool. "We will not have green inside our tents."

"Why not?"

"It is very bad luck," Rose says. "Everyone knows that."

I raise my eyebrows but take the scarf off.

"Leave it at the door."

I do as I am bid. I back into the tent slowly, holding the bread and honey at arm's length. Betty follows.

Rose says, "Give it to her now. She has been good!" Her voice is weak with relief.

The elephant explores my fingers with the delicate fleshy end of her trunk, then she takes the bread and honey and puts it in her ancient mouth.

"*Elephas maximus,*" I say to her without thinking, and wince. An old habit.

Rose stokes the brazier in the corner and soon it is throwing out heat. The air is dim and straw-scented. She takes up a broom and begins to brush Betty's flanks. The elephant leans into it with pleasure. She looks at me with something like a wink, twitches and sighs. I slip into Betty for a moment, her old sunlit mind. She does not see time in the same way that we do. She is beyond such things as life or death. She remembers long-ago worlds that have ceased to be.

"She hates the cold," I say.

"I know," Rose replies. "I do too. We will all go south as soon as may be. You would like to go to Spain again, Betty, would you not?" She strokes the leathered shoulder. "She had a brother," Rose says. "He died last winter. She hasn't been right since. They are awfully big on family, elephants."

"Someone has beaten her," I say. There are marks on the elephant's hide, old scars encircle her legs like rope.

"Ma does that if Betty won't move. I don't understand why you do it," she says to the elephant. "You know what happens if you don't obey. Can't you just be good, and then you won't get hurt?"

Betty sighs into Rose's yellow hair.

"They take them from their mothers when they are young," Rose says. "They tie them to the ground, starve them and whip them with wire, with a curved, sharp hook, until they forget that they are elephants. They are afraid of the wire and the hook for the rest of their lives. Why else would Betty agree to live with us and stand on her hind legs in the ring?" She pauses. "Ma says, *Be grateful, that is how we eat.* But I am not grateful."

"Sometimes I am ungrateful towards Uncle." The words are out before I know it. It feels bad and good at the same time.

Rose goes surely about the tent, getting water for Betty, putting brushes in order, sweeping, folding blankets, talking all the time. There is something strange about the cadence of her voice. Every word comes out with a slight hesitation, as though she has forgotten what she is about to say and recalls it at the very last moment. She sees me notice and flushes. "I stammer," she says, shrugging to show that she does not care. But I can see that she does.

Rose sits in the straw and takes an apple from her pocket. It seems easy and right to sit next to her. I offer her my knife.

"A shilling and half an apple," she says. "Not handsome payment."

"I cannot eat the apple," I say. "And do not give me the shilling just yet." There will be no reason to stay, once I have been paid.

"I couldn't live behind a gate like that," Rose says. "Are you quite happy there?"

"Yes."

"They told me in the village that you drink babies' blood," she says through a mouthful of white apple. "They say you made a bargain with the devil and will live for ever. That you can do flying, and so on."

"Well," I say, "I hope I do not need to tell you what to think about that."

"Are you their gaoler? That is another thing they say in the village. That you keep them prisoner."

"I hold the key," I tell her. "But they do not wish to leave. Only Dinah . . ." I shake my head. It makes me sad to speak of it. "Dinah is very beautiful," I say. "Like a pint of cream. So she gets bored."

Rose shrugs. "If you need help, I will give it. I owe you."

"Why?"

"I do remember you from Inverness. I was only pretending that I didn't."

"Why?"

"It quite shook me up to see you again," Rose says. "I didn't think you were real. Sometimes I see things that are not there. You would call them ghosts." She gives the apple core to Betty.

I put my hand over my mouth but I cannot contain a little snort.

"What?" she says.

"There's no such things as ghosts," I say. "Everyone knows that."

She looks irritated. "If you don't want to hear the rest—"

"I do!" The Impure cannot help their superstitions, after all.

She gives me a mistrustful look. "That day," she says, "I had been thinking of doing something . . . foolish. Then I saw you in the bus queue and I felt happy, as if I recognised you somehow. As if you were a part of me. That man had a copper's grip on you." She speaks with the voice of experience. "When you made a run for it, I thought, if she wants to go, why not? And when you ran it seemed like a sign that I could escape, too. I didn't need to do the foolish thing."

"What foolish thing?" But in her mind I can see. An evil-smelling brown bottle. Her body cold. I smell the earth as they shovel it on top of her.

"I had a disappointment," she says. "I don't want to go into it now."

"I am glad that you did not do it," I say.

Betty groans softly and waves her trunk. She kicks at her stomach with her hind legs as though in pain.

"That apple was too green," Rose says. "I should have known."

I am aghast. "It is not the apple but the honey. It is only to be taken on Altnaharra, from the Adder's hand. Perhaps she will be punished. Perhaps she will die."

"Goodness," says Rose. "She has a stomach cramp, that is all. Look, she is settling already."

Outside, the camp is waking. The clank of buckets. Someone shouts for beer.

"I must go." I am filled with the awareness of danger. "Uncle would not like me being here. Oh, I should not have come."

"Don't cry," Rose says. I had not realised that I was doing so. She strokes my back, as Dinah strokes Haystack during a thunderstorm.

I have made a mistake. "You are not a sign." I push her harder than I mean to and her head strikes the wooden tent pole. A snail of dark blood crawls down between her wide, surprised eyes. Bloodshed. I seize the shilling from her hand and run.

*　*　*

Uncle waits behind the gate.

I offer him the battered brown shilling on my palm. He places a gentle hand on my brow. "You are deeply troubled, my Eve."

I nod. "But I know what I must do, Uncle." I give him my arm and we climb the hill slowly. When we reach the castle I settle him in his chair in the Hall.

Abel comes in, the scent of peat on his skin. "Are you all right, Eve?" he asks. "You were gone . . ." He tries to take my hand but I avoid it. He is on shun.

I fetch the bucket of pine tar. I settle it over the fire and when it begins to smoke I daub my mouth with warm sap. Relief begins as it hardens.

I go to the cellar. As I close the trapdoor above me and climb down the ladder I feel only gladness. Wane. I lie on my back on the freezing stone and prepare to let Him into my heart.

I do not know how much time passes. He does not speak. Will He be silent for ever? He has abandoned me. *Perhaps*, a little voice whispers, *He was never there in the first place.* The sign that brought me back to Altnaharra was just a girl with a snake in a basket.

I am sorry, I tell Him. *Guide me in my doubt*. But still He does not answer.

* * *

Who is singing? I wake slowly, reluctantly. I recall where I am. Wane.

Something stirs against me in the dark. Cold skin, long fingers. Something is down here with me. I hear a sound, the clicking of its teeth. It is beside me. I scream through the gag that seals my mouth. I crawl and stumble on my weak legs, my head strikes the wall. Stars dance in the blackness.

Thin fingers grasp my ankle but I kick out. I struggle up the ladder with shaking limbs, heart pounding in my ears. I throw open the trapdoor. Beyond the cellar door it is a cool Altnaharra night.

I fumble for the lantern on the floor. I strike the match and the wick glows blue. I raise the lamp.

Something lies half-in and half-out of the pit. It wears Elizabeth's woollen dress. Its face is rotted away, green and brown. It watches me with eyes that are wide, cornflower blue in the corpse flesh. It drags its body further into the light, moving from side to side like a worm.

I thought I had screamed my loudest before but I was wrong. My throat is raw with it and I cannot seem to move.

The thing writhes out of the dark onto the cellar floor. It uncurls and stands upright, blue eyes shining. It comes closer, peering with its melted face. The air is filled with excrement and rot. Its fingers are cold as they curl about my throat. It is close enough to kiss in the flickering lamplight: skin brown, crumpled, featureless. I can hear my sobbing, my voice crying out, high and unrecognisable.

There is something blunt in the thing's hand. It drives this hard into my ribs and back, leaving burning islands of pain. This brings me back to myself. I take the thing by the throat and squeeze.

A short, high peep, like the call of a young bird. I know whose laughter it is.

Baby Elizabeth's face is daubed with pine sap. She wags her wooden spoon, smiles up at me, short peeps coming fast from her mouth. The brittle mask cracks where it is thinnest, shedding fragments on the floor.

* * *

Dinah's fingers are light on me, cool ointment on my skin. I am covered in tiny bruises, dark pockmarks. The end of the handle of Elizabeth's wooden spoon.

"She was just trying to joke with you, Eve," Dinah says. "She is only a baby."

"Fourteen turns," I say.

"Let it go. There is so little pleasure for her in this world."

I recall uneasily Elizabeth's eyes, blue in the brown mask. It was not a joke. It was punishment for the bath. She will bear watching.

I marvel at His ways. He gave me an answer during Wane after all. He reminded me of how much I am needed at Altnaharra.

* * *

Mission. I see him as I cross the market square. Chief Inspector Black sits comfortably in a canvas chair between an ironmonger and an orange stall. I try to feel surprise but cannot. I thought he might be here again. From somewhere the thought comes: *it will be good to have someone to talk to*, which does not make sense. I have people to talk to, and more sensible than him.

"I saved your place," he says, rising. "Allow me to help."

The tent goes up quickly with two pairs of hands.

I settle on my stool. "Why have you brought your own chair?" I ask. "You are not staying."

"Oh, come," he says. "Our last talk was so stimulating."

"You are making fun of me."

"I am interested, Evelyn, in what you say you can do. I will ask you questions."

"In order to disprove me."

"Naturally. Tell me, have you always had it, this . . . eye?"

"I may not speak of it."

"I have been polite," he says gently, "but please recall that I am a police officer. You will answer my questions now, or you will come down to the station and answer them there. If you cooperate with me, perhaps all will be well and I will go away. Who knows?"

I look at him as he sits smiling in the sunshine. I do not think he will go away. "It was given to me three turns ago," I say.

"Good," he says cheerfully. "We understand one another. Have you, at any time, received a blow to the head? Brain damage?"

"No." I am strangely affronted. "I am not damaged."

"If I were to think of a number between, say, one and twenty, could you guess that number?"

"That is not how it comes," I say.

"Does a voice speak to you?"

I think. I would not say this to him but it is pleasant to discuss the eye as if it were an ordinary thing, like how long candles will last or how to launder blood out of linen.

"It is like being lost at night," I say. I think of running through the forest, the clutching branches. "I catch glimpses. A tree I recognise. Stars I know. It is trust and luck both. A sudden knowing. I do not control it. It comes unbidden."

"What a great gift," he says. "To be granted such knowledge that others lack. It makes you unique, does it not? Almost godlike." He smiles, showing a white, wolfish canine.

"It does not always seem a gift," I say. "I saw Mr. MacRaith's murder. I was in him as he woke. I went with him to his death, into the dawn."

"Indeed," he says. His hat brim keeps his eyes in shadow. He strokes his lip with a finger. For all my power I do not know what is in his mind.

"You say you do not care what happens to others," he says. "But you busy yourself a great deal with the affairs of this world. Tell me, does he send you here to market—or is it you who wishes to come?"

"I would remain on the isle always if I could."

"Yet you wished me to look for your murderous mother," he says. "That was why you gave me those details. You think a girl is going to be killed and you care enough to ask me to prevent it."

My head feels hot and muddled. "Have you found her?" I ask.

"It was not very difficult. The woman is in fact named de Vere, that was the truth, and she seems very law-abiding! But the daughter is pretty." He pauses. "I will keep my eye on them," he says. "When I can. My colleagues would say that I am mad. Perhaps they would be right."

"Thank you," I say.

"I do not think you a liar," Christopher Black says gently. "I can see that you believe in your gift. Do you know what autosuggestion is? A man named Émile Coué discovered it. It is used to treat shell shock. One resolves to believe a certain thing—*I am not in pain*, or perhaps, *I can read minds*—and the body obeys.

"You can read people—the tiny tics and tells. The skills of a confidence trickster. That, and a wee, mental sleight of hand. I can see that it would be possible for you to believe in your own magic. A harmless fiction, some would say. But your uncle has set himself up in place of the law and that will not stand."

"Chief Inspector," I say, "do you have nothing better to occupy yourself with than us?"

He smiles. "You say you were in MacRaith's mind when he died, as he walked into the dawn. But Hector MacRaith died at noon. He was found in the afternoon."

His words taste of metal. "You are lying."

He laughs. "All right, fair is fair. A small test. Can you blame me?"

"What you are saying doesn't make sense," I say. "*Why* would I invent the eye?"

"To satisfy the great need that lies at the heart of us all."

"Which is?"

"To be loved. To belong."

"That's too easy," I say. "It's not worthy of you."

"Nevertheless, it is the truth."

"Your leg is paining you, Chief Inspector. I can tell."

*   *   *

The next time Dinah tries is high tide, just after noon. I find her basket half-full of seaweed, abandoned on the shore. Her sleek dark head is twenty feet out, bobbing in the waves. She is nearing the centre of the channel where the tide sucks everything down into its greedy depths.

I cast myself into the water and cut through it like a fish. I think I will never reach her. The waves break over my head. I grasp her slippery heel and then her arm.

Dinah flails and kicks me.

I push her head beneath the water and hold her there until she stops fighting. When I allow her up for air she is pliant, docile. I put her arms about my neck and tow her towards the shore.

On the rocky beach I hold her as she weeps.

"The riptide would have taken you," I tell her. My voice shakes with fury. "You would have died. Never, ever do that again. Do you hear?"

She looks at the black gate, half-submerged in the lapping sea. "What a thing," she says. "Is it not? A gate with no walls. Do you ever wonder, Eve, where the walls are?" Once, Dinah's mind had valleys and mountains and great rolling plains in it. Now it is a flat place where little stirs. When did it change?

"You are cold," I say. I rub Dinah's arms hard, chafing them. "We should get you dry. I will say that you stumbled and fell in the shallows. We will light a fire in our room!"

She allows herself to be led.

*   *   *

Breakfast, half a pear, three mouthfuls. A glass of sheep's milk, six mouthfuls.

"The scallop beds will be rich," Uncle says. "Abel shall dive today."

Abel is shunned because he did not bank the fire properly last night. I watch him from the corner of my eye. He stares at his plate. His right eye is closed by a fresh plum bruise. He shakes at the mention of diving. Abel does not breathe well. He never has since he was small.

"I could dive," I say. "I am better than Abel."

"No," Uncle says. "You cannot be risked." In low tones he says to Nora, "Do you remember when we chose Abel at the poorhouse in Tongue? We thought he was a girl. We tried to return him when we found out, but they would not take him back. One of you pitied him. He did not wish to go back to the orphanage, so we kept him. But he is not necessary."

Nora bites her lip and busies herself with the dishes.

The wind cuts into us. The wind is like a live thing today, it finds all the gaps in our clothes. I fill the bucket with seawater to hold the scallops. Abel ties the rope about his waist in silence. He dives from the rocky shelf, piercing the water cleanly with hardly a ripple. I begin to count. The scallop beds lie some feet beneath the surface. Forty-one, forty-two. The water is cold and black. Sharks come there. Fifty-nine.

Abel bursts through the rough skin of the sea, wheezing. His hands are full of scallops. He puts them in the bucket without a word. The scallops watch me, each of their hundred eyes a jewel. Through each one they see their death. They swim, their shells making hopeless denting sounds against the sides of the bucket. The sky lours over the sea, unending. I shiver. Abel dives again. One, two. I see shards of ice floating in the water. Thirty-five, -six, -seven, -eight.

The count passes sixty but he does not surface. Ninety-one, -two . . . A hundred. I take up the slack on the rope and pull it hard. It goes taut as though caught on some heavy object below. I kick off my shoes and my skirt and jump. The water is so cold that for a moment my heart seems to stop.

Below me Abel is floating, spread-eagled in the dim brown light. A curious fish noses at his yellow hair. His face is blue. The rope is trapped under a rock on the sea floor. The water grows heavier and heavier as I swim down. When I reach the bottom the blood is singing in my ears. For a terrible moment the rock will not move, but at last it gives and the rope comes free. Abel does not bob up to the surface, which means he has water inside him.

I pull him upwards, his flesh slippery in my hands. We break the surface and I take a long, ragged breath. A wind roars through my head. I pull him roughly from the sea, onto the rock.

I shake him and beat his white chest until he makes a strangled sound. Salt water pours from his throat.

"Abel," I shout. "What were you thinking?" I cannot stop hitting his chest even though he is breathing again. I am so afraid. The stone could not have placed itself on top of the rope.

"I wanted to see what you would do," he says. He coughs, shivering under the lash of the wind. "You broke the shun. I will tell."

"You would have died."

"You should have left me," he says. His hands curl into my hair. "You are weak. You are not fit to be the Adder. I see your face when you set off to market. You love them, the Impure."

"I make us warm and safe," I say. "I feed us. While you sit in the dark, shunned, doing nothing. Making up lies about me."

"He tests me because he sees power in me," says Abel. His voice has the old boyish tremor in it, but I am too angry to care.

I laugh. "He does not want you here. He never did."

Abel screams and pushes me from him. He picks up the bucket of scallops, then throws it at my head. It flies wide and sails over the edge. From below, the report of it hitting the water.

Abel sits down on the rock and sobs, his bare white back heaving. Below, in the sea, the scallops have swum away.

* * *

Abel does not come to supper. I go to look for him.

By the woodpile the axe stands in the block. White sheets lie in a pile nearby. But no, it is Abel.

I turn him over. His face is flushed and his eyes are vast and black. He is hot to the touch.

I run back to the kitchen.

"Abel is ill," I say.

Uncle says, "Keep him away from the castle." I wait but he says nothing more, returns to his liver and onions. I see that Elizabeth has eaten the egg from my plate.

* * *

I take blankets to Abel. He is hot but his whole body shivers. His eyes are glazed like something already dead. I wrap him as best I can and gather driftwood. I build a fire by him. It crackles, spitting red into the night.

"I am sorry," I whisper. "I should not have fought with you." I must be better than the others, if I am to protect them.

"Here," Dinah says. Firelight plays on her face, on the cup in her hand. "It was all I could take without Nora seeing."

Abel moans. He does not want to drink the milk. Some goes in his mouth but most spills on the ground. I look at it with regret. I am hungry.

"We should stay here with him," I say.

Dinah nods. We lie on either side of Abel, protecting him.

We do not sleep. We put damp cloths on his brow. We give him water from the well. He shivers and sweats.

The night wears on. The seals call in the dark. We count the stars overhead. We tell stories about them to Abel. This one is friends with that one. They are both envious of the big one because it is so green and bright. Abel stares up into the dark with his black gaze. We are afraid to let him sleep in case he does not wake up again.

"I wish there were willow trees on the isle," Dinah whispers. "Alice once told me that you can stew the bark for fever."

Dinah must be worried. She has forgotten that we do not speak of Alice.

"It will be all right," I say. I hope it will.

Dinah says, "I recall a day. It must have been summer. We were swimming, the four of us. Not racing, but playing in the shallows beneath the hall windows, which were open. Uncle and Alice and Nora were sitting in the windows. I think that one of them was smoking a cigarette. They were talking, watching us but not really. We joined hands in a circle and ducked underwater. We did not discuss it. It was something we all decided to do together. And there we all were, transformed by the water, our hair floating about our faces. Mouths puffed out from holding our breath. We moved out into the deep. The water grew colder, darker, but still we held our breath. My heart was beating fast, I felt dizzy. But still we all held on to one another's hands, moving towards the open ocean. And then we saw something drifting, white and long, curving through the water ahead.

"It must have been a ray or a shark but it looked like a woman. A drowned woman, dressed in white. We tried to scream. We turned to swim back to the shallows as fast as we could. But Abel did not turn. He kept swimming away from us, towards the white thing. I had to pull him back to land and he fought me all the way.

"When we reached the castle walls the grown-ups had not noticed that we had gone. They were still sitting and laughing in the sun. We did not tell them, but we stood in the shallows and hugged one another. I remember how Abel's back felt under my hand. I could feel his heart beating right through him. I thought, *We must take care of him. He always wants to go too far.*"

I nod in understanding and squeeze Dinah's hand. The story is an act of power. Dinah hopes it will pull Abel away from the edge, as she pulled him to safety all those years ago.

He is with us, too, beyond the firelight. I catch the gleam of black scales as He moves, surrounding us in His great coils.

You will not let Abel die, I tell Him. The night birds call.

*　*　*

Dew studs the blanket with gleaming pearls. Dinah's hair is in my face. Every muscle aches and my bones feel as though they have been ground to flour. I groan and rise.

"Eve?" Abel is watching me. "Why are we outside?" He is pale but there. He coughs. "I am thirsty."

I fetch water from the well. I watch him drink it from the bowl. My eyes are greedy for the sight of him. I cannot get enough.

Dinah wakes. When she sees Abel she begins to cry. "You stupid slug," she says. "You frightened us."

"Oh," Abel says. "You girls are always fussing."

"You really are better," Dinah says. "Quite your ungrateful self."

I hold Abel. Dinah puts her arms about us both as if we were one big person. He cries quietly into my neck. I wish it were not mission today. I do not want to leave them.

* * *

Chief Inspector Black stands in the market square, a dark rock in the moving sea. He holds a file under one arm. As soon as I see his face, I know. "She is dead. Mrs. de Vere's daughter."

He nods. "She was set upon as she walked her dog yesterday evening. A knife through her throat. Quick, it is to be hoped."

I cannot catch my breath. The cobbles are shifting and fluid beneath me. Poor impure girl, killed without a thought.

"Will you arrest the woman, Mrs. de Vere?"

"There is no evidence. A robbery gone awry, they are saying. The dog was a whippet. They killed it first so it would not bark." He sighs.

"I wish she could have been saved." Tears rise, and I wipe them away angrily. Abel is well but I am still in the lee of that fear.

"Sit on the stool. Breathe. Be calm. I have a story to tell you."

I say, "I am all right."

"Good. Do you know what horse racing is?"

"Yes."

"There was a famous race at Ayr some years ago. It was tightly contested, hundreds of thousands of pounds laid in bets. Do you—"

"I know what a bet is."

"The jockey who rode the favourite, tipped to win, had a strategy. He held his horse back behind the crowd to save its wind. He planned to come out late in the race, blazing ahead with his horse still fresh, while all the front-runners had tired themselves out. So he lagged behind, and when the third and final lap came, he began to close the distance. He was coming round a corner, and should have speeded up, but he didn't. Instead of urging his horse on, he pulled it up to a walk.

"Why?" I ask. "Why didn't he go faster and win?"

"Later he said that a feeling came upon him. Intuition. Whatever you like to call it. When he rounded the blind corner a scene of devastation met his eyes. Broken-legged horses crawling across the grass. Two men trampled to death. Everywhere blood and bodies, human and horse alike. There had been a tangle at great speed, and the horses were all so close together that they took one another down. Somehow, the jockey had known."

"He had the eye," I say. It can happen among the Impure, though not often.

"No. They looked at the photographs of that jockey, galloping towards the blind corner. He was a very famous jockey, accustomed to having all eyes on him. But in the photographs it was plain to see that every head in the stands was turned away. No one was watching his great spurt of speed, or cheering. The crowd could see around the bend to the carnage beyond. His unconscious mind made sense of this before his mind did. Intuition saved his life—a series of rapid, unconscious perceptions. But the effect seemed magical."

"Perhaps," I say. "Or perhaps he had the eye. I know you enjoy these exchanges, Chief Inspector, but I have work to do."

"When you saw me this morning the first thing you said was: *she is dead*. How did you know?"

"I saw the girl's murder in your mind," I say. "The knife. The dog."

"Tell me, Evelyn, did you notice the file in my hand?"

I look at it without interest. It is brown, battered.

"You cannot see the name on it now," he says. "I have turned it away from you. But when you approached me it was turned outwards so that you could read it." He turns the file over. It is labelled in block capitals, *DE VERE MURDER*.

"I did not see the file. I knew by the eye that she was dead."

"You do not know you saw it, but you did. For if you could read my mind, you would know that there has been no murder. Indeed, there is no de Vere family that I could discover. I gradually fed you this small invention. I let you think I had found them and was watching them. I wished to see if you would be led to a conclusion—and whether you would then attribute it to your 'gift.' The answer to both questions, it seems, is yes. You are not a liar, as I have said. You observe and you collate, all beneath the level of your attention."

"You are right. I am not a liar. You are." I feel as I did when Abel gave account of me, all those years ago. Stripped bare. Fear runs through me in tiny cold currents.

"I had to find a way to show you," he says. "I cannot allow you to deceive yourself any longer. Believe it or not, I have your best interests at heart."

"You tell yourself that," I say. "Did you even look for that woman or the girl she is going to kill? No. You were too busy thinking of the trick you wanted to play."

"When will you listen?" he says fiercely. "No one cares what happens to you. Who—with all the sorrow that has come upon this country in recent years—would lift a finger to help you? Godless women and children on the edge of the world. You are worthless, of no interest. He could kill you and the world would not blink. I am the only one who will notice whether you live or die."

I lean in close enough to see the flecks of gold in his iris, the small place on his neck that he missed while shaving. I speak softly, as one must speak words of power.

"I have told you that I am not her," I say. "Hear it. Know it. Your sister is dead. She is not waiting for you in the hereafter. You have lost your God, so you know this to be true. She is white bone. Dust on a cold wind. Gone."

He makes a small sound as if I have struck him.

"You are seen," I say. "Now leave me alone."

* * *

Home. The sound of the gate closing behind me has never been more welcome.

I go to the Hall. Uncle welcomes me with honey and I give him the coins. He puts them in the strongbox bound with iron. The sky is fading into black through the tall windows.

Dinah comes into the hall. "Eve," she says. "I heard your voice." Her face is blotched. As I watch, her mouth distorts and tears bleed down her cheeks.

"I have not told her yet, Dinah," says Uncle gently. "Do not take on so. It is not the tragedy you make it out to be."

Nora is here, too, holding her stomach with a grimace. "Do not upset yourself and everyone else, Dinah," she says. "It is as He wills."

Elizabeth makes a cheeping sound, sitting in shadow. Has she been here all along? She hits Uncle with her wooden spoon. He pushes her back with a powerful arm. She staggers and falls silent to the floor.

I look about the Hall.

"Where is Abel?" I ask.

Uncle says, "Abel has been granted a great honour. He has gone to the sea. He awaits us in the deeps."

Nora found him. I see it in her mind. His straw-coloured hair floating beneath the surface by the scallop beds. He had tied a bucket of stones to his ankle and leapt from the clifftop, holding it in his arms. Nora pulled his white, bony ankle to the surface and freed him of the chain, but the sea roared and seized at them with strong hands. Nora broke free of its clutches, fearing for her life. Abel was taken down, away, into the dark.

Do I see it, or do I merely wish that she tried to bring him back to shore? I do not know why it is important, that someone tried to hold on to him at the end.

I hope he was not afraid. I hope he did not change his mind as the sea closed over him. I hope he did not wish for me to swim down and release him as his lungs filled with water.

I go down to the Wane place. I close the trapdoor. I stay in the dark for some time. I do not count the days.

* * *

I am still weak. I took a piece of the darkness with me when I left the Wane place this time. It curls and flexes inside me, a fist clenched about my heart.

Abel is everywhere since he died. Nora forgets and sets a place for him at the table. Elizabeth looks for him to mend her bird crates. She cries when she cannot find him. I do not know how to explain it to her.

I have tried to find peace. I have tried to hear His voice in the ocean. I know Abel is with Him, now. But all that runs through my mind, like rabbits, endless, is the events of that day. The bucket, the rope, his fever. Uncle's words. *We did not really want him but by then it was too late.* They were as good as a knife.

Uncle cut Abel's heart out, but I was the one who left him to go to market. I have the eye. I must have known somewhere in me what he might do. Abel cannot tell Uncle lies about me now. He cannot say that part of me longs for the impure world and its people. Did some small, selfish part of me let him go to his death?

We will see Abel again when He comes. But I want him here with us now.

* * *

The evening air is broken by sound. It does not seem human but like a dog, set alight by a spark from a fire.

Dinah is in the shallows by the gate. Uncle holds her by her hair. In his other hand he holds a wax paper parcel: Jamie MacRaith's delivery. Link sausages swing in the evening air, grazing the sea. Dinah screams and tries to seize the sausages. It is not the meat she wants but the paper they are wrapped in. Inside, the parcel is covered in awkward boy's writing. Uncle raises the message away from Dinah's grasping fingers, holds it high in the last of the light, the name at the bottom just legible: *Jamie.*

Uncle pulls her up the hill. I follow. He does not let go of Dinah until we reach the Hall. She sinks to the floor, weeping. Nora looks up from her knitting, startled.

"All that talk of dreams and doom, Dinah," says Uncle, putting his hand on his brow as though he has a headache. "When all you wanted was to go to him."

"I do not want to end up like Abel," Dinah whispers.

Uncle shakes his head sadly. "Abel was not strong," he says. "He is better off where he is."

"You do not know what it is like beyond the isle, Dinah," I say. I cannot lose her, too.

"I know that Jamie is there," she says. "And I know that the world is not what you think, Eve. There is kindness, too."

"It does not matter, Dinah. You will end if you leave. When you die you will become ash and dust. You will not return to the ocean. Do you not wish to see Abel again? Do you not wish to be together, all of us, for all time?"

"Is that what will happen?" Dinah says quietly.

"Yes," I say. Fury rises in me. "It is." It must be.

"I am beside myself with worry about you," Uncle says. "It is not fair. Nor is it fair to give this MacRaith boy false hope. You must end it."

Nora is white. "John . . ."

"I will find a way off the isle," Dinah says, "and you cannot stop me unless you kill me."

Uncle stares at Dinah as if he has never seen her before.

"John," Nora says again. Something is happening inside her. She pants, bent double, one hand clawing the wall. Fluid pools about her feet. Her stomach ripples like the sea.

"Get away," says Nora. She slaps my hands. "Do not touch me."

I pin her wrists behind her back. Nora screams. I raise blood on my finger. She squirms and curses. She is afraid that the baby is dead inside her.

I cannot believe it. I raise another drop of blood to be sure. It is so. The baby does not want to come out. Its small fists are balled in anger.

"It is alive," I say. No one knows what to do for a moment.

Dinah comes to Nora. She puts an arm about her, takes Nora's weight. "Build the fire up, Eve," she says.

Uncle smiles with great warmth. "We have waited," he says. "She has tried to come in from the ocean many times and now she will succeed." He rises. "This is not man's work," he says. The door closes behind him and the four of us are alone. Nora sobs.

Dinah puts her long red hair up, purposeful. "Now," she says to Nora, "let us make you comfortable."

"Dinah, we do not know what to do." I feel faint. I had never considered that Nora might have an actual baby.

"He will show you," Nora says through clenched teeth. "The great snake."

He does not show me. When I try to give Nora a chip of ice to melt on her tongue I accidentally poke her in the mouth with my finger or drop the ice. When I try to make her comfortable, I pinch her somehow. When I offer her bread for the third time, Nora groans at me, "Go away, Evelyn, just go."

Dinah, however, seems to understand what Nora needs without being told. She gives her water to drink when her mouth is too dry, she helps her to walk around the hall at intervals. She warms stones in the embers of the fire and wraps them in cloth, making warm compresses to ease the muscles of Nora's back. She soothes Nora with sure hands, rubs her feet. She cools her brow with fresh water. She is like old Dinah. She smiles at Nora's thanks.

"Perhaps I should go and find Uncle," I say as Nora heaves and gasps.

Dinah turns to me. "Eve," she says. "We bring his Children in from the ocean. This power is given to *us*. You will not refuse the honour." She leans in close to my ear so that Nora cannot hear and hisses, "I am sorry that you are not good at this. But I am. You can stay back for once. Stoke the fire. Hand me what I need. Now give me that knife." She cuts a sheet in two with a rending sound.

I stay back. I stoke the hearth and hand Dinah things when she asks. We are tired and objects seem to disappear from my hands. A bobbin of thread vanishes from my pockets. Dinah mislays three blankets. I seize Elizabeth by the ear and pull her from her place by the hearth. The blankets are arranged in a nest beneath her.

"Stop it," I say. "We must help Nora now. We will play later."

Baby Elizabeth looks at me for a moment, then hits me hard on the forehead with the back of her wooden spoon.

*　　*　　*

Time ceases to move forward. Instead it circles about us, dreamlike, as it does during Wane. Starlight, dawn and sunlight fall through the windows in succession, but we pay them little mind. When we need water, towels or food we call through the door. These are left outside, presumably by Uncle. Apart from these requests, we do not speak. Dinah and I do not have much in common with Nora except our purpose here.

On the third night, in the small hours before dawn, she comes into being by the light of the fire. It is an act of great power. She is not there, and then she is, dark head first. Four people in the room, then suddenly five. She tears Nora from within, screaming all the way out. Nora screams too. The baby is wet and wrinkled and glutinous and Dinah catches her easily. She ties off the cord and dries the baby gently. Nora and Dinah bend to her. Blue eyes open. A starfish hand opens and closes, as though grasping at shadows.

"Oh my," Dinah says. "Oh, hello."

Nora kisses Dinah. "You brought her forth from me," she says. "You have done Him the highest honour."

Elizabeth stares at the baby. She shakes her head once, slowly.

Uncle is there in the firelight. The baby starts and cries out at the cold he brings with him.

"It is a girl," Nora tells him with tears in her eyes.

He smiles and touches the baby with a finger. "Feed her. She is hungry."

Nora has forgotten all her suffering. She wears a new face that I have not seen before. She looks rosy and young.

"You have done well, my Nora," Uncle says. He gives us honey from his hands. "The name that has been waiting for her is Mary."

The benison leaps in yellow spears across the dark. Mary's eyes follow it like newly opened flowers. "His grace coils about you," Uncle says. "You may rest now."

He takes Mary from Nora's arms. He kisses the baby's small, worried brow.

"Adder," Nora says, "please, I wish to hold her . . ."

"You have given the isle a child," he says. "It is good."

"No," says Nora. She weeps. Her mouth is twisted and ugly. "John, give her back."

"You may be part of the raising of her. One part of many, of all of us. But first we must break the false bond that ties you. The stifling affection of motherhood."

"She is mine," says Nora. Her eyes are black and shiny.

Uncle grows as tall as a conifer. Nora shrinks in his shadow. "There is no *mine*." He speaks quietly, distant thunder over the sea. "No man or child can belong to another. Do not speak the corrupt language of family here. Come forth, Dinah."

Dinah comes, eyes lowered.

"You will have care of Mary," he says. "For the first month you will bring her to Nora to feed. After that, she will have ewe's milk.

Nora must be protected from the impure feelings that wish to guide her. The child is ours—not hers."

Dinah nods, solemn.

Nora wails and claws at Uncle but he holds her. "It will be all right," he says. "You will overcome this."

"You will not take her from me," says Nora to Dinah. "Not after you laboured with me these days and nights."

Uncle puts Mary in Dinah's arms. She is crying.

"Evelyn," Nora says, swallowing her tears. "My baby is crying. Could you please bring me the baby? Would you?"

I step away from Nora slowly. I watch Dinah and Mary. They stand at the edge of the firelight. Dinah rocks Mary gently, paying us no mind.

"Hush," Dinah says, "hush, little one." Mary's cries soften into hiccups and then nothing. Dinah gazes down at her. In Dinah's eyes are worlds and time. She hums softly. Mary takes Dinah's finger in a small fist.

Dinah says, "Yes, that is right," in answer to a question I cannot hear. She smiles, bright and broken. "Oh," she says. Tears gleam on her face. "Oh." She bends to the baby in communion, for the giving and receiving of secrets. She breathes in, deep and long. "The smell," she says to me. Mary takes a strand of Dinah's dark red hair in her fists. Dinah has a special kind of eye now. She can hear the baby's thoughts.

"We will go upstairs," says Dinah. "Our child must rest. Keep Nora comfortable here. I will bring Mary down in an hour for feeding."

I watch them leave. Dinah trails peace behind her like a soft banner of blue. Uncle has given her the one thing that could keep her here on the isle.

Uncle says, "Eve, look to Nora. She will be hurt if she crawls on the stone like that."

I kneel and take Nora softly in my arms. She cries and hits me. I do not feel it.

I watch Uncle from a cold, still place. His face speaks of old pleasure revisited. The knowledge comes to me simply, like catching a ball thrown high. He has done this before. Parted women from their babies.

Nora's grief as Mary was taken from her arms. The look on Alice's face as she tried to take me from Altnaharra in the night. *Darling, come.* The same need; tenderness beyond anything. No wonder Uncle fears this power. It is the greatest I have seen. The word thrums under everything. The *M* at the beginning, the soft *r* at the end. The dream that plagues me is no dream, it is a memory. She rocked me, she sang to me. Alice was my mother, and he took me from her.

Uncle's gaze settles on me like chains.

*   *   *

That night I take the newspaper from under the mattress. It is not safe there. I cannot trust anyone. I keep the picture in my cuff with my knife.

I try to recall every detail of Alice's grey eyes, her kind hands, her strong nose, her voice. Her young face, rendered in newsprint, is fading, disassembling into smudges and dots. I hope I will not need the picture soon.

Ten days until mission seems long. I stay close to Mary and Dinah, fussing over the baby and fetching things. I make it seem as though they cannot do without me even for a moment. But I feel Uncle's eye on me, thoughtful.

Nora mends slowly. Much of the time she sleeps. Dinah and I feed her gruel with a spoon.

"Remember who you are," Uncle tells her. She nods, silent.

At first when Mary is brought to her for feeding Nora will not let her go. I pin Nora gently to the floor as Dinah pries the baby from her arms. We run, closing the heavy door behind us and turning the key in the lock. On the other side, Nora weeps and beats the door with her fists.

Uncle is there, smiling. He tickles Mary's cheek with his finger. She looks at him with big eyes.

"The false feelings that now prey on Nora are treacherous," he says to us. "They could make her want to steal Mary away from the isle. Or Nora may begin to think that the baby is bad and wish to harm her. Or she may harm herself. We must be kind and understanding, and wait for the impurity to pass. She will recall who she is, in time. Do you understand?"

Dinah nods, serious, slightly awed. I try to mirror her exactly. The tilt of her head, the widened eyes.

Uncle goes in to Nora and closes the door behind him.

"What is wrong, Eve?" asks Dinah. "You are quiet."

"I think the milk at breakfast was old," I say. "Do you not feel it?" The pretence of being who I once was is wearing on me.

"Oh," says Dinah with a ripple of revulsion. She cannot bear milk that is off. "Perhaps I do, a little. We should lie down." Dinah's favourite thing, these days, is to lie in bed and play games with Mary.

What Uncle says to Nora we do not know, but the next time we come she is pliant and quiet. She touches the baby only when necessary: to support her head or to guide her to the breast. Dinah stays close, anyhow, watching.

Uncle decides that Nora needs occupation. She is put to dealing with the goods and orders at the gate. Dinah is not to go near the gate again. Dinah writes the note to Jamie MacRaith with a still face, at Uncle's direction. When it is done she returns her attention to Mary and says no more about it.

Dinah and Uncle walk about the castle together, with the baby. I see them from the windows. They talk. Uncle holds a sheaf of papers in his hand. When they return he locks the papers in his strongbox.

It says something that ends in "and Testament" on the first page. I watch all this with my eyes lowered, seemingly absorbed in folding the laundry, sweeping floors, stirring the pot on the range.

Nora's dislike of me has distilled into hatred. I see it pure and fierce in her eyes. I have no friends at Altnaharra. Perhaps I never did.

Five days until mission.

*　*　*

Breakfast. Dinah eats bread and honey with one hand and soothes Mary with the other. Three mouthfuls. They sit in my stomach like pebbles.

"I suppose that Mary shall go to school in a few turns," says Dinah. "Who will take her? I do not like it. What if the Impure try to corrupt her? She is only little. At least we had one another to keep us safe when we went. What do you think, Nora?" Dinah always consults Nora politely on the subject of Mary.

Nora does not answer. Her fingers pluck delicately at her bread but she does not lift it to her lips.

"Mary will not go to school," Uncle says.

"Surely she should know her letters and numbers, and so on?"

"What does she need to know that we cannot teach her?"

"Will they not come for her?"

Mary stares with round-eyed refusal at the bottle that Dinah is trying to give her. She pushes it away with a firm hand.

"The corrupt world does not know of her existence," Uncle says, smiling. "She will be the purest of us all, for she will never leave the isle, from the time she was taken from the ocean to the time when she returns to it."

*　*　*

Mission tomorrow. Our room is hung with drying cloths and small woollen clothes, as it always is these days. The window is shut. Dinah does not mind that any more. There is a fire in the tiny hearth. Water steams in a pan on the coals. Dinah hardly notices me. She says *shh*, in an absent way, alert to the tiny sounds of the baby.

Nora comes to blow out the candle.

"The Adder does not summon you tonight," she says to Dinah and me. Dinah nods, expressionless. My relief is warmth after cold, like water drying on my skin in the sun.

I wake from the dream of white rabbits. The dark is lustrous and deep. There should be only three people breathing. I can hear four. Dinah sleeps peaceful beside me.

A white figure bends over Mary's cradle. It reaches into the crib with a thin arm.

I leap from the bed, falling in a tangle of bedclothes. I grasp the white figure, which has a reassuringly solid form. "Dinah," I shout, "light the candle!"

The candle ticks and flickers in Dinah's hand. It plays over the hollows of Elizabeth's cheekbones. Elizabeth blinks, her azure eyes upturned, empty.

"She is sleepwalking," I say.

"What is she holding?" Dinah asks.

I pry open Elizabeth's fingers. It is a long iron nail, gleaming at the point.

"Oh, Eve. Get her away." Dinah's face is filled with fear.

"I will lock her in tonight."

I lead Elizabeth back to her room. She is docile. When I push her gently down into bed, she does not resist. I draw the blanket up. "Goodnight, Baby Elizabeth." But of course Elizabeth is not the baby any longer. "I know what it is to be angry," I say, stroking her thin blond curls. "What happened?" I whisper. "What happened to stop your mouth?"

I sit with Elizabeth until her breath comes regular and sweet. Too sweet. I look under the bed. A honey jar, empty. I bend. Six jars are rolling on their sides in the dust. And a root, half-chewed. I know that woody purple flesh. I know the scent.

I lock Elizabeth's door, but I do not go back to bed.

The night is quiet. Below, the sea laps at the cliff. My hand searches in the crevice between two boulders. It should still be here. It must be. If someone had found it, there would have been questioning and punishment . . .

My hand meets something wet that slithers into the earth at my touch. But then there is the old oilcloth, the solid shape beneath my fingers. Something is growing on it. I wipe it off as best I can.

The *Kingdom Animalia* smells like low tide. The leather is rotten and the pages are coming away from the binding, but it is still legible. When I find the page I need I tear it from the book.

I need two more things. I find the first one nearby in the cold moonlight. The other I find in the cellar. I stow them under our bed. Dinah snores, a comforting sound. Mary sleeps, small fists balled.

Doubt is like rot, spoiling everything it touches.

* * *

I get off the train in Inverness. Now I should go out of the station. Across the road. Left, left, right and at the end of the street will be the market square. But I do not do that. Instead I take a deep breath and look about me. A policeman stands in the corner of the station, regarding the crowd. Red face. Shining buttons. Peaked cap. I sense his ill health as I approach, I feel him in my mind all fat and buttery. How can people live like this?

"Please," I say politely. "Where is Orme Place?" I have kept the words safe in my mind for years, since Alice gave them to me that day.

Left, right, to the end of the street with the name of a tree, second left, cross the square. My heart is pounding. What will happen? Perhaps she will pat me on the head and say, "I am so sorry, Eve,

I have changed my mind. I do not want you after all." Perhaps she will laugh at me. "Did you think I meant it? A thing I said only once, three years ago, to a child! You must be mad." Perhaps she will look at me without recognition and say, "Who are you?" I think that would end me. Family is powerful. Uncle is right to be afraid of it.

Black, jagged numbers are blazoned on the vast white faces of the houses of Orme Place. I go to the green-painted door of number fourteen and knock. I tap at the shuttered windows. I go round to the back where straw blows across the empty stable yard. Nothing. The house is closed, empty.

Foolish of me to think that Alice would be here. No doubt I have remembered the number or the street wrongly. Or this was where Alice once lived but she has moved. Perhaps Alice meant something completely different by the words "Orme Place." The newspaper clipping must have been one of Christopher Black's elaborate tricks and Alice died, after all, on that dark night during the bad summer.

I go to the shining front door of number fourteen Orme Place. I raise the letter flap gently and take from my pocket a spray of purple blooms. I push the crawler flowers through the letter box. That is all I can do.

There is only one place left to go. I make a little growling sound in my throat. I do not want to ask him for help, but there is nothing else for it. I walk briskly along the white row of houses. At the corner of the street there stands another policeman. They are quite helpful, I am finding. I make my good eye big and I put on a smile.

"I wish to go to the police station," I say.

* * *

"Chief Inspector Black?" I say to the man at the desk. The police station is full of brown and grey air. No joy has ever been felt here by anyone.

He says a word that sounds like *seal* and laughs. This one is made of tobacco smoke and has red, rheumy eyes. Thin.

"I want Chief Inspector Black," I say again. The Impure are sometimes very slow.

"You cannot have him," he replies. "He is not here."

"I will wait until he comes back," I say. There are no chairs. I think about sitting down on the floor but instead I lean against a wall.

The thin face peers at me. "Not here means not here," the man says. "He has not been with the force since he was drafted in '17. Nor will he be again. So move along, lassie. One of us has a bad back and reports to file before tea."

Oh," I say. "He is no longer a policeman?"

"Out." The man points to the door.

I hold my ground. "Where is he, then?"

"How would I know?"

"I have to find him." I make my voice tremble, and both eyes well up. It comes quite naturally. All the doubt and fear of the last few days rise within me. Suddenly I am not pretending any more. I cover my face with my hands. The thin man comes out from behind the desk and puts an arm across my shoulders.

"What's all this?" he asks uneasily. He does not really want to know. He wants me to be far away. "Och, come now."

"Chief Inspector Black—"

"Mr. Black."

"Mr. Black is my—" I taste the unfamiliar word. "Brother. We have been estranged for many years. But our mother has passed away and I must tell him."

"He said he had a sister," the man says, "who died young."

"What a cheek," I say indignantly. "He is always telling people that I have died. But here I am, very much alive as you can see!"

I chose a good story. The man does not quite believe me but he has a feeling that I am bad news of some sort, and he likes the idea of Christopher Black being given bad news.

"I suppose he might still be at his old address," he says. "We have that on record. But you did not get it from me, you ken?"

"No," I say. "Of course not."

He gives me the address and, on seeing my blank look, directions. Cities are quite simple in the end. Left, right, left, straight. Left again. If only life had such instructions.

The houses grow thinner and are lower to the ground. Even the rain here seems grey and tainted as though already used. I cannot feel the benison at all now. Being cut off from it makes me feel that nothing will ever be good again. I shiver in my thin cotton. The door of number nine is blue, dented as if by stones. A pane of glass has been replaced with cardboard. Red letters are daubed across the blue in a childish hand. Someone has tried to cover them with white paint but they show through like ghosts. An *S*, perhaps, and a *W*. The step is swept clean.

I knock. There is no answer. I try the handle and it turns. I go in.

A white room, curtains drawn. A small stove in the corner, embers dying. A table, a cold cup of tea, filmed over, half-drunk. A heel of bread, crumbs scattered across the scrubbed wood. Next to the bread lies Christopher Black's wooden leg. He is reaching for it.

"You," he says. He has not prepared a face for me. He is afraid. He thinks that he might be dreaming or that I have found him by witchcraft. It almost makes me laugh. What a time for him to begin to believe in the eye.

"I went to the police station," I say. "Chief Inspector."

"I see. You have come a long way to triumph over me."

I sit at the table and tear off a piece of bread. I eat it. It is the first food I have eaten off the isle in three years. I wait for the ceiling to fall in, for His wrath, but nothing happens. The bread is good, it has caraway seeds in it.

The walls are covered with drawings and paintings. They are all of the same girl, caught in pencil, hair falling over her brow. She looks troubled, resolute, as though she is setting out on a difficult journey. She sits beside an azure lake in a straw hat. Swans sail behind her head. She looks up at someone, just out of view, with love. A large pen drawing of what can only be her eye stares at me from the wall opposite.

"Is that your sister?" I ask.

He nods.

"I do not look like her at all," I say. "That was all in your mind, I think."

"Certainly you are nothing like her."

"What did you do to make the policemen shun you?" I ask. "I can tell that it was bad. The man at the station called you a seal."

"A seal?" He says it to himself. "A seal . . . Oh, I see. Not a seal. An SIW."

"What is that?"

"A self-inflicted wound. I shot myself in the foot." He looks at his empty trouser leg which hangs limp from the knee down.

"Why?"

"To make them send me home from the War."

"Was it that bad, the War?"

"Yes."

My thumb traces the outline of my eyepatch. I recall the plunge, the dark, the knife. I think I understand. "Did they find you out?"

"They could not prove it or they would have executed me. There was a court martial. But they knew. Everyone does. The children follow me. They come in the night with stones. They paint words on my door. I had to resign."

I am trying to steel myself with dislike for what I must do next. "Why did you lie to me?"

"I suppose I wanted someone to look at me in the old way," he says. "As if I were still worthy of respect."

"But I never looked at you that way," I say.

"I was the youngest Chief Inspector in Inverness." He wears a fixed expression and his voice is smooth and cold. "I had an excellent record. Everything before me. The police was supposed to be a reserved occupation. When my number came up it should have been easy to make my case for exemption. Do you know why they denied it? Because I had become unsteady. Overly preoccupied with a certain John Bearings, against whom no criminal case could be made. I had lost my touch. Trust in my judgement was eroded. I would be more use over there, according to them. I should never have gone to War. I should still have my leg. And the reason that I do not is you."

"I did not make you chase us," I say. "Is there any more bread?"

He puts his head in his hands. Then he laughs, a tired sound. "Have this," he says. "You are too thin." From a cupboard he brings a loaf and a piece of cheese, daffodil yellow.

My mouth sings with its sharpness. "You must eat if I eat," I say. "Otherwise He will come for us. The great snake in the ocean."

He raises a sceptical eyebrow.

I make my voice shake. "Please. I cannot eat unless you do."

"Very well."

Really, people will believe anything. I take the little jar from my pocket. I give us each a teaspoonful of honey. It falls through the air in a slow, golden stream. I keep my face still. It is very hard for me, to watch him eating Altnaharra honey. I want to snatch it from his impure lips.

I feel it at the first gentle touch. The golden light in my heart.

It takes hold of him a moment later. His head nods slightly. His pupils swell and take up his eyes. He is the colour of birch bark.

"What do you feel?" I ask. But I know. It is strange to see the benison in his eyes.

"All the world is shining," he says. "A wave is coming to take us.

Soon it will be here. What is this?" he asks, struggling back to himself. "Did you come here to kill me?"

"A test," I say.

"How can you stand it?" he says. "So much beauty."

I smile too, because it is soaring through me. But beneath it is the darkness where my heart once was. I was right.

* * *

The effect lasts an hour or so. Afterwards we are weak, with sore heads. Our fingers tremble.

"What did you give me?" he asks. Some of the old light is in his eyes and he looks almost happy. It is the chase.

I take from my pocket a handkerchief in which are wrapped some more of the vivid purple flowers. "These grow in the ruins of Altnaharra," I say. "Uncle planted them there. I think they have the benison in them. It must be added to the honey somehow."

On the table I spread the page torn from the *Kingdom Animalia*. "This says that the flowers are *Rhododendron ponticum*. Are these the same ones?" Half of me hopes he will say, *No, these are quite different, you silly girl.* The other half knows that he will not.

Black gives a whistle. "How dim-witted I am," he murmurs to the wilting blooms. "Oh, I should have thought of it." He takes the handkerchief from me. "They bloom in late summer in Asia Minor and produce a hallucinogen called Grayanotoxin. It is a very old poison. Wars have been fought with it. The bees pass the poison from the nectar into the honey."

"The bees are not dead. We are not dead." Even now I want to argue. "How is it possible?"

"Poison or drug, it's only a matter of dosage," he says. "I expect the bees suffered a great deal in the beginning, before they grew accustomed to it." He examines the rhododendron flowers with careful fingers, a policeman's eye. "How often do you eat the honey?"

"Every day, a little. More when we worship in the stones." I am cold. I have gone to Uncle's arms for comfort all my life. Where will I go now?

"Just enough to keep you under the influence," he says. "Not enough to incapacitate you—that he reserves for special days. It is clever. It is a form of assault to drug someone. He could be charged for that, I think. If the others would support you."

"They will not," I say. My stomach is a worm. "I took my eye out for him. I thought I must pay in flesh, as he did with his leg."

"Have you heard of polio?" he asks. "It is a sickness that withers limbs. That is what happened to his leg, Eve. There was nothing holy about it."

Christopher Black lays the flowers on the table then goes to the sink in the corner and washes his hands carefully. He comes back and sits down. He is very solid and still, expecting me to fly apart. It is then I understand that the worst is yet to come.

"Tell me," I say.

"John Bearings was already known to the Met," he says. "As I thought. He left India under a cloud, and then trouble began in London. They would not tell me what he was suspected of when I enquired. And when they will not say, it is usually one thing. With girls so young . . . their accounts cannot be relied on. Not enough to bring charges."

My heart beats hard and sluggish. Each detail of the room assaults me. The white walls, the scent of dust, the vague sounds of children shouting in the street.

Black says, "Evelyn. I must ask. Did he ever—?"

"No," I say. "Uncle has not asked the duty of me." *Not yet.* I cannot breathe. I want to pant like a dog.

"Breathe slowly," he says. He brings me water to drink.

"You gave me this." I take the newspaper from my sleeve. "Did you know she was my mother?"

"I wanted you to know she was alive," he says.

"You should not have let him take me," I say to the picture of Alice. Alice's dark eyes look back. My eyes. It is like talking to myself. "You should not have left me there alone." I can almost feel her arms around me. Longing feels just as it sounds—long and endless.

"I tried to find her today," I say to Christopher Black. "The house was empty. I left her a message. I do not think that she will get it. Where will I go? Who will I be?"

He says, wearily, "If anyone has the answers to those questions, it is not I."

"If there is no serpent in the ocean," I say, "what is there? Who orders the world? Who looks after us? Is it your God?"

"No one," he says. "There is nothing."

"That cannot be true."

"Believe it," he says, savagely. "We are alone."

I leave him, closing the door behind me.

* * *

The train to Tongue surges like my blood. I think of Alice and my dreams. *Mother*. How foolish. I will never have a mother, just as I will never be at one with Him and the ocean. This is all there is.

The carriage is packed with tired bodies. Hair oil and sweat. Cold red noses. A bowler hat nudges my cheek, a foot treads heavily on my instep. The carriage is packed tighter and tighter as it travels north, everyone fleeing the town. My ribs are compressed by the weight of the crowd. A long pheasant feather tickles my nose. The owner of the hat, a plump woman, draws her shawl about her. Gold, the colour of toasted tobacco. The woman stares at me with too-large, pale blue eyes. She takes the flesh of my arm between finger and thumb and gives me a long, painful pinch. "Push me about, indeed," she says. "Wee madam." The marks left by her fingers sing on my arm.

I want to hurt her. And why not?

The train stops with a scream as it always does, in the tunnel before Tongue. Some signal is broken here. Everyone groans, shouts and grasps for purchase. A wiry, dirty arm snakes about my waist and squeezes. The carriage lights flicker. I push the thin, dirty arm off me and slip my knife from my cuff. A good feeling is beginning. Perhaps it is not so bad to be alone in the world. Perhaps alone can mean free.

The woman in the pheasant hat leans on me. Her face is averted. I press the blade gently into my forearm, two quick, shallow slashes. It still comes, the old pain-sweet comfort. Not everything has changed.

The blood trickles onto the woman's shoulder. I pull my sleeve down and fold my arm, closing the small wounds.

"He cut you," I say. "With his knife! Oh, catch him, catch him!"

For a moment the woman's eyes rest lazily on the blood that darkens her golden shawl. She does not understand what she sees. Then she screams.

The carriage explodes. Panic, bodies pressing, shoving. There is no space to move. It is chaos. The good feeling rises higher in me, like walking a taut wire across a deep ravine. Someone falls, knocking the breath out of me. I am pinned to the wall and something jabs my eye. A pheasant feather. A faint mineral scent and the acrid smell of fear. My mind hums with night thoughts. I cannot breathe. The darkness fills my eyes and body. The sound of screaming, of weeping, everywhere. An elbow jabs my mouth hard, breaking my lip. I taste blood. It is like the fight in the schoolyard, it is like benison, it is the knowledge that nothing I do matters. The good feeling reaches its pitch. Dark coils tighten, tighten and I fall.

At Tongue the crowd presses towards the doors, straining for release. I duck low into the sea of legs and crawl on my hands and knees out of the carriage. Behind me comes the wail of the woman with the pheasant hat, *He stabbed me!* The station guard is summoned but I float with the tide of people out of the station, into the cold dusk. Haystack whickers at me from the paddock nearby.

The pleasure drains away, leaving me gritty and nauseous in its wake. My mind and flesh and blood are frantic with unfamiliar signals. I should not have done that. Where now? The thought of returning to Altnaharra makes the very skin walk on my bones.

I think of grey, cracked skin and a timeless eye, an amber beech leaf caught in golden hair. I have not deserved it but she said that she would help. Perhaps she will tell me to go away. But I must try.

I lead Haystack to the mounting block. He pushes me hard with his head and I stumble, skinning my hands on the flinty ground. I mount, slap him hard on his quarters and urge him east. He protests, turning with his whole body towards Altnaharra, where he knows that Dinah is waiting for him with hay. I curse him and pull hard on his left ear until he turns away from home, towards the foot of Ardentinny. As we go, I practise apologies. Nothing seems good enough.

The early moon shows the clearing through the trees. I give Haystack a thump on his shaggy quarters and he hurries on.

The clearing is bare, churned earth. A paper bag drifts on the wind, a white ghost. Gashes where poles were driven deep into the ground. Wheel ruts where heavily laden wagons lumbered slowly away. The circus is gone.

I put my face to Haystack's shaggy neck and weep. My very limbs seem laden down by fear and doubt. "Help me," I whisper. "Please. Help me." There is no answer.

"Well, we cannot stay here all night," I say to Haystack at last.

Then I do the only thing I can, which is to go forward. I urge Haystack on, following the cart tracks. Perhaps the circus did not leave long ago; perhaps I can catch them. Haystack grumbles and resists, then valiantly rises to the challenge and summons his little rolling canter.

Suddenly he stumbles in the pockmarked earth. I fly over his head. The world spins in sick rotation. There is a stunning blow to my back. Surely my lungs have been knocked clear out of my chest. When I try to sit up, the world staggers and slides.

Haystack shivers a few feet away. A flap of tan hide hangs loose, exposing the white patella. His reins have snapped in two. When I reach for the trailing ends, he throws up his head and trots past me heading west, towards Altnaharra. His hoofbeats recede into the distance. I struggle to rise, to follow the track of the circus south. I must get right away or Uncle will come. He will come and give me honey again. I crawl. My limbs grow faint until they are no longer there. Somewhere, a nightjar welcomes in the darkness.

* * *

"Eve." Hands are cool on my brow. I have taken my eye and I am walking through the dark, held tight by His coils. No, that was then, not now. I am in a hole with the white rabbits. No, not that either. I am flying through the dusky air, and I am sad because someone has picked all the roses . . .

"Evelyn." Dinah's voice again.

I look about me with an aching head. The hall is lit with flame. The sound of the sea. Altnaharra. I am back and everything is wrong, wrong. How did I ever feel safe here? It is the warmth of the tiger's jaws, just before they close.

"Uncle was so worried," says Dinah. "We all were. Haystack came back in a lather, with his bridle broken."

"Dinah," I whisper. "How did he find me? How did Uncle bring me back?"

She gives me a strange look. "You came back, Eve. We found you unconscious outside the gate, not an hour ago." She gives a little smile. "Now you are safe again."

"No, Dinah, that cannot be . . ." I sit up. My head swims. I try to see what is in her eyes, but they are unreadable. Something is missing. I put my hand on my collarbone. The great cold key to the gate is gone.

Uncle is in the doorway. He seems vast as the ocean. "My Eve," he says. "You are returned to us. That pony has always been wilful, now he is a danger. Something will be done."

"The key to the gate," I say. "Forgive me, Uncle, I must have dropped it. Perhaps the cord broke when I fell from Haystack."

"I have taken the key in my charge," Uncle says. "I will carry that burden now. You have suffered it long enough. Come. There is great news, and this is no place for it. We must be under the sky."

Dinah helps me out of the castle, down the rise to the stones. The night is cold, clear. In the circle, flaming torches lick up against the dark. Nora is there, and Baby Elizabeth.

Uncle brings forth the bowl. Honey drips from his fingers. When he comes to me I take the honey from his hand into my mouth like the others. I pretend to swallow. It pools under my tongue, agonising and sweet.

"A great day is upon us," says Uncle. His voice is changing. He shivers. The benison is everywhere. Snakes of light writhe about him. I must have swallowed some honey despite my efforts. "He has spoken," the Adder says with eyes of burning coal. "He has told me the hour. It will be eight days hence: at the turn. Hogmanay, in the calendar of the Impure. He is coming. The world will be washed away. These are the final days."

Nora gasps and holds on to Uncle. She has tears in her eyes. Dinah smiles. Elizabeth comes close and takes me tightly about the waist. She seems faint with excitement.

"We have locked the gate for the last time," Uncle says. "When next we see the world, it will be new." He goes to the shadows at the edge of the stones, then pulls Haystack into the light. Haystack's neck is extended, taut as the length of rope. He skids on stiff legs, neat hooves leaving furrows in the earth. His eyes roll, showing a ring of white about the brown.

"This creature was once a friend to the isle," says Uncle. "He worked in the service of the Children. But then he threw our Evelyn and injured her. He has forgotten his purpose. We will give him a new one."

Uncle strokes the pony's neck, which is dark with sweat. In his other hand he raises the hammer high. It casts a long shadow across the grass, the stones. "Thank you," Uncle says to Haystack. "You are the Flesh Price that will make the isle safe." He brings the hammer down on Haystack's shaggy crown. Once, twice. It lasts only a few moments but they tick by in too-slow succession, blood red and filled with the odour of flesh. The sound is awful. Dinah cries out and hides her face. Elizabeth breathes into my waist.

I watch. I will not close my eye. I will not give Uncle the gift of my fear. "The isle is sealed," Uncle says. Haystack's blood shines on him in the torchlight.

The Adder comes across the circle. The flame dances in his eyes. He takes my throat in a warm, bloody palm.

"Swallow," he says.

DINAH

1931

MARY is ten. We go to the forest, as is our tradition.

Rose lines a basket with clean gingham. In it she places boiled eggs, a pinch of salt in a twist of newspaper, bloater paste sandwiches, ginger ale, three apples, half a plum cake.

The path is scooped out between high banks. Overhead bare branches interlock against the blue. The trees bear only sparse pennants of auburn. The leaves fell early this year.

Mary swings between our hands, solemn. "I am going to look after animals when I grow up," she says. "Like Rose." Rose helps on a farm. Calving and medicine. "It is called a veterinarian," Mary says. "Sister Margaret says that there is a college. I will go there."

I see my fear mirrored in Rose's face. There are too many ways for the world to blunt Mary, to show her what her place is. I did not even want her to go to the little school where the black and white nuns welcome her at the gate each morning. I was afraid she would not thrive. But she does; she comes home shining.

"Let us find all the animals we can, today," I say to Mary. "That will be good practice for you."

The forest is alive. We see dung beetles shining like jewels. A furious robin keeps pace for a hundred yards, chasing us off. Crows sit in judgement on a leafless oak. Starlings move overhead in mesmerising clouds. A young roe deer on skittish legs. No people.

"A *Cervidae*," Mary says. "That means deer. It would be better if I could see them from the inside." It is something any child might say, isn't it? But to me Mary's face looks dark and small, as if the person in there had slipped away for a moment. Those fears are always stirring just beneath the surface, too. How much of me is in her, how much of the other one? Sometimes blood tells.

We spread the blanket in a small clearing, open to the sky. Mary eats the plum cake first. It is allowed, because it is her birthday. "How did my father die?" she asks me.

It is not the first time, but the question has power today. She understands that, even at ten. On this day each year the past grows vivid, obscuring the present like woodsmoke. It is harder for me to lie today.

"He was killed in the War," I say. "Lots of girls and boys are missing their papas, you know."

"I know," she says, worried.

"But you have me."

"Look," Rose says. Something pours through the grass. Round orange eyes, scales marked like sunlight on bare earth. She moves slowly, great with eggs, looking for somewhere beneath the leaf mould.

I take her up in my hands. I support her swollen length.

"Come," I say. "You can hold her, if you like."

I place Mary's hands on the grass snake, gently, so as not to bruise the cargo she carries within.

"She is beautiful. Does she have little snakes inside her?"

"Dozens of little snakes inside dozens of little eggs."

"They will come out of her like I came out of you."

"Yes," I say. "Just like that. A snake lived with us when I was your age. His name was Hercules. I was afraid of him. I shouldn't have been. He was only a snake."

Mary looks at me, startled. Usually I do not speak of the past. She strokes the snake's head. "Can we make a little snake come out? I would love it for my own."

"They are not ours to take." I set the outraged grass snake down and she slides away from us into the fallen leaves.

We play hide-and-seek. Rose is the best at it. She seems to shrink at will, fitting into hollows half her size, shinning up branches slender as wands.

Mary grows tired, bullish.

"If you sleep now," I tell her, "the day will go on when you wake up. If you don't it will be over, and we must go home."

Her lip trembles but at last she lies down and puts her head on my knee. Her hair is a pool of gold in my lap. I stroke her. I feel the moment when it happens, when her small tired body gives itself up to sleep.

"She is clever and kind," Rose says. "She likes animals. She is very like someone I used to know."

"She gets all that from you."

Sometimes I catch Mary in thought, eyes wide, mouth solemn. She looks so like Rose that my heart nearly stops. How is that possible?

Rose smiles and the moment is full; there is no need for further words.

When Mary wakes we share apples and drink tea from the flask. Then we eat sandwiches. "It's all in the wrong order," Mary says, gleeful.

"Don't get used to it," Rose says. "We're back to normal first thing tomorrow."

Mary sticks out her tongue. "I am going into the forest to discover a new animal," she says. "They will name it after me."

"If you cannot see us," I say, "that is too far. You turn around. You come back straight away."

"Yes!" She runs, pigtails flying.

"If I had not given Altnaharra to him," I say to Rose, "I could have sold it and sent my daughter to school."

"You couldn't have," Rose says. "You know that. The bargain was made."

"I meant it," I say. "She is yours as much as mine."

The sun caresses us. I have learned to store such moments, to catch them just as they are: the down of hair on Rose's forearm, Mary scuffling through red leaves at the edge of the clearing, the weight of plum cake in my stomach.

Mary strides towards us across the grass. My eyesight is weak these days. I do not see what she is holding until she is quite close.

"Mama," she says. "I have found another one. Look!"

She holds the snake gently, as I showed her. The unseasonable warmth is drawing them out.

"I see that, darling." I stand and go to her slowly.

The snake thrashes his muscular coils. His narrow tongue flickers black. His jaws open wide to show the pale pink sheath. It is more frightening than the fangs beneath it, somehow. Mary's eyes are wide.

"Do not be afraid," I tell her. "Be still. That is very important." I take the snake firmly behind his head and I lift him from her hands.

"We will let this fellow go now," I say. "He is not the right kind." The adder arches in my grasp.

I look into his red eyes. Everything I have been running from is there, waiting. I say, "The Adder has found me."

"No," Rose says. "He is dead, Dinah." Her voice fades. I am alone in the dark. *Uncle.*

*　*　*

Mary is crying. A pink finger and thumb fill my vision. Rose holds the smelling salts under my nose. Their acrid sting runs through my body.

"I hate her," I say to Rose. "Evelyn. I hate her so much that I am *scalded* by it. I wish she had never been born. I wish . . ."

Rose strokes my brow. "I know," she says.

I push her hand away.

*　*　*

When we reach home I go directly to the chest where Rose keeps the planchette and boards. It is locked. Mary pokes into everything. I hold out my hand. "Give me the key."

Rose looks as though she might cry. I suppose she thought all this was behind us. She bends to Mary. "Go into the garden," she says. "Find me the last of the wild strawberries."

"Mama is angry," Mary says.

"No, she is not."

But I am. Rage is racing through me. It gnashes bright teeth. When the kitchen door shuts I say to Rose, spitting each word, "Someone else will do it for me, if you refuse."

Rose says, "You know why I say no."

"I accept the risk."

"What happens to you happens to all of us," she says. "Do you accept the risk to Mary? To me?"

I sit down, suddenly tired. "It weighs on me like a corpse. I drag it everywhere. If she has only hate for me . . . still I must know."

Rose turns her flat green gaze on me. "I am tired of being the one who must always say no. Who must wheedle you out of it, time after time. If you want it so very much, I will do it." She turns from me. "Take Mary down the road to the farmhouse. See if the Dennys will give her supper. I will not have her in the house for it."

"Rose . . ."

"It will be ready when you come back."

I make to kiss her. She pushes me away gently. "Don't ask me to comfort you."

Mary comes willingly. They have kittens at the farmhouse.

Mrs. Denny wipes her flushed face and says Mary may eat with them, of course. I watch my daughter trot into the bright, loud kitchen. Dogs' tails wag and children's legs swing from wooden chairs. A scent of bread and lamb. Tired people ending the day together. Perhaps it would have been better if Mary had been born to the Dennys instead. But I am too selfish to wish for such a thing. She is mine. *I will make it right, darling,* I promise her silently.

*   *   *

When I open the door to the cottage I can feel it. The other place is close. A cold wind blows through the rooms, flicking the pages of books and rattling doors. It tugs at my skirt with curious fingers.

In the sitting room candles flicker on tables, the floor, before the mirrors and the windowpanes. Rose kneels in the centre of the room, the rusting tea tin by her side. A small round mirror is before her. A thin knife by it, gleaming wicked.

Rose puts a finger to her lips. I sit before her without speaking. She opens the tea tin. She takes a pinch of the ashes and scatters them across the mirror. She motions for me to do the same. Rose holds a candle aloft.

The ash is white, powder-soft in my fingers. There is a low drumming in my ears. Shadows gather about us. They are doors waiting to open. The air is filled with the scent of the sea.

I take up the knife. I prick my finger. Blood falls in shining drops, a dark blemish on the silver. I unclasp the silver chain that hangs about my neck and place the locket on the mirror's flickering surface.

I bend over the mirror. Beneath the scattered ash and the drops of blood there is the silhouette of a head. Someone, face rippling as if through water.

I lean in closer. The mirror figure does the same. She approaches me through time. I forget to breathe. Light plays on hollow cheeks, an empty eye socket, a shadowed brow. I gasp and she gasps too. Candlelight flickers over her skin—or is there something underneath it? Crawling over her skull. The barriers between things shake. A hand reaches for mine, fingers aching to touch, living to dead. Her will fills the air, the room. No quiet spirit, she. No soul at peace.

Images chase across the mirror. A chain, at the end of it a bucket full of stones. Mist reflected in pools of rainwater, stones in a circle like the fingers of a cupped hand, thick strands of honey falling in the grey light. The memory of touch. We were together then, all of us. The drops of my blood spread across the mirror, covering it in darkness.

I think the words, or hear them. *Hello, slug.*

I sweep the ash from the glass with my hand and catch the silver locket in my palm. I flip the mirror facedown. It seems to hum at my touch. I am dizzy, breathing too hard. Our sitting room is about me, known and warm, but I am also in a dark cellar where little flames burn, feeding on dead flesh.

"It is not real," I say. I turn the mirror faceup. Blood is smeared across its bright surface. It is just a cheap thing. "After all your warnings," I say. "Nothing. You have no power after all. Or perhaps you keep her away. Are you so jealous of the dead?"

"What a thing to say to me." Rose's mouth purses with hurt. Her patience is unbearable. I hate her for agreeing to this.

"You need me to be incomplete," I say. "You wouldn't know what to do with someone whole."

"And you force me to save you," she says. "Over and over, until I am exhausted."

"Sometimes I hate this place so much that my blood sings with it," I say. "My heart beats out the very word, *trapped, trapped, trapped.*"

"Clean this up," says Rose quietly. "I will fetch Mary. It is her birthday, after all."

"I suppose I have ruined it."

"Yes," Rose says. "As you well know." She takes the bloodied mirror from the room. In the garden I hear glass breaking.

Some things lie deep in the chasms between two people, and they should not be touched or looked at. We haven't fought like this since the beginning.

* * *

The dream always comes after the worst days.

She stands on the cliff in the silver light, the blood and matter drying on her. Behind her, we lie dead.

Below, her true brothers and sisters call. She bends and buckles and cries out in pain. She looks wildly about, seeking to flee, to resist the call of the sea. She runs to the car and drives towards the mainland, rattling over rock and turf. But the whooping call of the selkies is too strong, and without her say-so her hands steer the car slowly east, off the narrow causeway.

The little car plunges into the deep. Eve's hair floats about her head like weeds. Her legs fuse together, her toes push out, the bones elongating into finials, a tail. Her arms shrink and grow into her sides. Her eyes become black shining balls. Her waist swells and bursts her skirt, popping the buttons. Her bones break and break again. Over and over it happens, each part of her remade. Grey pelt creeps up over her feet, hands, arms. Last it covers her face, rolling over her expression, wiping it away like the tide, leaving behind a rounded snout, whiskers.

She is plump and sea-ready; her cries have become barks. She rolls towards the car window, her body awkward and wrong in the confined space. The mortal parts of her that she does not need are piled sadly on the seat. Crabs are already coming to return the corpse to nothing.

Evelyn pushes herself out of the little window, out, out into open water. She moves her sleek body and looks back once with her round eyes, at the husk that was her human form. She gives a little sigh and pushes off, arcing into the ocean, carving the water. Her brothers and sisters are waiting. The seals move swiftly away from the land and the thing that was Evelyn goes with them. The *Eubha Muir* returns to the sea.

* * *

I wake weeping, though not with sorrow. He promised that we would go to Him in the deep. Instead I am imprisoned here, far from the ocean. The unfairness of it leaves me breathless. My anger is so strong that I see it drifting in veils before my eyes.

The skin between the worlds is thin tonight and I feel her near. Her dead hand lies atop mine. She is angry, too. Her breath cold in my ear.

"I miss you," I say. The word *sister* was forbidden on the isle, but that is what we were. Perhaps I will never have the answer to my question. Never know if I am forgiven.

I go to the pantry and sit down on the stone floor. I take the lid off the barrel of rice, scoop up the milky grains and let them run through my fingers back into the barrel. I do this over and over again until my hand and my ear have achieved a rhythm, and the shushing and falling of the rice is like a waking dream. I close my eyes. This trick has served me well over the years. If I pour just so and let my mind drift, it sounds like the sea.

* * *

Rose and Mary lie tangled together. Rose's brow is furrowed: care pursues her through her dreams. A cardboard puzzle piece is clutched in Mary's damp fist, not to be relinquished even in sleep. So tightly we cling.

I lie down in their warmth. "I should not have made you do it," I say quietly to Rose. "I am sorry."

They do not wake.

CHRISTOPHER BLACK

1931

HE stops under the open window of number fourteen, Orme Place. The sashes are thrown up to let in the night. Music spills out into the cold street. The gentle strains of a violin.

Through the swags of silk curtain, Christopher Black watches. The cigarette smoke is so heavy that the figures look like wraiths in a fog. A red silk dress, a peacock feather. Long black satin gloves. A bare back, smooth as ivory. A string of pearls runs down the spine like a river. Red liquid winking in glasses. Most pungent is the excitement that comes off their bodies, seeping from their skin.

The man who admits him wears long white socks. His hair shines like a pile of currant buns. He wears some kind of paint on his face to hide his scars.

"Miss Seddington is expecting me." Christopher Black proffers his card.

The man ushers him through the bowels of the house. Somewhere ahead water is running. The carpet yields to black and white tile. They come out into a hot place that seems to be made of panels of night. Flickering lanterns hang in the branches of unfamiliar trees, paper lampshades casting coloured light: blue, yellow, pink and orange. Birds sing in the artificial glow. He catches flashes of long green tails. There are white stone figures draped in stone linens on plinths. The three-tiered marble fountain stands in the centre of the conservatory, water tumbling in shining sheets.

She sits alone on a bench beneath a fig tree. Her eyes are ringed with black, her fair skin is powdered and rouged, her dark hair as smooth as lacquer. When she moves her bracelets chink together. They are gold, inlaid with black stone. Her black silk dress shimmers in the light. Beside her on a table there sit a small brass bell, wrought in the shape of a woman in a ballgown, a cigarette case, a lighter fashioned like a silver seashell, a pillbox inlaid with lapis lazuli and a glass of water.

"Mr. Black." She does not rise to greet him. "A tall dark stranger crosses the threshold after midnight. That is good fortune, they say, for the coming year. Is it luck that you bring, I wonder?"

He feels the urge to bow or sink down on one knee. He resists. "This is quite the setting."

"I come here to listen. I miss the sound of water. But you did not visit me to speak of that. I only agreed to see you to rid myself of a nuisance. You have made yourself as persistent as a disease, loitering about."

He sits down beside her uninvited. "It was ten years ago," he says abruptly, "almost to the night, that they were killed. Do you never wonder whether you could have prevented it? That thought visits me each day. It is on my conscience. For I believe that I could have." His voice catches. He clears his throat.

"She thought that you were her mother. Licentious, the goings-on at that place!" Alice raises her eyebrows and he stops, winces, recalling that she was part of it all. This is going badly. "Anyhow," he says, "she seemed to change under my eyes that day. Her voice, her face. How much are our beliefs built into us? What did she lose when she lost hers? My apologies. Where was I? She came here to this house, but it was all closed up. She said that she had left you a message. Did she do so?"

"I received no note," she says. "If I had, I would have thrown it away. I have no truck with anything relating to Altnaharra."

"I was a defeated man that day, Miss Seddington. I had nothing to spare for others. The beliefs he fed those children—pagan odds and ends, profanely cobbled together. Snakes and oceans and the end times. Nonsense. But they were all she had, and I took them from her."

He draws a deep breath. "A week later they were dead and she had done it. I had no position. I could do nothing. But I followed the story in the papers. I read everything. I asked favours of the colleagues who would still speak to me. Some even granted those favours. I have seen the police report.

"Doubt, Miss Seddington. Doubt is in me like a tick. It will not let me rest. The last time I saw Evelyn she was strange, unlike the girl I knew. But not as strange as the evidence. It does not add up. Those bunglers who investigated were not curious. They were happy enough to close the book on it, having found their culprit. And dead, too! No need for a trial. They could not see that it did not make sense. They did not *know* the victims."

"You knew them, of course," says Alice. "Pray, share your insight. I long to be illuminated." She looks at him with steely eyes.

He examines her face very carefully, like a traveller studying a map. "The beef," he says. "It troubles me. Except for John Bearings, they did not eat meat. So why would they order a whole side of beef for Hogmanay? They would not—at least, not for the purpose of eating. And where did the beef go? Was it left on the isle? Did Jamie take it with him, as he rode back? It is not recorded. Two explanations occur to me. One: Jamie MacRaith was supposed to discover the scene, so he was summoned with an order so large and expensive that he would not fail to deliver, even in wind and rain. Or," says Christopher Black, "no beef was ordered at all. It was a clumsy excuse for his being there, fashioned after the fact. And if that is the case, what was Jamie MacRaith doing at Altnaharra that morning?"

"Your opinion only. Things change. Perhaps they began to eat meat. Or perhaps they wanted it to smoke and preserve it for the winter, or to feed to the chickens. Or to conduct a ritual. That's not evidence."

"I know, I know," he says, smiling. "Many explanations are possible. Very well. We will leave that aside. By the way, I have noticed a handsome car parked behind the house. An older woman drives out in it sometimes. Your mother, perhaps? Green. A Daimler. Very nice. The motorcar they found off the Altnaharra causeway, the one in which they found Eve's body—that was green." He clears his throat.

"Forgive me," Alice says. "Are you suggesting that the car my mother bought new from the factory two years ago was used to commit a murder in 1920, eleven years before it was even built?"

"Ha! Perhaps it was put into Mr. Wells' machine."

Alice regards him blankly.

He clears his throat. "Merely the car caused me to reflect on possessions and habit. My father had an old grey mare at one time. She was an awkward bit of horse, if you ask me, but he loved her. More than any of his family, for certain. When she died he was inconsolable. He buried her under the apple tree. I mention this because, for the rest of his life, he was kinder to grey horses, and he always tried to buy a light one. It was a habit he had formed. Now, of course, motorcars are the new horses."

She laughs aloud. "What precisely are you accusing my mother of?"

"I was wondering," he says, "whether she liked green cars. In particular I was wondering if the AC she reported stolen in January 1921 was green."

"You would have to ask her."

"I would much rather ask you." He smiles.

"I don't really notice cars. I am not much help, I'm afraid."

He frowns. "No, you can't be. Dinah is the key. She alone in all the world knows what passed that night. But Dinah is gone. Did she walk out of that inn after the inquest and dive straight into the sea? She might as well have done. I have looked for her, and you must believe me when I say that I know how to look." Black takes an envelope from his pocket.

"I received a strange letter in the autumn following the murders. It was postmarked 17 November and signed, *D*. To all appearances it is from Dinah Bearings. Is it genuine? I do not know. Is that her writing?"

"It could be," she says. "I never saw Dinah's writing more than once or twice. There was not much call for it on the isle."

"Whoever the letter is from, Miss Seddington, it is truly puzzling. It unsettled me—which was the intention, I think. It describes James MacRaith's discovery of Dinah among the bodies. The scene is conjured in such detail. We hear not only Dinah's thoughts but Jamie's, too. We are told what he eats, what he thinks, what he reads.

"I have met young Mr. MacRaith twice. Once during the War before he was called up, and once after. He struck me as very different at our second meeting. His eggs had been somewhat scrambled, you might say. He was reading a manual on sheep-breeding and there were no other books in sight. He did not seem to know who Edgar Rice Burroughs was when I asked. Nor did he recognise the name Agatha Christie, although, according to Dinah, he had books by these authors out on loan from the library. Not to mention that *Tarzan and the Ant-Men* was published several years after the murders. Why add these details, if they are not correct?" He pauses. "Those are, as it happens, two writers I enjoy."

"Perhaps Jamie had forgotten. Or Dinah was embroidering."

"Possibly. Some weeks ago, I received another letter from the mysterious 'D.' It is even stranger than the first. Why now? I believe that the anniversary of the murders has provoked strong feelings in the writer. As it has in me. Read the lines I have marked. The inquest. The account of my behaviour there. I asked Dinah a question about her missing locket."

Alice takes the letter. "I cannot see any mystery," she says. "Though I cannot fathom why you would ask such a question."

"Ah," he says, pleased. "You have put your finger on it. It is a point-less question. Quite unlike me, I think. What could have possessed me to interrupt official proceedings with such a mindless enquiry? It is baffling.

"Here is the thing, Miss Seddington. I did not ask that question. That exchange with Dinah never happened. I was not at the inquest. Guilt kept me away. Shame. I deeply regret it, but I remained in Inverness that day. May I?"

He does not wait for her reply but takes a cigarette from her case. The silver seashell clicks out flame.

"Now," he says, "why would Dinah invent such a thing? It cannot be to deceive me—I *know* that I was not there! Whose eyes is it designed for, this fiction? The transcript of the inquest is publicly available. It shows that I did not stand up and say those things. So if Dinah's intent was not to mislead, what was it?"

"How mysterious! I fail to see what light I can shed."

"I wonder if perhaps you would tell me where she is."

Alice's smile is dazzling. "So sure of yourself, Mr. Black," she says. "I envy it. Shall I explain to you why I cannot—and will not—answer your question? One moment." Alice takes the lapis box from the table. She swallows a small white pill with a sip of water.

"I fled Altnaharra," she says, "to a mother who had long thought me dead and had made her peace with it. My father had died in the meantime. Of grief, my mother informs me. I killed him. She is very clear on that point. She has since remarried. Whatever illusions I had cherished of a fond reunion were quickly dispelled.

"The first thing my mother did on my return was engage a doctor to examine me. Not for my health, you understand. I am not the first gently bred girl to run away from home and return with a case of amnesia. The doctor confirmed what my mother suspected; that I was no longer marriageable. To compound things, he suspected that I had borne a child, or conceived one.

"My mother has not said a single unnecessary word to me since that day. We could not return to London, to society, so we stayed here. When there is company, I remain out of sight. I dress like this in case I am glimpsed. But I am not to mingle. I do not leave the house unless accompanied by Mother. I do not go to parties or concerts or other houses. I have not been touched with affection by another human being in years. I am embarrassing. I am valueless. I am unmarriageable and unportioned. When my mother dies a distant male cousin will have this house and the money. I hope to be allowed to continue to live here, but it is not at all certain. Otherwise, I genuinely do not know. I could not teach or be a governess. Mine was a very public indiscretion.

"Every three weeks I am taken to a special place for ladies of my calibre. It is out in the country, far from anywhere. There is a waiting room full of lilies. My mother sits in a pretty upholstered chair and reads periodicals. The room is full of mothers of wayward daughters, sons who have been caught, shall we say, on the back stairs. No one meets another's eye and no one has an appointment under their true name. My mother, for instance, becomes one Mrs. de Vere. A heroine from a novel she once read. She finds it mysterious and glamorous. The name 'de Vere' makes her feel as if she is having an adventure. It stops her asking herself: *If this deed must be committed under a name that is not my own, should it be done at all?*

"While my mother sits with the other Mrs. de Veres and reads about grades of raw silk and what colour of mink is fashionable, I am taken to a room. The decoration is very tasteful but they can never quite eradicate the scent of burnt hair. Accidents do happen. In the centre of the room is a chair with restraints, and beside it the machine.

"It is not as you might imagine. The shock is like a deep, dark place where there are no names for things. I am no one, there. For a time afterwards I remain in that place and from the bottom of my well I watch the world pass by. It is peaceful. But each time I leave something down in the darkness. A memory. Another detail gone for good. The name of the dog belonging to my best friend when she was six. The second boy I danced with at my coming-out ball. And that is peaceful, too. I wish to let it all go.

"We spend the night there in a room with more pretty wallpaper. In the morning the chauffeur drives us back to Inverness. If the house is dark and shuttered, that is where I have gone. I am somewhere in a room with flowered walls, at the bottom of a well.

"Now." Alice releases smoke from her mouth in a delicate water-fall. "If I knew where Dinah Bearings was I would ask them to burn that secret out of my brain, even if it took every other memory with it. I despise her, them, Altnaharra and myself most of all."

She leans forward in her chair. "You come to me beating your spoon on your plate like a child in the nursery," she says. "*Nanny, I cannot finish my puzzle!* Worse, you think that you have a right. Everything created, including myself, must serve your urge to *know*, at any cost."

Alice rings the little brass bell that sits beside her. "Go, please. I am not a free woman, but a few privileges remain to me, and one is that I need not listen to this."

Christopher Black rises from his chair. Now he does bow to Alice, an ironic half-bob. He gives her a white smile.

"You do know where she is," he says. "I thought so. You are quite right about me, by the way. I must pursue. It is my damnable nature. You cannot prevent it. I am as inexorable as the stars. Good evening, Miss Seddington."

Green parakeets scatter before him as he goes, crying like broken music boxes. It is a good exit, suiting his mood. Later he will wish he had forgone it and stayed to ask more. Alice Seddington will be dead of a heart attack within twelve months.

HOGMANAY

1920

WHITE *knitted wool*, the note at the gate says. *Ten ells. Pure as driven snow. For Hogmanay. Not a day later, or there will be no payment.*

Sarah Buchanan snorts when she sees it. For Hogmanay, indeed. Eight days for twenty ells? To card it, clean it, wash it, bleach it, spin it, knit it on the loom? But she has always had the talent of doing the undoable and she needs the money. So she tucks her hair into her cap, says goodbye to the white skin of her hands and locks the front door. She works without thought, biting an oatcake here and there when she remembers, seizing a few minutes of rest. And seven days later, it is done. Her head aches from the lye. Her arms and hands are reddened and burnt. She can barely see, she is so tired. But there it is, ten ells of pure white wool, neatly folded looking soft as mist in the firelight. All that remains is to deliver it to Altnaharra. After that Sarah will sink into her bed and she will not raise herself up from there until market day.

She winds her golden hair into a knot. She ties it tighter than she needs to, twists hard, pinning it with ruthless ferocity so that her eyes water. She puts up her hood. In the glass her face floats pale above her black dress. There is no Sarah there. She has purged hope, love, feeling, become a slip of flesh. A blank, person-shaped thing. She does this whenever she goes forth from the cottage. She leaves herself behind so they cannot hurt her. The looks, the taunts. Children running after her horse, screaming *hoor*.

William sleeps on a blanket by the hearth. He is three. He will be apprenticed to the shoemaker in Tongue in a few years. He is a good boy. He always seems taken aback at the fact of his own existence; his wide, surprised eyes. She is apprehensive of her feelings for him— the joy he raises in her is too strong, too much fierce pleasure clawed from sin.

Hector MacRaith was six months murdered by the time his son first drew breath. And Hamish Buchanan dead on the scaffold. Father and grandfather gone in one swift blow. One the killer of the other.

Sarah touches William's head now with a feather-light finger. There is none of Hector MacRaith in him. Instead Sarah sees her father. She traces Hamish Buchanan's strong jaw in her son's face.

The scratch comes at the windowpane and Sarah tuts. Early. She goes to the door. "Come," she says, her voice hushed. "I'll be off directly." Jamie MacRaith comes in with the sky all over him in glistening drops and a cord of wood on his back. The storm is nearly upon them.

"I have no use for this," he says, indicating the wood. "You might do me the kindness of taking it off my hands." Sarah raises an eyebrow and nods for him to set the wood down by the fire. She is always doing Jamie such favours. Whenever he calls he brings something. A plucked chicken, a new axe, a set of knitting needles, a saddle for the colt.

He goes to the settle where his brother sleeps, lifts a lock of his dark hair and blows briskly into his ear. William wakes with a start and swats at him.

"Go away!" he says, delighted.

"No," says Jamie. "Your ears are so dirty, I shall have to clean them out." He blows into William's ear again and William shrieks with laughter. He flings his arms about Jamie and hugs him. For a moment Jamie's face is twisted, almost violent. Sarah recognises that look. Her own face wears it sometimes. Love, closing like a tourniquet about the heart.

She banks the coals so they will not flare up again and spit red sparks at her child where he lies. She douses all but one candle, a wick floating in a bowl of goose fat. She wraps the precious white wool in layers of stiff oilcloth.

"You will be back directly?" Jamie says, spreading his wet greatcoat before the fire. "Put the wool in the basket and speed home. Get away from that place as soon as you can."

"What are you saying? You think that they will *not* ask me to stay for tea?"

"I should go with you," he says. "I do not like it. Or I should take the wool and you stay here."

"You cannot come," she says, "for I will not leave William alone. And you cannot go for me, I do not trust you with my crisp ten-shilling notes."

He smiles but his heart is not in it. "If the gate is open, do not go in," he says. "Leave the wool in the cage."

"What an odd bee you have trapped in your bonnet, MacRaith," she says. "That gate is never open."

Sarah supposes that it is strange, her friendship with Jamie Mac-Raith. She was his father's . . . what would you call it? And then her father killed his.

Sarah's mother had died shortly after Hamish Buchanan was hanged. Sarah could have sold the cottage then, left Loyal, started elsewhere. Loyal is a village of a hundred souls, with perhaps four or five topics of conversation. They whispered about her and when her belly began to swell, eyes followed her everywhere. They did not stone her in the street, but no one would speak to her. Former friends shunned her. The shopkeepers would not let her in to buy a penny twist of tea—she was made to call her order from the front step and place the coin on the floor, so that their hands would not touch her sinful one. Sarah began to feel that she did not exist. It was like death, in some ways. Still she did not go. She resolved to be a thorn in their sides. She would not leave her birthplace because of them. Perhaps she was afraid. Sarah has never been further afield than Tongue.

She managed. She fished with her father's nets in the pools at low tide, holding her pendulous belly with one hand as she bent to catch crab, shrimp and lobsters for the Saturday market. Then she bought wool with her pennies and taught herself to use her mother's old loom. She picked woad on the chalky riverbanks. She learned the hot and careful business of dyeing. She made ends meet. She birthed William by herself at this very hearth, with a cauldron of hot water for company. He was a dark-eyed, plump-lipped baby, and the bonniest thing she had ever seen. Sarah was no longer alone. They managed together, he and she.

Jamie had come back to Loyal when the War was over. The first thing he did was visit his father's grave. The second thing he did was call on Sarah Buchanan.

Sarah was dyeing wool and singing. Jamie must have knocked but she didn't hear. She looked up and there was a giant in the doorway. When Sarah saw Jamie's face she knew, like a sliver of ice in the heart, that he had come to kill her. She threw the closest thing to hand, which was a pot of yarn soaking in cochineal. It missed his head and exploded against the wall in a bloody bomb of warm, wet wool. Jamie put his hands up in supplication. "Stop," he said, "I did not die at War and I will not be dyed now!" He was given to this sort of pun.

LITTLE EVE

Sarah had regarded him in bafflement. "We had best get that off you," she said after a moment. "Or you will be pink until Tuesday." She took him quickly to the burn at the back of the cottage, where she doused him with cold bucketfuls.

"We are kin," Jamie said to Sarah, spitting water and shivering. "Because of him." He nodded at baby William. "We should know one another. We need not let the past stand between us." In the end Sarah had decided to trust him. The fact was she had no one else and she was so lonely that sometimes she thought she might break in half.

The village tongues wag. Sarah knows what they say. But they are wrong. There is nothing of that sort between her and Jamie.

They never discuss it. The murder, the execution, fault and where it lies, his father's hands on her.

She recalls her dreams with bemusement. She thought she would be in the pictures and wear fox furs and drive a Rolls-Royce and live anywhere but here. Life has not turned out as she had hoped. But she has a stubborn streak a mile broad. She has Jamie MacRaith, who re-lieves some of the labour of her life. And she has William. He makes up for everything. On balance, Sarah Buchanan finds herself to be a lucky woman. She drops a kiss on William's forehead. He rubs it off. "No kissing," he says absently. "I'm too big." The tourniquet on her heart gives another little twist.

Jamie says, "Weather's turning. You'll be drookit when you get there. Go now or," he says hopefully, "not at all!"

"I'm gone," Sarah says. "This is but the ghost of me!" She throws her shawl about her, swift and elegant. The hard years have not taken all her grace.

The horse scents a storm in the air. He does not want to leave his stall. "Nor I," she says, and hits him with the switch. "Choice is not our lot."

The rain begins as she crosses the moor, handfuls of cold thrown in her face. She throws her cloak over the precious package on her back. What do those loonies need ten ells of wool for, anyhow?

*   *   *

It is two hours' hard ride to Altnaharra and she is drenched by the time she reaches the isle. But mercifully the wool stays dry.

She leaves the pony at the foot of the causeway. The tide boils about her boots. Out to sea, a jagged line of light joins the waves to the burning sky. Thunder rolls in a moment later, cracking the world in two. Sarah gasps and closes her eyes, then wades towards the black gate.

The money awaits her in the wire cage, damp ten-shilling notes bound with twine. Sarah takes them with cold fingers. They mean a new shirt for William, bags of flour, hay for the colt. She puts the parcel of wool in the cage, her duty discharged. She may go home now and rest. She gives the gate a mischievous push. She will tell Jamie she tried to open it.

Something is written on the corner of one of the ten-shilling notes. Two tiny words in pencil. *Help us.* Years have passed, but Sarah knows the writing. How often did she peer, trying not to breathe as she read the answers over Evelyn's shoulder? A raindrop splashes on the words.

Sarah Buchanan will not tangle with the peculiars of Altnaharra. She will turn around, go home and curl up beside her son and sleep until Kingdom come. She will.

But for those two little words.

She regards the spired gate for a moment. She could swim around it if it were summer. But the Arctic sea in winter is not forgiving. It is a clever arrangement, she acknowledges. The cold ocean serves as walls.

Sarah makes the money safe in her pocket, tucks her skirts up and grasps the spars of the gate. She scales the gate as she does everything: neatly, quickly and well. She drops down into the shallows on the other side. Sea slops over the tops of her boots and she grimaces as the freezing water soaks her woollen stockings. There is a little beach, covered in blue shingle. The rain is as thick as mist. It fills her ears, coats her eyelashes, runs down her neck in streams.

Sarah makes her way carefully across the shingle and begins to climb the slope. The weather has made the ground slick and treacherous. Once she startles and looks behind her. Surely there was a sound, like a footfall. But there is nothing except the driving grey rain, like a hail of arrows, and the thunder out to sea.

*   *   *

Evelyn's letter had told only the truth. Through the hard years she has come to understand that it was a kindness. When Sarah saw the words spelled out on the paper, *she has his child in her*, she realised it was true.

It changed everything. Before, she had felt nothing. Then she was filled with a biting, restless rage. She knew that Hector MacRaith must have no claim on the person growing inside her.

As night fell Hamish Buchanan had locked Sarah in her room. She had waited, listening to the murmurs of her parents' voices next door. Her mother tearful, her father bewildered. They had both looked older since that letter came. At length the voices grew quieter, the breaks between their murmurs longer. They were tired, her mother and father. And there was the catch to bring in tomorrow.

Sarah knew the tricks of the lock on her bedroom door. She picked it with a hairpin, then went down through the silent cottage. Hanging on the wall beside the front door was the scythe her father used to mow the little meadow behind their cottage each autumn. Sarah plucked it from the wall.

She knew that every morning Hector MacRaith milked his cow in the pasture at the edge of the village. She curled herself into a ball in the hedgerow and waited for the dawn.

She does not clearly recall the act itself. It was a blaze of light. But she recalls coming to, looking down at what she had done. It seemed like a painting or a stained-glass window, not like something that had really happened. She had thrown the bloodied scythe into a deep pool at a wide bend of the river.

Her father had been waiting for her when she came in, staring at the bare place on the wall where the scythe had hung. Hamish Buchanan used to tell Sarah that he loved her more than life itself. He proved it, in the end.

Loyal still blames Eve for everything. Sarah wonders what Eve would say if she knew the truth, which is that Sarah would have killed MacRaith eventually. The letter merely drew the time down upon them. Perhaps Sarah will tell Eve that, one day.

Something moves behind her on the dark hill. Sarah stumbles. She falls forward, cheek to the wet earth. The world goes white.

*　*　*

Dinah and I empty the storeroom deep in the bowels of Altnaharra. The cellar is dark and cold. We carry up provisions until our hair is full of spiders and our arms tremble. Everything I brought back from my missions to Inverness, all the proceeds of the cold hours in the market square. Blocks of butter, urns of ewe's milk, rows of shiny tin cans, bags of flour, oats, cheeses in string bags. I can imagine the taste of the cheese, its soft crumble in my mouth. We had only five mouthfuls of bread and butter this morning. To be kept are clay pots of honey, sealed neatly with wax and string. Put those aside, Uncle says. Have them ready. Soon there will be nothing left in the cellar except the trapdoor to the Wane place. We take everything down to the stones, feet slipping on the icy winter earth. The stores look strange sitting on the poor grass beneath the lowering sky.

Snow circles in flurries. Nora fells the little twisted trees and chops them in the frosty air. She builds a pyre in the centre of the stones. She is animated. Her cheeks are high and pink.

Haystack's corpse lies against Cold Ben. His dark shaggy neck is bent at too acute an angle. He looks very dead. Out to sea the storm clouds are as high as castles and lightning dances in their depths. The storm will be here soon. Uncle says He will be borne to us by it.

I roll a barrel of salt fish across the cellar floor towards the light. Dinah is beside me, thin arms straining. Her eyes are dark with exhaustion.

"What does Uncle want done with these?" she says in a small, calm voice.

"They are to burn," I say quietly in return. Once, burning was only for the dead. No longer. The stores are offerings to the sea.

"I thought that this food was to sustain us while the world changed," Dinah says quietly. "What shall we live on after He comes?"

I touch her hand lightly, just once. *I do not think he intends us to live*, I want to say.

I can no longer see. The eye is gone. It dropped away with my belief. I have begun to see other things, however. I am uncovering memories, writhing like worms exposed to light.

I kneel before a keyhole, peering into the gloom. A fistful of yellow dress is caught in a thin hand. The scent of chalk and damp paper. That is how it happened, of course. I saw them through the keyhole. There was no night land, no stars.

I hold a pink ribbon in the moonlight. Amy. Later, in the circle of stones, I use Nora's grief to silence her.

Uncle is telling me what to write to Mr. Buchanan. He makes me repeat the words aloud as I write them. Some of the words make me feel ashamed, and Uncle insists that I say those ones more than twice.

Other memories remain but with new shades of meaning. I recall sending Nora into the rain to cast off her stillbirths. It was not to preserve the isle, but because I do not like her.

When I turned the key to the great iron gate, helping Uncle to imprison them all, it was not for their protection. It was so they could not leave me, as Alice did. So that I would not be alone like Sarah Buchanan.

I gave them baths and shoes and woollens not for their welfare, but so that they would be grateful. I never thought of them, not really. Only of what I wanted from them. I see myself as I am for the first time.

I do not need the eye to know that Dinah does not trust me. Who would?

"Come, my pups," Uncle says from the cellar door. "Much to do, much." He is everywhere. In the castle, on the shore, before the gate. Wherever I turn Uncle is watching, kindly. He carries Mary in a sling across his chest. He keeps a caressing hand always on her: on her fragile, downy head, on her small back, enfolding her arm. Dinah's eyes follow them wherever they go.

* * *

We are all to be vested in white for His coming. At Uncle's direction I count out the money for Sarah Buchanan. Without looking down I slip a stub of pencil from my pocket. With my left hand I write two words on the corner of the ten-shilling note. *Please*, I think. *Help us.* I try to imagine that the eye is real; that my thought is travelling towards Sarah across the moonlit moors. I do not hold out great hope.

I walk with Uncle to the gate. It looks different when one does not hold the key. The metal screams open. I put the money in the wire cage. Ravens call overhead.

I look about at the sea, the sky, the isle. It will all go on after I am cold and dead.

I no longer dream at night; of Alice or anything else. Perhaps this is how the mind prepares for death. Closing off the pathways and thoroughfares, one by one.

*   *   *

We take the bed linen from our rooms. We break the bedsteads down for kindling. We tear down the curtains, make piles of our clothes. Elizabeth weeps and holds her carved wooden bird away from Nora's grasp.

"It must burn, Baby," Nora says firmly. "We must be pure. That means everything, now." There is a light in her eyes that I have not seen in years. Nora is longing for Him.

Elizabeth weeps. She climbs up the pyre on her hands and knees to place the bird at the very top. Does she know what is coming? I hope for her sake that she does not.

We take out our knives. We raise the little globe of blood from our fingers. Uncle throws a pine pitch torch into the heart of the pyre. The flame roars and dives. Cans burst in the heat, the scent of burnt bully beef is everywhere, like roasting flesh. Over the sea, thunder speaks.

There is a second, taller pyre erected beyond the stones. It is covered in oilcloth to prevent the rain soaking the wood. Uncle does not say what it is for.

*   *   *

The storm rattles the windows of the Hall. It is evening but it might be any time of day. It is as dark as Wane.

We stand against the wall in order of age: Nora, Dinah, me, Elizabeth. As usual Dinah and I leave a space between us for Abel, then we remember. Our bodies will not absorb his death. Dinah steps closer to me, narrowing the gap. I can read nothing in her face.

On a blanket in Uncle's lap, Mary catches firelight in her fists. She is hungry. She stopped crying yesterday. I do not think that is good. My hunger is in the hollows of my bones. Almost all the food was burnt on the pyre. We have had only a few mouthfuls each in days—and the honey taken from Uncle's fingers. He comes tomorrow.

Uncle sits in his winged chair. He eats chicken and potatoes with a spoon. His beard shines with grease. Nora stands behind him, a gaunt shadow.

I try to hold truth in my mind. Christopher Black's face as the benison took him. Betty's trunk touching Rose's golden cheek. Alice's hand on my head in the dark. *Darling.* These are hard thoughts to cling to, spiked and painful. Easier to wish for the great snake. Easier to let the benison stroke my mind. Easier to love Uncle, who smiles at us now with such hope. Why should I not?

Uncle sees my look and smiles. "Soon," he says. "We will be together with Him soon, my sea-pups."

Nora takes Uncle's plate. I catch the scent of gravy. I think of breaking the chicken bone in my teeth, sucking forth the marrow. I bite the inside of my mouth until I taste iron. *Bloodshed.* There is no power in it. There never was.

Nora returns from the gate. Her arms are full of piles of soft white wool. Sarah Buchanan has been and gone, then. And even if she saw my message on the ten-shilling note, why should she heed it? What does Sarah owe to me, her father's murderer? Still my heart beats hard with hope.

"All to your final tasks," says Uncle, taking the key from Nora. "Then we will retire."

"I cannot sleep." Nora's eyes are alight.

He smiles. "Try. We must be fresh on the morrow."

Dinah puts vegetables and barley in a pot to make broth overnight. She puts unleavened dough in the bottom drawer of the range. There will be bread and broth tomorrow morning. It is the last of the food.

Nora fashions the white wool with her needle. Baby Elizabeth goes around the castle walls, picking up maimed birds, wounded fugitives from the weather. She takes them to her room to nurse. I bring the quivering hens into the Hall, one under each arm, put them in their pen in the corner.

Who will need eggs in the coming days?

In the centre of the hall there are great coiled lengths of rope and buckets of pitch. There is a pile of young tree trunks, stripped and split to form stakes, each a little taller than a person. My mind blurs with honey, hunger and exhaustion. Are they coming, the crofters, to burn us on the stones? Witches waist-deep in barrels of pitch. I count the stakes. Four. Who will live?

Uncle comes in, humming, wet with rain. When did he leave? He stares into the fire, eyes distant. He nods a little, as he does when sleep is creeping over him. If I am to try, it must be now. Time is running away into the night. Can I snatch Mary from Uncle's lap? That would free Dinah. I need a chance, and then it will be up to them what they do.

"Did you close the gate after you collected the wool?" I ask Nora.

"Yes," replies Nora scornfully. "And I locked it too, thank you, Miss Pertness."

"Not properly, then," I say. "I can hear it swinging in the wind." I try to believe the words as I say them. I push my mind outwards, as I do in the little white tent on market days. I try to make them hear the mournful song of steel hinges, the crash, through the wind and rain, of the gate slamming against its post, constant. I will Uncle to hear it too.

"No," says Nora, "it is not open, Evelyn. You never believe that anyone can do anything right but you."

The groan of the gate, the thump as it hits the post. It is only in my mind, I remind myself, but it sounds real.

"It *is* open," says Dinah unexpectedly. "I can hear it too."

Uncle raises his head. His monocle gleams. "We all go," he says. "Together." He gathers Mary up.

We run down the hill towards the shore. The storm is raging. Raindrops the size of farthings strike our flesh. The sea is tossed into black and white towers, the waves rearing to twenty feet and smashing themselves against the isle. Uncle does not need to kill us. We will die anyway in this storm. A great wave will drown the isle and us with it.

Below on the shore the gate is swinging in the gale. I cannot help but wonder if I opened it with my mind. *Or perhaps,* I hear in Christopher Black's cool tones, *you heard the gate without noticing.* Perhaps that is what caused you to settle on this plan. I shake my head to banish him.

Something lies over the threshold, preventing the gate from closing. It has begun to float and bob in the choppy rising tide. The gate batters Sarah Buchanan's corpse. She lies across the entrance to the isle, a grim sentinel. When I come close I see that her right eye is gone, pulped to a jelly.

I have missed my chance. Death has begun.

* * *

Sarah is laid on the table in the Hall, white and cold. I cannot stop looking at the place where her eye was. The skin around the socket is bubbled as if by flame. I have never seen a corpse before. It is clay, roughly shaped like Sarah, but it does not seem anything to do with her.

"Did something . . . eat her eye?" asks Dinah. "A crab?" No one answers this question, because an animal did not do it. A person did.

"It looks like the trying, John," says Nora. "When Hercules bites, the flesh looks burnt, like that."

"How could a snake bite her in the eye?" Dinah asks. Her hands tremble.

"It is beginning," says Uncle.

Sarah must have climbed over the gate. Or perhaps he asked her in. Either way it happened because of my note. Another death laid at my door.

Uncle strokes Mary's back. "He is clearing the corrupt from the earth," he says. "Nora has made ready the robes. Let us now don our whites." He cannot take his gaze from Sarah's corpse. A flicker of something deep in his eyes. What? Doubt, or pleasure.

We strip, shivering. I catch Dinah palming her locket.

"Burn them," Uncle says. We put our clothing in the hearth. The damp clothes burn slowly, filling the hall with smoke. The lice die with a sharp crackle. Baths could never rid us of them completely. The smell is noxious. Uncle did not think this through. It gives me a tiny satisfaction to watch him wipe his streaming, reddened eyes.

We put on our white garments. They are strange and shapeless, slack white skins. Dinah helps Baby Elizabeth to tuck up the hem about her waist and roll the sleeves up.

"The morning," Uncle says, "will see us renewed!" He goes up the darkened stairs. Storm light flickers on him and on Mary's face, peering over his shoulder.

* * *

Dinah and I sit in our room by candlelight. We do not speak. We keep our eye on the door, waiting for Nora to come and blow out the candle.

Dinah takes out her locket. She rubs her thumb back and forth across it, making it squeak. I put a hand over Dinah's. "Please," I say. "Do not fill our last night with that sound." I meant it as a joke but it is not funny. Dinah turns on me a gaze so filled with fear and feeling that I take her in my arms.

"Dinah," I whisper. "He killed Sarah." I am crying a little.

Dinah's arms hold me tightly. "I know," she says, no louder than a breath. I hear the tears in her voice too. "And, Eve, Eve, tomorrow . . ."

"We must think," I say stupidly. "After she blows out the candle, we will think of something."

She nods, eyelashes wet against my cheek.

"If by some chance you make it," I say in her ear, "go south. Find the circus. There is a girl named Rose. She might help you. Tell her that I am sorry, if you find her—"

Dinah says, "We will go south together, you and I."

We start at the creak of the door and spring apart. Nora is tranquil, smiling. Her strange, flat eyes are vibrant. "Candle out," she says.

We try to make ourselves comfortable on the cold stone floor. It will be a miserable night. "I wish he had waited until tomorrow to burn the beds," I whisper to Dinah. She gives a startled giggle.

"Dinah, the Adder calls for you this night," Nora says.

Dinah is not quite listening. She nods and continues to try to arrange herself comfortably.

"Did you not hear what I said, Dinah? The Adder calls. Make yourself ready and come." Nora puts a bar of black carbolic soap on the floor. She puts a bowl of water next to it. Some slops over the side. There is a cloth floating in the bowl. The soap smells like cut grass. Dinah sits up and stares at these objects as though she has never seen their like before.

"Five minutes," Nora says. "No longer." The door closes gently behind her with a click.

"We must go now," I say to Dinah. "We must leave Mary. He would not hurt a baby." I do not know if I believe it.

"I will not go without her, Eve."

"What, then?" I ask. "What, Dinah? How do we get her from him?" I want to hit her for being so stubborn.

Dinah is silent.

"No," I say. "Not that."

Dinah says, "It is the only way."

I reach for her, horror in my heart. She pushes me away gently. "Get Elizabeth. I do not think that Nora will come but I will try to make her."

"Dinah, you cannot do this."

"Get Elizabeth." Dinah takes up the cloth.

*   *   *

The corridor blinks white and black in the storm. There is a thin line of light under Elizabeth's door.

"Now it is time for medicine," a fluting voice says within. I start. It is a woman's voice. Amused, beautiful. Someone is in Baby Elizabeth's room. I peer through the crack in the door.

"The medicine the Adder gave us," the voice goes on. "It will make us both well."

I push the door open silently.

Elizabeth is pale and fragile in the candlelight. She goes to a cage and opens the door carefully. The gull's eye is dark in its pure white head. She reaches a hand in. Soft wings flutter.

"You are nearly mended," Elizabeth says to the gull in those strange, melodious tones. His orange legs paddle, confirming it. "But you cannot go out in this horrid storm. Oh, no." She quickly rebreaks the bird's legs between finger and thumb. "You stay with me now, birdie," she says sternly.

The gull's orange beak parts, closes, drinking air.

"I will make you better." Elizabeth produces a syringe and pretends to pierce the bird's shivering sides. She scratches her arm with the needle and depresses the plunger. Something viscous drips from the tip.

"Baby Elizabeth," I shout. "Do not! Please!"

"Evelyn," says Elizabeth. Her blue eyes are full of hurt. "How could you? You are spying on me." She begins to fit.

"Baby . . ." The scratch on Elizabeth's thin arm swells and blisters under my gaze. I hold her thin frame tightly. "I would have stopped you," I whisper. "But I did not know your voice."

Elizabeth gazes skyward. There is a clicking in her throat, some white discharge between her lips. There is nothing to be done. She dies quickly. All about is the soft sound of startled birds.

I stroke Elizabeth's bony forehead. I close her long-lashed eyelids. I suppose it is kind of Uncle to poison us before burning us.

There comes a great roar from Uncle's room.

Dinah screams.

I run out into the hall. The Adder's will is all over the stone walls. It crackles in the air and in my lungs. It is in the green-black sea outside, it is in the storm.

Footsteps. Dinah runs. In her arms she holds a screaming Mary. Uncle stumbles behind her. He falls. His arm comes forth, long fingers wrap around Dinah's ankle. Dinah screams and kicks at Uncle. He pulls her towards him. In a moment she will fall or drop Mary on the stone floor.

We must reach the front door.

I slip the knife from my cuff. The Adder roars with eyes of flame. His pupils are vertical, pointed, black in golden irises. I stab and saw at the fleshy web of his thumb, gasping at the blood that runs all over us. Altnaharra thunders with pleasure, the very earth shivers. Uncle's thumb comes off with a soft, horrible sound. He howls. Dinah hits him, hard.

We run down the stairs and burst out of the door into the night. The storm is in my bones, the lightning drapes the world in blasts of white. The sea breaks like falling towers, within me, without me. I know it is the lingering effects of the drug but my senses are alight, I smell the blood in my veins. The isle is awake and I am awake, too. We are galvanised by death. The sandy path beneath my feet, the little scrubby hills and the waves. Beside me Dinah is panting, clutching the baby to her.

The dead are with us. Elizabeth, her thin child's lips parted, face white and staring, the gull clutched in her hand. Sarah Buchanan is here, her hair streaming out behind her like a banner in the rain. Abel's drowned face is blue and swollen. He runs with silent ease, as he never did in life. Hector MacRaith's thin head rolls, bounces on the path ahead, the dark bloody stump of the neck, the white bone. Which of us is a dream, which real? All I know is that I must not die at Uncle's hands. Anything but that. I run.

Smoke billows over the slopes on the eastern shore. Nora's gardens are on fire. Bushes burn, black skeletons inside clouds of flame. The fires send long red tails upwards into the dark. How can everything burn so, in the driving rain?

I hear screaming. From each dark hive there pours a river of orange. Thousands of tiny bright points, hovering in the acrid air, sizzling in the deluge, racing out to sea, blazing, crackling as they sink. The bees are burning. He is sacrificing it all. The smoke catches in my lungs and Dinah coughs hard beside me. She tries to shelter Mary with her thin shirt.

"The church," she shouts. "We need shelter."

* * *

We take shelter under a ruined arch. About us, the storm beats like a drum. Each shadow, each blade of grass stands out, branded on the world.

"What happened?" I must ask.

"It is all right," Dinah says. "Shh. Eve, it is all right. I hit him over the head. I told Nora to come but she was wailing and calling me a traitor. I do not think that she will."

"What now?" I say.

"We could stay here until it passes," Dinah says. "I hit him hard. He will be out for hours."

I shake my head. "It is an Altnaharra storm." They go on for days at a time.

"We are two and he is one. What can he do to us if we stay together?"

"He has a poison," I say. "I do not know what it is. It only takes a scratch to kill you."

"Where is Elizabeth?" Dinah asks. She looks at me. "What has happened? Please. Please, just tell me."

"Elizabeth is dead," I say. "Uncle gave her poison in a needle. She was playing with it. You know how she likes to heal birds." I do not feel equal to describing it further.

Dinah sits down on a stone. She weeps. Mary's face crumples in her lap and she cries too.

Best get it all done at once. "The benison is not real," I say. "There is something in the honey."

Dinah nods. I do not know if she has understood me. "I think we should kill him," she says. She says it as one might say, *the pears will be good this year*, or, *put a log on the fire*.

"No," I say, startled. "We must get away."

"What then, Eve? We have no trade, no education, not a penny between us, no knowledge of the world. Where would we go? Where but here do we belong? If we stay we will have the isle, you and I. Uncle has made a will and testament. Altnaharra is left to me."

"That cannot be right," I say. "Why would he leave it to you?" My heart is beating fast but time is moving slowly.

"He said you had served the isle well, but you were not the heir. You have never even had your time. He said you were not really a woman. I was going to make a plan," Dinah says. "I meant to save you all. I just needed time." She wipes her wet face.

We have held hands in the dark of Wane, worked beside one another in the rain, hands bubbled with blisters. We have clung together in the night. Shielded each other from the toothy bite of winter. Her dreams make their way into mine. We are as close as human animals can be. I know each familiar feeling that chases through her eyes. So as I watch her now, I understand.

"He meant you to live," I say. "Just you and he."

"And Mary," she says. "He promised that if I . . . went along with it, she and I would be spared." Dinah reaches for me. Rain pastes her hair flat to her head.

I do not take her hand. "You agreed."

"I had no choice, Eve."

There is a screaming in my ears, my head. Thunder shakes the isle. Or is it my heart?

"I never meant it to go this far," Dinah says. "I thought there would be a chance for us all to get away. But he would never put Mary down, not for a moment . . ."

"I understand."

"Do you?" Relief in her voice.

"Yes," I say because I do. What magic brought me back to Altnaharra after Haystack threw me? None. It was my longing for Uncle. He has divided our souls within us. Even now, I wonder, *How is Uncle's thumb? How long must I go on Wane for cutting it off?* I want to comfort him and bind the wound with honey. Would that part of me have agreed to murder, as Dinah did?

"He lives in us," I say. "We cannot help what we do." The screaming in my ears reaches a pitch. My hands close about Dinah's throat. She claws at me weakly. Somewhere a baby is crying. I am so angry, not even with her, really, but with everything. I have one need, which is to see the moment when Dinah leaves her body, to see her eyes change from living to dead.

Other hands on me. A sharp clip to my ear and my head rings with stars. Nora pulls me off Dinah. She is slick with rain and blood. Nora says, "John is looking for you. He is very disappointed."

Dinah did not hit him hard enough. Uncle is coming.

Dinah coughs, clutching her throat. My fear reflected in her eyes. She makes a noise like a wounded stag and crawls away from us. Her hand slips on the stone and dislodges something wedged between two mossy blocks. She falls, clutching at the object. The lid of the tin box springs open and they spill out.

Dinah lunges back as the first snake darts forth. It fastens on her neck. More adders pour out from the darkness of the tin box. Four, five. Nora and I run to Dinah but it seems to take too long. The snakes are all over her, writhing. They are not like Hercules, accustomed to human touch. They are wild. Fangs sink into the delicate underside of her arm. Dinah screams.

We pull the adders off her. Nora makes a *tsk* noise as she is bitten on the thumb. The adders writhe a moment on the slick stone, then slip out of sight.

"Why would anyone do such a thing?" Dinah says. "Keep snakes in a box?" She is grim, waiting for pain, for sickness.

I examine the two sets of punctures, the neat eyes of blood in Dinah's arm, her neck. The wounds are clean. There is no blistering on her or on Nora.

"How do you feel?" I ask.

"All right," she says, cautiously.

"The adders had no venom in them. I think that Uncle has been milking them of their poison."

"Adder venom does not kill," Dinah says.

"One bite, no. But a hundred? How long has he been harvesting it?" I shiver.

"I do not understand," Dinah says. "It was to be burning, not adder poison."

"I thought that I was privy to his plans, once, too," says Nora. "We are not."

"I am not like *you*," says Dinah, lip curling. "I was only going along with it because of the baby."

Nora looks at Dinah with sympathy. "There is always a reason to go along with it," she says. "When he told me that Eve, and later, you, would be the Adder after him I accepted it. When he showed me the will with Dinah's name on it, I accepted it. When he said that we would burn, I accepted it." Her voice breaks. "But I do not think He is coming from the ocean. And I find that I do not want to die."

"Nor I," Dinah says. She crawls over to us and takes our hands.

"Nor I." All three of us are crying, but it does not feel bad.

"I do not think we could kill him," I say.

Dinah shivers. "What if he calls for us, and opens his arms?"

"Where do we go?" I whisper. The isle is Uncle and Uncle is the isle.

Hail starts to fall. White globes of ice bounce on the black stones, strike our faces with stinging blows. We huddle into the slight shelter of the ruined arch. Mary begins to cry again.

"Can you quiet her?" I say. "That noise will bring him."

"Certainly, Eve," says Dinah through tears. "Shall I just smother the baby? That would solve everything."

My ankle is beginning to ache. I must have twisted it when I was wrestling with Dinah.

"It has to be the cliff," Nora says. "We must jump."

"Mary cannot go off a cliff into the sea," Dinah says.

I say, "I will swim across alone and come back with help."

"Help from where?" Dinah asks. "Even if you make it, reach Loyal, who would help us? No, we must stay together."

I recall Christopher Black's words. No one will blink twice at our deaths.

Nora wrings her hands. "Please," she says. "Do not fight."

The hail is falling harder, bruising our flesh. It is driven in all directions by the wind, it ricochets beneath the arch where we are huddled.

"We must find better shelter," Nora says. "There is only one place."

I look at her. She is right. "If we take the ladder off the wall then he cannot get down to us," I say.

"What do you mean?" Dinah says. But she knows. "No. I cannot. No."

I stroke Dinah's wet hair. "You can. You have weathered more than this. You have been on Wane for five days in the past! This will only be for half a day, a day. You will not fail."

"No," Dinah says. But she knows we must.

*　*　*

The stone steps to the cellar are lit by lightning. We go down. The trap-door yawns at the centre of the bare storeroom. Open, as if waiting.

I help them down the ladder into the Wane place. It is quiet here, I hear the stream running cold along the wall. I look down at them. White faces upturned, eyes gleaming in the dark.

I unhook the ladder from its supports and lower it down to them. Nora leans it against the wall.

"See?" I say to Dinah. "When the storm stops and the tide turns we put the ladder back up and run for the mainland. In the mean-time, you are safe."

"Could Uncle jump down here?" Dinah asks me.

I look at the drop from the trapdoor to the floor, measuring. "I do not think so. He would break his legs."

"We must take the bolt off the trapdoor," Dinah says suddenly. "Do not give him a chance to lock us in."

I go cold at the thought. I unscrew the bolt from the trapdoor with my knife and take the bolt off the storeroom, too. He cannot lock us in but nor can we lock him out.

"We must stay silent," I say. "I will stand guard up here. If I give the alarm, do not put the ladder back for any reason."

"Very well," says Nora.

I close the trapdoor on their pale faces, small in the darkness below.

I wonder where Rose is now. Does she think of me? I wonder if I will survive the night. What happens then?

The storm is an orchestra of sound outside. I go up the shallow stairs, to watch. I stand in the shadow of the storeroom doorway. Altnaharra is a battlefield. Hail and lightning strike the ground. I scan each shadow in which Uncle might hide. He will not harm us. I promised.

I am not paying attention to the quiet cellar behind me. I do not hear the trapdoor creak open. I do not hear feet approach across the sandy earth, up the steps. I do not feel the dark figure stand tall behind me, arm raised high, stone in hand. At the last moment the hair on the back of my neck stands up as the stone whistles down to meet my skull. I try to turn, to see, to fight, but it is too late. The darkness closes over.

*　*　*

I am lying in the stone circle. My feet point towards the centre. Sarah Buchanan lies to my left, dressed in white.

Uncle is on my other side. He is dead, his lip curled in a rictus. One of his eyes is gone, the flesh bubbled about the socket. The dark figure bends over him in the hurricane.

"Oh, you are awake," the murderer says. "Well, it does not matter." Hercules' head pokes out of her cuff. He is curled about her forearm like a gauntlet. His tongue tastes the air.

"So you are the Adder now," I say.

"Yes," says Nora. "I have waited. I have suffered. It is my time. He would have replaced me with Dinah. He promised her power, as he promised it to me. But he would never give it up." Nora's eyes have yellow flames in them. "Better to take it."

She comes across the circle, kneels at my side and places a cool hand on my face. She offers me a bowl. "There is no need to suffer." Rain strikes the surface of the honey, pools on it.

"Never again." I press my forearm against the wet ground. I feel the outline of the little knife in my cuff, where it sits pressed against my flesh.

"As you wish," she says. "I hate it myself. One dawn, during ritual, oh, ten or so turns ago, I did not eat mine. I pretended to be caught up in the benison. You were all lolling and talking nonsense. And I watched. It was as I had suspected. I saw what he did to you while you were out. You know, they used to call it mad honey, and I think it made me mad. Or at least the things I saw did."

"You are lying," I say. She must be. I rub my sleeve against the grass. The point of the knife snags on the cloth, makes a little tear.

"They would not let him take any more children from the poor homes in these parts. Word spreads even up here. It became my task to give children to the isle. He let Dinah be, more or less. He needed her whole so she could take my place. But you, no. He was amused that you were so afraid of it. The duty. He had already taken what he pleased."

"No," I say.

"I think you have the memory of it somewhere. You can never bury such things deep enough. Baby Elizabeth stopped speaking after he started with her. I did not need to kill Elizabeth, I merely gave her the needle. She has been walking towards death for many years."

The blade tears through the sleeve. It has cut my arm. I try to slide it down, within reach of my fingers.

"If you let me go I will serve you." Perhaps I would. There is a deep part of me unfilled. The hole left by Uncle.

"That is kind," Nora says. "But you are already serving me. I need a murderer. I have written to the police. I have sown the seeds. They will know you have done it. They were never fond of you in these parts. You write filthy letters. You caused two good men to be killed. Jamie MacRaith knows you for a murderer. I told him. He is a good boy, to buy me these needles. He will come to the isle sooner or later to see if I am all right. I left the gate open for him. And he will find that you have killed us all, except me."

"Good," I say. "That is a good plan. But I think it is better to have a murderer who is still alive. A chase. I could run far from here." I have nearly worked the knife down to within my grasp. My fingertips slip uselessly on the handle.

"You would not get a mile," Nora says gently. "They would catch you and then you would talk."

"I would not be caught," I say. "I would go to Alice. She would help me. Yes, I know that she is my mother."

Nora looks at me. Raised brows over blank grey eyes. "Alice, your mother?" she says. "No. She could never carry them to term. All the babies were mine, though only three of you lived."

She reaches down and gently takes the knife from my fingers. I tremble when her hand touches me. She puts my knife into her sleeve.

"But I look just like her," I say.

"You may like to think so, but I cannot agree."

"You are not my mother," I say. My hand searches the ground. A stone, a stick, anything will do.

"No," she says. "I am not. But it is my task to rid the world of you, since I brought you into it."

She raises the needle high above my remaining eye.

I stagger up. I try to run for my life. But the grass and the ground are no longer in any sensible order. My legs paddle with the slow grace of a nightmare. Nora's hand clutches my hair and pulls my head back. I feel everything about me: the night, the stars, the scent of death, the call of the seals below. Nora's hands stroke my throat.

"I have often wondered why you exist," says Nora in my ear. "Now I know. I must have birthed you for this very reason, to fill my need this night. I promise that this is better than what he had planned. This will be quick."

If there is any grace or god in this world, I pray silently, *I beg for mercy*. No answer comes.

But there is one power that remains. It is not from Uncle, or from Him. It is my own. I am Nora's greatest secret. And I know what to do with a secret.

"I was your first," I say to her. Her hand flexes on my throat. My heart is hammering in my ears, but it is important not to rush. "You met the knife boy on your nights off. He was poor and you thought you loved him. You were fifteen." My mind races, struggling to re-call what I overheard between Alice and Nora all those years ago, the day Alice gave me the address in Orme Place. "You had to leave London before you began to show but you had nowhere to go. You did not want to lose your baby to the poorhouse. So when Alice ran away you went with her, came north to Altnaharra. Uncle told you that you would be free. He said it did not matter that you were not wed. We were not slaves to the bonds of family, here on the isle.

"You called me Amy. You loved me, even though you say that you did not. He allowed a photograph to be taken of me. The Uncle I knew never would have allowed it. Perhaps Altnaharra was a happy place once.

"I do not know when he decided to take me from you. But he saw the power of it—the bond. If it could be broken, he would be at the centre of everything. You say you were glad when he took me. You are lying. You crept to me at night and sang to me, the song you made up for us. *Love will find a way* . . . I remember it. I dream about it. You, the song. But he must have caught you one day. Or perhaps you simply grew tired of resisting. He turned your love for me into something else. He gave me a new name. The name of an ancient monster. I suppose it amused him."

Nora cries out. I am in her soul. "Leave me alone," she says. "Stop talking."

I throw myself backwards, knocking Nora to the earth. I take her head at the base of the skull, as one would pick up a snake, and dash it against Cold Ben. It splits like fruit.

I lie for a moment, the weight of the dead woman pressing on my heart. Light rain patters over my cheeks, eyelids, lips. But the rain has stopped. It is Nora's blood dripping gently from Cold Ben where he leans across the darkness.

* * *

I groan and come to, limbs numb. Above me the sky is changing. The world is emerging from the battle of the storm.

Something is different. Cold Ben lies fallen on the grass beside me. There is a great scar in the earth where he was uprooted.

Nora's corpse is heavy. I push it off, shuddering. I take Hercules from her sleeve. He hisses. In his mouth there gleam the pearly tips of two new fangs. I put him down on the grass and he slides away, red eyes staring. He is not *Vipera berus* or part of Him in the ocean. He is as he has always been. What he was before names.

I run from the stones up the hill towards the castle. I stumble. The ground and sky are humming.

"Dinah!" I call. "Dinah!" My breath is ragged in my throat.

I tumble down the stone steps, pull the door open. The cellar is wreathed in shadow and moonlight. The trapdoor in the centre of the floor is closed. My heart pulses in my throat, a warm plum. I go to the door. I take hold of the handle. For a moment I stand there, perfectly still. I cannot, but I must. I lift the trapdoor. It creaks gently. I look down into the Wane place.

There she is in the dark below. Dinah. Her sides do not move. She is beyond all dreaming. The reekling has been here.

I imagine it; the two of them huddled together for comfort in the dark beneath the ground. When did Dinah understand that death was not coming from above? That it was there with her? Trapped beneath the earth. But she had always known it would come.

Dinah's arm is outstretched, fingers spread wide on the cold stone. Who did she reach for? But I know.

I wish Nora were alive so I could kill her again. And again and again.

There is a weak, high sound. I stagger back from the edge of the pit, skin thrilling. I have my wish because now Nora will rise from the shadows with the shining needle. The small cry becomes a full-throated wail. It is coming from the far end of the cellar.

Mary is wrapped in a blanket. I hold the baby to me. "You are good," I say. "No, do not cry. Oh, you are being so good." I must find food for us.

* * *

In the hall the coals still glow red. I bank them high, shivering. I strip off the white clothes, now drenched in blood, and dress myself and Mary in old nightclothes I find in Uncle's cupboard. Only his things have not been burnt.

In their pen in the corner the chickens have laid one egg. I take it.

Dinah's broth is on the stove. Her dough has risen. I put it in the oven and heat the soup. It seems years since yesterday evening. I recall Dinah's giggle. We were about to die but she laughed at my remark about the beds.

I cannot think about Dinah.

I break the egg into the hot soup, then I cool it, pouring it back and forth between two cups. I feed Mary broth and egg in tiny sips. I take the bread from the oven. It is half-baked but I cannot wait any longer. I soak it in broth and try to put it in Mary's mouth, but she will not take it. She seems to be very sleepy, not hungry at all. I hold her and rock her. "Please do not die," I say aloud. "Please."

I eat bread in yeasty fistfuls. I drink ladle after ladle of broth, hot and steaming. My mouth burns, loses all taste and feeling, but still I drink. I catch sight of a spectre reflected in the window. Hunched, hair flat on a bulging cranium, eyes wide and bloodshot, limbs skeletal and trembling.

When my stomach is as tight as a drum I sink down beside the great iron range, Mary in my arms.

The great snake came after all. He must have come, because the world is at an end. I think of what Nora told me. What Uncle did to me. She was lying to give me pain. But something stirs in the depths. Half-memories, vague images made of fire and eyes and hands. It happened, I think.

I seem to be at a great distance from myself. Tears are coming from somewhere. Me, I suppose. They fall on Mary's face. Her little mouth turns down.

"Sorry." I wipe the tears away gently. "No more crying. I promise."

I lie back with Mary on my breast. Our breathing slows. The world is winnowed down to this: the dark, the rain, the baby's heartbeat.

*   *   *

I wake, skin screaming to the sound of gunshot. Outside, the dark electric air has softened into grey cobweb. Dawn is not far off. Through the brightening world there comes the unmistakable sound of an engine. It is not gunshot—it is the exhaust of a motorcar.

I seize Mary and go to the kitchen window. Two yellow headlights sweep across the sea. Someone is driving across the causeway to the isle.

My first thought is to hide. But where? I cannot go back to the Wane place.

I find what I want in the dresser. I stand by the kitchen door, holding Mary to me with one hand, the meat cleaver in the other.

The car rumbles closer. I think of police and prison. Could they have come so quickly? I grip the cleaver. They will not take me. The car is driving up the hill, bounding over the rough ground. As it comes into view through the window, I see that it is small and green. It is not a black lorry, which seems good. The car comes to a halt in front of the castle as though this were quite an everyday thing to do.

The door opens and a tall figure gets out.

I squint hard through the glass. Something in the angle of the chin, the set of the shoulders, is familiar. I drop the cleaver. It hits the floor with a great clang. I put Mary down in the empty log basket by the range and tuck a blanket over her, then I run from the kitchen along the corridor and out of the great front door.

The visitor pauses in the act of taking off her hat. A little everyday gesture.

"Alice?" I say.

"Evelyn?"

We go cautiously to one another.

"What are you doing here?" I say weakly.

"I got your message," Alice says. "The flower through the letterbox. I knew it must be you."

"You will wish you had never come," I say. "They are dead. All dead. Nora killed them. I could not stop her."

Alice puts a hand to her mouth. "My God," she says.

I take Alice's index finger and twist it hard to the point of breaking. I feel the fragile joints creak. Alice cries out. I twist harder. I learned the trick from Abel and learned it well.

"You left me. I wish you had gone to the fire, as Uncle said you had." My breath is coming too fast. I release Alice's finger and sit down on the icy ground. "I thought you were my mother," I say.

"Instead I am h . . . h . . ." My mouth makes the shape but will not say it, *hers*.

Alice's hand strokes my back. "It does not matter who birthed you," she says. "You were, you are mine. I would shed blood for you. I would tear flesh for you. Whatever needs doing, I will do it."

"Too late," I say. "It is all too late. What Uncle did . . ."

Alice holds me and rocks me. "It is all right," she says. "Darling. I will make it all right." She tries to keep the tears from her voice.

*   *   *

It had begun in a small way, as these things often do. It was autumn. Jamie was leaving the sausages in the wire basket at the gate when the slot at the back of the cage slid open and a pair of bright eyes looked out at him. He was as surprised as if the gate itself had sprouted eyes. He hoped against hope that it was Dinah.

"Hello," he said cautiously.

"Hello," said the eyes. They were large and grey and made him wonder what the rest of the face was like. It was not Dinah.

"I am Nora," she said. "I expect you are James MacRaith. Dinah said that you were a fine-looking young man!" Jamie blushed.

She laughed, though not at him. "Do not worry, my love," she said, sympathetically. Jamie had never had a mother.

The next time he came she was there again. "Our little assignations," she said. But it did not make him uncomfortable, as girls' jokes sometimes did.

Nora told him about her childhood in London. "Dad was the footman," she said. "He opened a door once, for the old Queen. Fancy that! He died, but I had been working in the kitchen since I was nine, so the Seddingtons kept me on. They were decent people. It was a shame about Alice. How she turned out, you know. Unsteady."

Jamie told her about the War, and how difficult it was to learn a new trade, especially butchery. He did not enjoy it. "Who *would* like it?" he asked. "Killing."

They met at the gate several more times before he found the courage to ask, "Is Dinah well?"

"Oh," said Nora. "Not too well, I fear."

"I am sorry to hear that. She was writing to me for a time. I thought . . . well, never mind what I thought. She said it was not the case." Dinah had said a lot more than that but Jamie did not wish to dwell on those hurtful things.

Nora was quiet for a moment. Then she said, "She was made to write that letter, Jamie."

"Who would make her do such a thing?" But his heart grew wings.

"She is in danger," Nora said. "She told me not to tell you. She said that you were very brave and that you would wish to help her, would risk your life for it."

"I would." He felt a pleasant ache at the thought of rescuing Dinah.

Nora said, "It is Evelyn. She has taken over the isle. I believe that she is plotting our deaths."

He was startled. He remembered Evelyn at school. A thin shadow. But did she not have a devious look to her?

"Will you post this letter?" Nora said. "It is to the police, asking for their help. You may read it."

"Of course," he said. "I wish that you would let me in. I could help you get away."

"She keeps the key." Nora looked frightened. "I must go. I have said too much."

Jamie read the letter. It said that Eve had long been unhinged. She wrote poison-pen letters as a child, filled with obscenities. She devised strange rituals requiring blood. She believed that she could read minds. She spilled entrails on the stones of Altnaharra at dawn to spy the future. She spoke of the end of the world. *I am afraid*, Nora wrote.

Jamie MacRaith did not like the police. When they came to Loyal during the War they made everything worse. It was due to their interference that everyone heard about his father's shame with Sarah. But still he took the letter to the constable in Tongue, a sleepy man who let his old sheepdog doze under the desk. It panted all the way through the interview, groaning with private dog pain. The constable read the letter slowly, spelling the words silently with his lips.

"And what do you have to do with this, laddie?" he asked. "You do not seem so well enough in yourself."

Jamie was more easily confused these days, that was true. Since the War. A shell blast had taken out a few of his teeth on the left. It had also scrambled his brains, and he did not think as clearly as he used to. He could put a dental plate in to replace the teeth but he couldn't put anything in his brain to straighten it out, worse luck. He liked habit because he could not always remember what had just happened.

"No need perhaps to interfere with quarrelling women," the constable said. He reached over his desk and touched Jamie's shoulder. The dog yawned. "I will note the letter and keep it on file, but we are shorthanded these days. Unless there are developments, there is nothing to be done."

The next time Jamie came to the gate Nora said that Eve had begun carrying a knife in her cuff. "She tells us that it will all end soon," Nora said. "And then she does this." Nora drew her finger across her throat, making a sound like a death rattle. "I am afraid, Jamie. Dinah is afraid."

"You must leave," he said. "Why do you stay?"

"I cannot leave without my daughter," Nora said. "Eve took her from me. Can you believe such cruelty? She is sick, you know, my little girl. And Eve will not let me out to buy the things I need to care for her." Nora began to cry.

"I will get what you need," Jamie said. So he wrote down what she asked for. Hypodermic syringes, with needles, ten of them. Chemist's bottles with tight stoppers.

She wept and thanked him. "Leave them at night, if you can," she said. "I cannot risk anyone else seeing."

She gave him a serious look. It was odd, seeing only her eyes. Like a floating presence.

"Jamie," she said. "If you find the gate open it will mean that the worst has happened."

* * *

Jamie sits in Sarah Buchanan's cottage with William. The storm rages on. Sarah has not returned. Perhaps she has taken shelter in a shepherd's hut, he tells himself. Perhaps someone took her under their roof. But he is filled with fear.

Jamie is startled by hooves, a commotion in the yard. He goes out to the lean-to. The horse eats hay hungrily, glad to be home. Its bridle is broken and the saddle has slipped under its belly.

"Useless beast," Jamie says. He shrugs on his coat. "I am locking the door," he says to William. "Do not open up for anyone except your ma or me."

William says "Aye," without looking up from his marbles, so Jamie takes him by his collar. "You do *not*," he says, looking deep into his little brother's eyes.

"Aye," says William, startled.

Jamie rights the saddle on the horse and ties a knot in the broken leather of the bridle, then rides the sweating beast as fast as it will go over the moor. He gallops through the oak wood where the bare branches scratch the dark sky. He fords the burn at the old black house in the ruined village of Forth, where, in another world, he met Dinah Bearings. He urges the stumbling horse faster along the sandy coast path to Altnaharra. He can hear its breath sawing in and out.

He leaps off the colt and wades across the causeway. The gate stands open in the half-light. He runs up the hill, sliding on the ice, the mud. There are tyre tracks here. They end at the portcullis that protects the entrance to the castle courtyard. He rolls under the portcullis without a thought.

There are two women in the courtyard. One is tall and pale, with eyes like steel. She leans against the castle wall, smoking a cigarette. The other woman is small and carries a baby. Both are streaked with mud and blood.

"Hello, Jamie," the woman with the baby says.

"Who are you?" he asks. "Where is Sarah?

"Wait," she says, but he runs into the castle, calling for Sarah. The rooms are cold and empty. No soul breathes there. He runs out the back way, down the slope, towards the ruined church and the standing stones. When he breasts the hill, he stops. It is some time before he understands what he sees below. The white, five-pointed star.

He cries out. Sarah's poor face, her lovely eye, her dead heart. He runs to her and falls to his knees. He shoos the gulls away from her corpse. "Oh, God," he says. He touches her. "Sarah, Sarah." Clarity comes, cruel and belated. It was Sarah he should have loved. They let the past stand between them.

The small woman is beside him. "I did not hurt her," she says. "I swear it, Jamie."

His tears are too painful. He strokes Sarah's cheek. "I wish that she was alive," he says. "Not you. I don't know you."

"I am Dinah, Jamie."

"No," he says, "you are not Dinah. You look like the other one,

Eve. Nora said that Eve would do this, and she has! Get away from me!"

The woman kneels beside him. "You have a choice. If I am Eve, I will be arrested. I will be forced to tell them that you purchased the needles and syringes that killed these people. I will be hanged, and I expect you will go to prison. Altnaharra will go to some distant cousin in England and that will be that.

"But if I am Dinah, Altnaharra will go to me. You have a little brother, do you not? He is Sarah's child. He has lost his mother tonight. She would wish him to be well looked after. If I am Dinah I will give the castle and the isle to you for life. There is no money but there is the land, the sea. Peat, grazing, fishing. You need not be a butcher any longer. Your brother would play in the halls that the MacRaiths have walked for centuries. All that would happen, if I am Dinah.

"If you agree, you must go back into Loyal at full gallop. You came here this morning to deliver a side of beef. You happened on the scene. You found me alive."

"I have done it all wrong," he says. If only he could wish himself back to the schoolyard. He would never look at Dinah with her wine-coloured hair and deep eyes. Instead, he would speak to Sarah, in her yellow dress. She would love him back and his father would not touch her. Jamie would not let it happen. It would all be different.

Jamie thinks of William playing with his marbles by the hearth in the locked cottage, waiting for Sarah to come home. William's surprised eyes, his round face, his still-unbroken trust in the world. Why should William pay?

"It is time to decide, Jamie," she says. "Who am I?"

Jamie looks at her. "You are Dinah," he says. His mind is full of holes, after all. Who is to say she is not? "Now leave me alone." He takes Sarah in his arms. The sun comes up over the sea.

* * *

I stand high above the water. The winter sun pours over the isle and the stones, as it has done for five thousand years on Altnaharra. It is not the first time that bodies have been laid here in offering.

I am Eve no longer. I am no one. I am in the process of becoming.

We put Dinah's body in Alice's car. I touch her cheek and kiss her. "You saw it coming," I say. "I should have listened." Dinah had been dreaming of our deaths since she could speak. If there is such a power as the eye, it was Dinah who had it, not I.

We push the green car off the causeway. It drowns in the water. Alice weeps as we do it. I have spent all my grief.

It is ready. I hope the trick will work. Give them a villain. No need to create her. She is already made. It remains only to set her loose.

Soon the police will arrive. Jamie has gone to bring them here. In a moment my life will no longer be my own. I will take up a dead woman's name and bear it until the end of my days. I will live, always waiting for the heavy hand on my shoulder. But I will live.

Alice comes down the hill from the castle. She puts her hand in mine. "I will go south now," she says. "You follow when the inquest is over. Are you sure that I should take the baby?" Alice is awkward with Mary, startled and stiff. I see that she does not really like children. Like does not always have anything to do with love, however. Mary will be safe.

"Better if she does not exist," I say fiercely. "She is the one good thing to come from this."

"I do not want to leave you again," Alice says quietly. "Please let me come."

She is as dear to me as an old dream from childhood. "No," I say, "it must all be new."

I look around at each cold face. My family. My gaze rests for a moment on John Bearings' corpse. He was quite a short man. I had never noticed.

"It is time," Alice says. "They will be here soon. I wish we did not have to do this."

"The wound must look new." I lie down in the place made ready for me. I become a spar in the five-pointed star of the dead. I take up a stone and make ready to drive it into the place where my eye once was. I prepare to survive.

EVE AND DINAH

1946

WE are going to be late. I cannot put my face on, my hand shakes so.

Rose takes the lipstick from me. "You don't need it," she says firmly.

My reflection has begun to be a stranger. Who is this anxious woman? Lines cut across her face. Only my eye remains the same. It tells me that I am still in here somewhere.

"How can I be so old," I say to Rose, "when you are the same as the day we met?"

The bus bowls through the spring day like a promise. Daffodils flow over the banks. The grass is bright, young. It is good weather for a wedding.

We reach the church in time. They are still outside on the steps. Dark-clad men, girls in blue and yellow and green. A white, narrow figure, still among the fluttering. The woman turns. Nora smiles at me, her old, small smile. The world goes dark. I feel Rose's hand on me.

"All right, D?" she says. "Keep it together."

And then it is just my Mary, coming down the steps. She does not look like Nora at all, not really. Her eyes are wider, her face rounder, her brows darker, her hair fairer. Purpose radiates from her at all times. A different artist drew her.

She takes us in silken arms. She is thinner than I would like. The years have not been easy. I could not protect her from everything.

"Mother," she whispers. "Auntie Rose. Is it too late to do a bunk?" She is hilarious, half-serious, a scent of juniper on her breath. Courage comes in various forms.

The church is cold. Light falls through the windows, golden, red, blue. Suffering people outlined against the sky. Thorns, nails, swords. Blood and haloes. Strange to find myself here in this place, at last.

Music swells. It fills the air, my heart. Mary walks down the aisle. Her fingers are white, clenched tight about her bunch of daisies. No one by her side to give her away. It is not uncommon these days. Before the altar, in pools of coloured light, Stephen waits. He is still, as serious as a carving.

He is not Mary's first. The first one had eyes like a cloudless sky and a nose like the prow of a ship. He wrote poetry and drank. He burned with restless, feverish love. He was killed in '43.

Mary went on afterwards, as one must. She met Stephen at the hospital. He is a doctor, she a nurse. He loves her abjectly, sensibly. Perhaps it will be enough.

She plays her part well, speaks clearly with no hesitation. He stumbles once, at the part about worship and bodies.

Afterwards there is lunch at the hotel in town. Mary is quiet, relieved, as if some great question has at last been settled for better or worse. Stephen's mother is red-faced, sorrowful. She drinks steadily, watching her son. She talks of WI meetings and ways round using sugar. She talks about lack. Stephen's father was killed early on. She is alone, too. Rose listens, attentive. Rose and I do not stand out as we once might have done. Everywhere, women are alone.

We all drink more than we should. We are celebrating on the ashes of the world.

I cannot see Mary in the dining room, so I go looking. Through the lobby, which smells of fried fish, past the man at the desk. I think of another hotel, far north of here, where many years ago Christopher Black chased me, just as I now chase Mary through empty rooms.

I see her through the window. She is sitting on the gate across the road, dress rucked up around her slender knees. Her eyes are closed, face lifted to the first stars. The smoke of her cigarette curls about her fingers, spirals up through the still air. White moths flicker.

In the unguarded moment before she has time to arrange it, her face is sad.

"Join me, Mama," she says. She moves aside to make room for me.

"Careful with the dress," I say.

"It's parachute silk," she says. "Tougher than it looks." She offers me a cigarette. Her lipstick is gone, her mouth pale and tender.

She puts her head on my shoulder. "Tell me again about my first birthday," she says. "How it was just you and me in the woods."

Rose comes out of the hotel. We wave to her. She crosses to us and I swell with love. She climbs onto the gate and takes a companionable cigarette. "Where's the other one?" she asks.

"What do you mean?" asks Mary.

"I saw you from the window. All three of you sitting on the gate."

"Just us," I say. "Sorry."

Rose shakes her head. "Young. Dark red hair. She had her arm around Mary. She was lovely-looking. Don't you know her?"

"No." Mary slides her arm about Rose's neck. "Too much sherry for you, Auntie."

A sound comes from me that is like a laugh. I dab stupidly at my eyes. "I know her," I say.

Dinah has shown herself at last.

* * *

This will be the last letter. How many days have I given you? The good outnumber the bad now.

I left Loyal the day the inquest ended. Snow was falling in broad flakes. I bought a cheese from the inn. They would not take my money. I did not argue. They told me not to go. The roads were near impassable. The circus had been held up for some days—they had made off barely an hour before. Snow was still falling.

I would not stay. I walked south into the blizzard. The road ahead was blank. All about me the world breathed. A robin sat in a tree, his head cocked. I expect he was wondering whether he could eat me. I followed the tracks of the circus wagons, which lay deep in the snow like the paths of low-bellied beasts. Uncle's iron-bound box was heavy in my arms. It clinked as I stumbled onwards.

Just after Tongue, between two mountain ash trees bent low with snow, I was gone. My footprints stopped on the snowy road and I disappeared.

That was twenty-five years ago. Still I see it before my eyes, the burning white of the snow. I feel snowflakes on my cheek, cold ghost fingers, an ache in my legs. Trouble and hope churning in me like water or blood. It should have been an ending. Instead it was a beginning.

No trace of me has been glimpsed, no campfire tale is told of me, no rumours of emigration to America, or a lonely death in a poorhouse. I am *vanished*.

There. It is finished. I am empty. You have it all. What happens now? Perhaps you become me. And I become someone who never heard the word Altnaharra, or the name Evelyn Bearings.

I have carried her with me for many years. It is time to set her free. Jamie MacRaith is dead. Perhaps you have heard. I can tell you how it was done, if you wish. I am willing to spoil the trick.

I began this as an exorcism but it is also a summoning.

AFTER Little Eve killed them she went back to the sea. Sometimes she can be seen there. The village children know this. They look for her in the foamy spume, the rolling shallows, the waves that slump on the shore.

Joan MacRaith is seven and Daisy MacRaith is nine. They were going to look at the circus that is camped at the foot of Ardentinny, but low tide laid bare the causeway and the isle looked so enticing. They may stay as long as they like because Ma and Pa are at Uncle Jamie's funeral. They are too young, said Ma. Time enough to learn of such things.

So there is no one to miss them or ask them dull questions about *where* and *when* and *supper*.

The Isle of Altnaharra is a little kingdom just for them, and the sheep and the gulls and the sea. They run on the soft, bright turf, through the great standing stones, chased by the wind. They tease and dare one another. Uncle Jamie was always very nice but he would not let them climb on the ruins or the standing stones or do a hundred other things they wished to do!

Daisy takes a silver length of driftwood and pokes one of the vast, ugly seals that litter the rocky beaches by the causeway. The seal turns a round, unknowable eye. It snaps at the stick and Joan and Daisy scream and run away, hearts pounding. They know that you can die of a bite from those yellow teeth, those powerful jaws. But it is summer and the seals are well fed and too lazy to pursue. Joan and Daisy climb to the highest point of the isle and lean out over the sharp cliffs that fall down jagged to the furious sea. They lean further and further, holding onto one another's legs to catch the faint drift of salt spray on their cheeks.

By noon Joan's arms and legs are tender from the sun and Daisy is half-crying with hunger. But it is quite *dwaibly* to go home.

"We could go in," says Daisy, who always starts things. "Out of the heat."

Joan looks up at the castle, which squats atop the hill. The stone is gapped and broken. It seems to crumble before their very eyes. Does Uncle Jamie's ghost live there?

Daisy and Joan go in through the tumbled arch where the portcullis once stood. It is suddenly quiet, the sea and the wind and the gulls muted. The Castle of Altnaharra breathes about them, cold and damp. The timbers groan as though remembering the deaths they have witnessed. Daisy takes Joan's hand and they squeal under their breaths. It is very exciting. They have never been here alone before. It was always *mind this*, or *don't touch that*. Everywhere the gentle smell of peppermints and Uncle Jamie's dogs. Now it is empty and strange. Theirs.

They hopscotch through bright puddles of sunlight that fall in through the decayed roof. It is easy to imagine that the dead are lurking in dark corners. That a murderer stalks their footsteps, slipping from shadow to shadow. That eyes peer out from under the rotting stairs. That a shape, too thin and sharp to be human, stirs in the depths of the great hearth.

The windows of the Great Hall give directly onto the green and glassy sea. The ocean rises and falls, the gentle flanks of a sleeping beast.

"This is the window," says Joan. "If you look out you can see her in the water below."

Daisy squeezes her hand and goes to the window.

"Don't," says Joan, who knows her sister well.

"Don't fash," says Daisy. Her eyes are dreamy. She pushes the broken, leaded window frame outwards. Flakes of rust float down, land in her hair like poisoned snow. Old cobwebs cling to her lips. She spits and bats them away. "Hold my legs, Joanie," she says.

Joan sticks her thumb in her mouth, which she hasn't done for years, and shakes her head.

"Just like we did on the cliff," coaxes Daisy. "Come on, be a pal." She lies down and slides her upper body over the edge, into air. Joanie runs to her and sits on her legs just in time.

Daisy laughs. Her face hangs above the water. The tinny scent of the sea is everywhere. It moves in fascinating ways, silk billowing. It kisses the stone with wet little sounds. The water is so clear that Daisy can see right to the sandy bottom. Weeds wave in unseen currents. Silver fish dart in circular clouds. The old stone sill presses sharply on Daisy's stomach. She can't quite breathe right. And that is exciting, too. She reaches an arm down towards the water.

"You have to call her," Joanie says from above. Her voice is brittle with excitement. "Danny McClintock said. Three times you call her and then she comes."

Daisy draws a long breath. What a tale to tell in school tomorrow! "Little Eve," she says to the water. "Little Eve, Little Eve . . ."

Nothing happens, of course. The fish swirl beneath her in circles. She feels slightly dizzy. Don't they hang people upside down to torture them? Is Daisy being tortured? "I'm coming up," she says.

The sun comes out from behind a white scudding cloud. Its light pierces the ocean. And then Daisy sees it. Through the clear water, beneath the busy silver swarm of fish, something long and dark curving. Something that has flowing hair and no legs; instead a sinuous, terrible appendage like a tail. Daisy makes a sound, trying to say *help me, Joanie*, but it doesn't come out right. Joanie doesn't hear, but the thing in the water does. It turns belly up. The fish scatter and the rotting fish-woman-thing is revealed. It looks at her with its white, dead face, deep eyes like holes in the world. Daisy begins to scream. Joanie starts to cry. Daisy feels her sister's grip loosening on her legs. Daisy slides towards the water.

Her legs are brusquely seized.

Someone pulls her up over the rough stone sill. Not Joanie, but someone with strong hands and long arms.

"You could have been hurt," the woman says. She is dark, and small for a grown-up. Her face narrows to a point at the chin like a fox. Her clothes are beautiful. Soft brown boots, a woollen dress the colour of light through a forest canopy. A black patch covers her right eye, like a pirate. They brace themselves for a telling-off.

"Daisy likes to be scared," says Joanie with a whine. "She wanted to see her in the water."

"Who?"

"Little Eve," says Joanie.

"I saw her," whispers Daisy. "It's true. She's down there." She gulps. She doesn't want to cry in front of a stranger.

The woman looks startled. She steps carefully over to the window. "Come here," she says. "No, don't lean out." She points. A long tarpaulin ripples in the current, trapped beneath a stone on the ocean floor. It is touched in places with silver fish scales.

"Not a murderer," the woman says. "But it could have killed you all the same." She puts a hand on their shoulders. "Come away from the drop. You should not be here at all."

"Why not?" says Daisy. "*You're* here." The natural resentment of the rescued towards the rescuer is setting in.

"That is different," the woman says. "I am old. Anyhow, if you really want to see her you should not look there. That is not where she went into the water. She drove off the causeway."

"Who are you?" asks Joan after a moment.

The woman says, "Didn't you call for me three times?"

Daisy's mouth forms a growing "o" and Joan wails.

The woman says, "That was a silly joke. I am sorry. I heard you playing earlier and it startled me. I thought you must be ghosts! I was quite white with terror! Aren't I stupid? So now we have each frightened the other and we are even. What do you say to that?"

"All right," say Joanie. She takes the lady's proffered hand.

Daisy knows that Ma would not like it, so she takes Joanie's hand back and holds it herself.

"My name is Dinah," says the woman, unruffled by Daisy's rudeness. "What are you fine ladies called?"

"I am Daisy MacRaith, and the little one is Joan." Joanie looks cross at "the little one." That will teach her to hold hands with strangers.

The woman smiles. "I thought you had a familiar look to you. Your Uncle Jamie lived here."

"Yes," says Daisy, suspicious. "He lived in the castle. He is just dead. We live in Loyal."

"Do you wish you lived here?"

"No," says Joanie. "It is old and smelly."

"Well, Joan and Daisy MacRaith, you seem very grown up. Perhaps you will help me with something that I must do."

* * *

The standing stones are buffeted by wind, which comes in hard over the sea. In its roar are other sounds: beasts calling, the ring of swords, children playing.

"Now I am going to show you a great secret. I had a sister once. She died. I have carried her with me for many turns."

"What are turns?"

The woman shakes her head and bites her lip. "So easy," she says. "To slip between then and now. I meant to say 'years.' Anyhow, it is time to let her go." The woman takes out a tin. It looks like an old tea caddy, rusted. She opens it, and white powder rises and scatters on the wind.

The woman who calls herself Dinah takes a battered silver locket from the neck of her dress. She opens it with a nail. Inside is a lock of hair. Dark with red lights in it.

"Such a lovely colour," says the woman. "So alike, we were, she and I, in that respect. But as you can see, hers was always the more lustrous red. And mine is greying now, of course." She smiles at Daisy and Joan. "We used to dive from this cliff. We would race. We could have a race now, we three. What do you say?"

"It is too early in the year to swim," says Joanie politely. "It will be cold."

"You think so?" says the woman. She leans in and bares white, pointed teeth. It is not a smile. "Perhaps you should learn what real cold is. Let us race to discover which of you is best!"

The sisters huddle together, staring. "We don't want to," says Daisy.

The woman looks away. She says the word that Pa says when he hammers his thumb. She says it quietly, though, to herself. When she looks back at the girls, her face is different. Tired. "I am being silly again," she says. "It has been too long since I was myself." She offers Joan the locket. "You can do it if you like," she says. "Throw it over the cliff. Let the ocean and the wind have it."

Joanie takes the dull silver thing. Daisy wants to stop her. The locket seems powerful, somehow. Fireside stories surface dimly in her mind, of curses and witches and hundreds of years locked inside hills. But Joanie grins and throws it into the sea and nothing happens, so perhaps it is all right.

The woman stands for a moment, touching the place on her

breastbone where the locket sat. Then she shakes herself. She makes a little surprised noise like Ma does when there's more in the biscuit tin than she had thought.

"There," she says. "She is at peace. So that is that. You had better go home now. I see an old friend coming this way."

Daisy and Joanie run. They splash across the causeway, drenching the velvet trousers of the man who is walking towards the isle.

"Take care," he says, urgent. "Please." He does not seem to mean the splashing.

* * *

I watch the sea in the fading glow. I hear his approach behind me, his step on the path.

Christopher Black says, "Shall I call you Dinah?"

"Eve," I say. "For old times' sake." Strange to hear that name again after so much time. It does not sound like me any more. "You understood."

"Well," he says, "I made a few wrong turns along the way."

"I knew that you would see, in the end, when and where."

"James MacRaith never read Edgar Rice Burroughs, but I did. It took me months to understand how Dinah Bearings could know that. Then I remembered the train journey to Inverness with Evelyn. You were pretending to sleep. I saw you watching me.

"The question at the inquest about the locket was to set my mind to work. If Dinah's hair were compared to yours under a microscope, they might have begun to suspect that you had taken her place." He sighs. "No one compared them, of course."

"They did not," I say. "You would have."

"I would. Of course, you might have thrown Dinah's hair away or replaced it with your own at any time, but . . ."

"No," I tell him. Some warm barrier in my throat. "I could never have done that."

"It was well done, the exchange," he says.

"Give them something to watch," I say, "while the real trick happens elsewhere."

He smiles. "More difficult than palming a piece of liquorice."

"We were roughly the same age, same height, and we both had red hair. No one in the village had seen her for years. We gave them a victim and a villain."

He shakes his head. "I could have come to the inquest and spoiled everything."

"I knew you would not. You blamed yourself too much."

"For many years. I expect you know that too. And has it brought you happiness, Evelyn, your stolen life?"

I smile. "Did you leave word with anyone that you were coming here? 'Open in the event of my death,' that sort of thing?"

"There is no one to leave it with," he says. "I spent my life in pursuit of one woman."

"I am sorry," I say.

"Don't be. You know, I joined up again in forty-one. They took me, no questions asked, as if the court martial had never happened. Despite the leg. I had some idea that I could make up for it all. Show courage. But they put me behind a desk in Brighton. I was never afraid, not once, throughout the entire thing. I am a nightwatchman at a girls' school now." He smiles. "I used to blame you for my life. I thought that were it not for you, I could have been something. Fulfilled all that early promise."

"And now?" I say.

"I would have made the same mistakes if I had never known you. And that would have been the sum of me." He smiles. "It is a kind of privilege, to witness the darkness."

"That is not the truth," I say. "I don't believe that is what you feel."

He shrugs. "Some days it is. Some days not. You don't have the right to all the truths, Evelyn. Someone told me that once."

I bow my head.

"You seem well," he says. "Different."

"I am a mother. I have people to love."

The wind combs his hair with cool fingers. He turns his face to the last of the light. "It is beautiful here," he says.

"I suppose so," I say. "Although that is not the word that comes to my mind."

"Will you come back?"

"Never," I say. "I will sell it and give the money to my daughter."

He is quiet for a moment. I feel him testing the air between us, judging. "Will you tell me," he says, "if I ask?"

"Let us see," I say.

"Did you kill them?"

"No," I say. "Nora killed them."

Relief pours off him like water. "I was right," he says. "I have been right all along. The Eve I knew could not have done it. Tell me how it happened."

"Let us sit. We called this stone Cold Ben, you know. He is the most powerful of them all."

He watches me intently as I talk. The sea light plays on the bones of his face.

"I killed Nora," I say when I come to the end. "I had to."

"I understand," he says.

"Her skull broke open like an egg," I say. "It happened here, in this very spot where we now sit. I felt her life pour out, flow away." I feel it again on my fingers. The scent of blood mingling with the earth. "I changed in that moment. You cannot be the same after such a thing."

"No," he says. "You cannot."

"So many questions asked about what I did that night," I say. "No one has asked, what did that night do to me? I had never killed before, never felt a life glistening on my hands."

I look at my upturned palms. The past overlies the present. Pink, clean palms with a scratch the rosebush made on my thumb yesterday in the garden. They are familiar hands, and mine, worn with work and care. A happy life.

Through them I see the other hands. Hers. Made for death. Nails rimed with black and red.

"To kill," I say. "Such a thing makes you comprehend yourself as if for the first time. It gave me such a liking for it. There is something of my mother in me, after all."

I take hold of Christopher Black's wrists. He struggles but my grip is as strong as eagle's claws. He looks at me with something like triumph. He has his long-sought answer. Death has found him, at last, here on Altnaharra.

"What will it be?" he asks.

What indeed? Will my hands wrap about his neck, will I dash his head like fruit on the stone as I did Nora's, all those years ago? Perhaps it will be the sea. I look into his eyes. He is not as afraid as he should be. Part of him came here for this.

"I do not give in," I say. "Each day I wish to, but each day I do not. I never let what is inside me out." I look down at where I grip his wrists. "I have frightened you." I release him. My fingers leave white ghosts on his flesh. "That is not what I want."

He gets to his feet, shaking. "What do you want?"

"It is a lonely thing to be a monster," I say. "And an unwilling one. I cannot burden those I love with it." I feel my old face surface for a moment. Eve, full of need. "Everyone who knew me is gone. Only you are left. Is it so wrong to wish to be seen, just once, as I am?"

Christopher Black rubs his wrists. He shivers as if my touch were cold. His heart is racing, I can almost hear it. His body is telling him to run. It knows what I am. He looks at the sun where it is sinking into the ocean. I see his thoughts. Evening will be here soon and after that, the chill night. No witness but the sea and the stones. Who would choose to keep a tiger company?

"Go," I say. "It is late." Loneliness closes over me, my shroud.

He sits down beside me. "It's not too late," he says, firm. "I can stay for a while." His warmth along my side. Kindness is a physical thing. My body receives it.

The globe of the world turns towards darkness. We watch together. I rest my head on his shoulder. At last it feels like a homecoming.

"One day I may have the courage to write the true story," I say. "How it happened. Is it possible to be healed of such things?"

"I don't know," he says.

Starlings pierce the fading blue, soaring skyward like a blessing, like a sign. Out to sea, black scales gleam in the last of the light.

ACKNOWLEDGMENTS

Ed McDonald has all my love and thanks, as always. You're the light of my life.

To my mother Isabelle, my father Christopher, to Antonia, Sam, Wolf, and River, thank you for being a constant source of love and joy.

Huge thanks are due to my amazing agents, Jenny Savill and Robin Straus, who were determined to see *Little Eve* reborn. You have my heartfelt gratitude, as ever, for everything. Michael Dean, many, many thanks for your tireless work and care in bringing my books to film. To Andrew Nurnberg and all at Andrew Nurnberg Associates, especially Barbara Barbieri, Rory Clarke, Lucy Flynn, Juliana Galvis, Halina Koscia, Sabine Pfannenstiel, and Marei Pittner, thank you. I am so appreciative of everything you do. Thanks to Danielle Metta for all your help.

To my wonderful US editor, Kelly O'Connor Lonesome—you've brought *Little Eve* back to life, and I can't tell you what it means to me. Anneliese Merz, Alexis Saarela, Michael Dudding, Jordan Hanley, Sarah Pannenberg, Kristin Temple, Jessica Katz, Devi Pillai, Lucille Rettino, and the rest of the fantastic team at Tor Nightfire and Tom Doherty Associates, thank you—you're all heroes. Thanks to the talented Katie Klimowicz for creating the beautiful, dramatic cover art for *Little Eve*, which goes straight to the heart of the book.

ACKNOWLEDGMENTS

To Gillian Redfearn, I'm as thankful for your friendship as I am for your keen editorial eye—you are a shining star. To Marcus Gipps, Rachel Winterbottom, and the lovely team at Gollancz, thank you for all your support.

I'm very grateful to the kind and talented Arzu Tahsin, who worked so hard editing this book for Weidenfeld & Nicolson in the UK.

To those who read early drafts, thank you for your encouragement and insight: Nina Allan, Laura Barnett, Kate Burdette, Emily Cavendish, Susan Civale, Edward McGown, Eugene Noone, Catherine Shepherd, and Mike Walden.

I'm deeply grateful to the jurors, advisory board, and directors of the Shirley Jackson Award. In 2018, *Little Eve* was awarded the prize for best novel—despite not being published in the US. That award changed the fortunes of this book and my career.

READING GROUP GUIDE

Guide written by Amy Root Clements

1. What causes the bond between Eve and Dinah to fluctuate throughout the novel? How might their relationship have been different if their survival had not been continually at stake? What are the most significant differences in their personalities?

2. What does *Little Eve* illustrate about the development of a child's sense of self? How does gender affect what Eve and Dinah believe about their place in the world? What is it like for Abel to grow into manhood in a household where Uncle has absolute control, and most of the inhabitants are female?

3. When Dinah is released after five nights of Wane, she flings her arms around Uncle, and the others join the embrace. "*Uncle* is the name for *home* in our minds and hearts," Evelyn observes. How does Uncle exploit the extremes of abuse and devotion, hunger and sweet honey, to manipulate his clan? How is he able to create a home from which they do not want to leave, despite the horrors?

4. What is the root of Mr. Black's bond with Eve? What injuries, emotional and physical, is he trying to heal in himself?

5.   When Mr. Black is with young Evelyn and sees the headline saying that Hamish Buchanan has been hanged, he says, "An eye for an eye." Evelyn thinks to herself that Hamish "paid the price for my power." In her mind, how is the balance of power maintained? How does she experience guilt, and how does she define justice and purity?

6.   How does Nora's status shift throughout the novel? What does her story say about the nature and limitations of maternal instincts?

7.   In what ways is Alice a prisoner in every aspect of her life? What does it take for her to finally be free? How does life at Altnaharra change after her departure?

8.   How did you react to the reality of Elizabeth's bird hospital?

9.   What does the novel demonstrate about truth and memory? How does the structure of the storytelling in *Little Eve* escalate the suspense?

10. Raised in the heart of the Loyal community, seemingly far removed from the secrets of Altnaharra, Jamie and Sarah nonetheless endured multiple tragedies. Who is ultimately to blame for their suffering? Who are the novel's most innocent characters?

11. What makes the time period of the Great War and its aftermath an excellent backdrop for this tale?

12. How is Rose distinctly different from the women of Altnaharra yet able to create a kind of kinship? How does the introduction

of Rose and the arrival of Mary create a new pathway of hope? What turning points do they spur?

13. In what ways does Altnaharra itself become a character in the novel? How does the natural world of the island, along with the history of the weather-beaten castle and its imposing gate, reflect the varied generations that have lived there over the years?

14. Catriona Ward masterfully depicts the contradictions of the human psyche. Discuss the ways in which *Little Eve* enhances your experience of her other fiction that you have read.